loving ro____

Magnolia Falls ~ Book 1

laura pavlov

This one is for my favorite fictional hero of all time…

"It ain't about how hard you can hit. It's about how hard you can get hit and keep moving forward." Rocky Balboa

copyright

Message from the Author:
Click the link below for content warnings.
https://dl.bookfunnel.com/t4bhrknjyp

one

. . .

Romeo

BURPING.

Farting.

Giving one another shit.

It was what we did best.

Me and the guys sat in the same seats we sat in every week for what seemed like forever. Creatures of habit or superstition—maybe a little of both. Boxers aren't like race car drivers in that way, though. No, you won't find stinky socks that a guy's been wearing for a year, but we do have our own beliefs that some may think are quirky, thus the seating arrangement. We'd been meeting at Knockout, the gym I now owned, where we'd been coming since we were kids. I'd grown up here.

Hell, in a way, we all had.

"Lots to talk about today." River quirked a brow at both Kingston and Nash. He took no shit and was the first to call you out if he had a problem with something.

"Are we still whining about the fucking coffee shop?" Kingston groaned. Kingston and River were the only biological brothers in the group, but we were all brothers in our own way.

In the way that mattered most.

Nash barked out a laugh. He and Kingston owned ROD Construction, which stood for Ride or Die, the words we'd all marked on our skin years ago. "Dude, it was a job. What were we going to do? Turn her down? We'd look like dicks if we refused to work on the project. We've done every renovation downtown since we opened the doors four years ago."

"Newsflash, assholes. You still look like dicks. That has nothing to do with the jobs that you take." River chuckled. "But I think you're just afraid of pissing off the Crawfords."

The Crawford family owned most of the real estate in Magnolia Falls, the small town we'd all grown up in. Their name was on the main drag street sign—also the schools in town, the library… the list was endless. They were rich as fuck, and we had our reasons for hating them.

But I'd sided with Nash and Kingston when it came to working on the building. The money was good, and their company was thriving. I wouldn't let my personal issues get in the way of them building their business.

Demi Crawford, who'd come home after being away at school for years, had decided to open a coffee shop right next door to my gym. The guys were there to do a job, not hang out with her. River didn't quite see it that way.

"I've told you that Saylor became friends with her while she was away at school, and according to the ray of sunshine who I somehow share DNA with, Demi's a cool girl. Her words, not mine. Obviously." Hayes rolled his eyes, referencing his younger sister, whom he adored and who was much friendlier than her broody older brother. "The Crawfords are no friends of mine, but it doesn't mean we won't occasionally have to work with one of them, seeing as we live in the same small fucking town as they do. I did have to put out that fire in their guesthouse last year, and you didn't shame me for not letting it burn down."

"Whatever. The job is finally done." River sipped his

coffee and leaned back on the leather couch in the back room, where we always held our meetings. "We can stop ass-kissing the devil now?"

"Correct. But I've got to tell you, she isn't the rich, bitchy girl you think she is," Kingston said, holding his hands up to stop River from jumping down his throat. "I'm not defending her. I'm calling it as I see it. She renovated the apartment above the shop, as well, and she's going to be living there. Not quite the princess in the tower that you seem to envision. That's all I'm saying."

"Oh, let me guess. You're going to try to date a fucking Crawford now?" River hissed.

"Take it down a notch, dickhead. King was out with me last night, and I can assure you, he's not looking to date anyone," Hayes said over his laughter. "He's looking to date *everyone*."

"Well, don't make me sound like an asshole. I just like to keep my options open. And no, I'm not looking to date Demi Crawford. She's far too sweet for me." Kingston waggled his brows, knowing he was getting under his brother's skin.

The disdain for the Crawfords ran deep for all of us. Rightfully so. But Demi wasn't really involved in that, and none of us knew her all that well, seeing as she attended the fancy private school in town, and we all went to public school.

On the days that we actually attended.

None of us had been scholarly, but we'd made it through.

River and I had both gone through a hard time after those months we spent in juvie, but we'd worked hard to get our lives back on track.

Once you'd been labeled a bad kid, it was tough to turn things around.

People love to judge—and judge they did.

"Those Crawfords have evil running through their blood. But we've wasted enough time talking about them. Let's move on to the elephant in the room, shall we, Golden Boy?" River turned his attention to me.

They'd given me the name, which had carried over into my boxing career. We'd been through a lot together. I was the youngest in the group. We'd become friends when they'd found me in the alley behind the gym, fighting off three dudes who were several years older than me when we were just kids. They'd jumped in when they'd realized that I was outnumbered, and we'd been best friends ever since.

"Yes. Who the fuck do we need to hurt for the latest shit that fuckface is pulling?" Hayes leaned forward, resting his elbows on his thighs. He was a firefighter, and it showed. He was big and tough and a total badass.

"He's just looking for attention." I shrugged, trying to act unaffected, when the truth was, this shit was getting to me.

Leo "The Flamethrower" Burns was a professional fighter. They called him The Flamethrower because he claimed his right hook was the kiss of death.

He lost the belt to Gunner Waverly a few months ago. It was the one single loss in his entire career, and he'd been whining about it to anyone who would listen for months. He wanted a rematch. Claimed it was an off day and that Gunner got lucky.

He was a big name in the industry. He had a huge following on social media, and the press loved him because he was completely out of control and unpredictable. He'd thrown a chair through a restaurant window when he claimed the hostess hadn't recognized him and tried to make him wait for a table.

The guy was a complete douchebag. And for whatever fucked-up reason, I was on his radar now. In an odd turn of events, the fight that had given me professional status a few years ago was against Gunner Waverly. He'd just become a professional fighter at the time. My father had pulled some strings, and Gunner had agreed to fight me. He wasn't a big name back then, and it had barely been news when I'd beat him. But I'd stepped away from fighting shortly after and walked away from the boxing world.

Gunner had gone on to make a real name for himself. He'd taken the belt from Leo, and Leo had been going on every news channel that would listen, demanding a rematch. Fast forward a few weeks, and Gunner Waverly got into a car accident and ended up getting his foot amputated.

I can't make this shit up.

He'd officially retired, and Leo hadn't stopped throwing a tantrum since it happened. The man had lost his goddamn foot, and all Leo could do was complain about not getting his rematch.

That was when I got dragged into this shit.

In an odd turn of events, it just so happened that the last fight Gunner Waverly had lost was to me. Hence the reason Leo was now fixated on redeeming his name by fighting me.

Leo was the last person to hold the belt before Gunner, and he believed I was the person he should fight to win his belt back. To prove to everyone that he was deserving of said title.

Even though no one knew who the fuck I was.

And I was just fine with that.

"He's a fucking prick. But if you agree to fight this asshole, you know that we will be in your corner the whole way," Kingston said, shaking his head. My boys had been at every single one of my fights since I'd started boxing in high school.

It was just the way we were. We always showed up for one another.

Ride or die.

"Damn. I remember that fight with Gunner, man. You dropped his ass, and everyone was stunned." River rubbed his hands together. "But this Leo situation is out of control. I know you're on the fence about getting back in the ring, but I've got to tell you… I'd love to see you shut this guy up."

I'd stopped fighting the day my father collapsed ringside a few months after that fight with Gunner, and he'd died a few hours later. I'd lost my desire to fight, and I'd started running the gym with my dad's partner at Knockout, Rocco, who'd since retired a year ago. He'd worked out a way for me to buy him out, and now the place was mine, and it kept me plenty busy. I trained a few fighters, overlooked the staff, and kept the lights on in this place. I made enough to live comfortably, but I certainly wasn't rolling in dough, and this fight would be a quick way to make some cash.

While my sister was away at school, I was doing my best to keep my mom and my grandmother moving forward since my father's passing. I'd been grateful when we'd moved my grandmother in with my mother because I didn't like the idea of either of them being alone.

"I don't know. I talked to Lincoln about it, and he said not to let his goading get to me. He's dealt with this shit a lot more than I have." Lincoln Hendrix was my older brother, who I'd only found out about after my father died. Our dad had left a letter for my unknown brother, and I'd tracked him down, and we'd been close ever since.

"I think Leo is enjoying the fact that you've got a famous older brother, too," Nash said. "He's really running his mouth. And I have to say, Cutler would sure love to see Uncle Ro in a real fight."

Cutler was Nash's son, who'd been one of us since the day he was born. He was almost six years old, and the dude was the coolest little kid I'd ever met. We were all four named his godfathers, and there wasn't anything we wouldn't do for him. Nash was basically raising him on his own, minus the occasional weekends his ex showed up to spend time with him. So, in a way, Cutler was all of ours. He started taking some boxing lessons from me a few weeks ago because he suddenly wanted to learn how to fight.

"Yeah. He told me last week that he wants to see me fight. I thought maybe I'd drag one of you into the ring with me and spar a little," I said with a laugh.

"I don't know. You might want to take Leo up on his offer. Did you see what he put out yesterday with that whole play on your name?" River changed his voice to sound like a little girl and did his best impression. "*Romeo, Romeo, wherefore art thou Romeo.*"

Leo had been interviewed on a major sports channel, and when they'd asked about his next fight, he'd pulled the *Romeo* bullshit. If I had a nickel for every time someone had said those fucking words to me—well, I wouldn't have to consider getting back in the ring again.

The truth was, this shit was wearing on me.

Everyone in town was asking if I was going to go knock his ass out because the asshole wouldn't shut up, and he continued to take a shot at me every chance he got.

"He's just trying to rattle you," Nash said. "If you want to get in the ring, I will fully support that, because seeing you destroy him would be fucking fantastic. But if you want to stay retired, you don't owe this prick a fucking thing."

"True that." Hayes held up his coffee, and we all did the same.

"I need to think about it. I don't know what the fuck I want to do." I cleared my throat and turned back to Nash. "Are you bringing Cutler over after school today?"

Nash and Kingston were working on a huge renovation for the city right now, and he'd be working late.

"Yeah. Thanks, man. It'll just be a few hours, and then I'll swing by and grab him after dinner."

"Sounds good. I'll let him play in the ring for a little bit and we'll grab some pizza."

"Cutler is a lucky little dude. He's got the coolest fucking uncles around. Imagine the swagger that kid will have by the time he's in high school." River barked out a laugh.

"Let's slow our roll, all right? He already never takes off that goddamn leather coat you got him." Nash raised a brow at River before turning to Kingston. "And now he's asking how old he has to be to get the *Ride or Die* tattoo because someone told him he'd have to get inked someday to be in our brotherhood. That was fucked up, King. He's not even six years old, and he's asking me to get a fucking tattoo."

Kingston held up his hands and smirked. "Dude. When he was over last week, I had my shirt off, and he wouldn't stop asking questions about it. He also told me he doesn't like his name and wants to change it."

"What is the fucking deal with his name? He told me it doesn't *feel like him*, and he's working on figuring out his new name. I'm probably fucking this kid up more than I even realize." Nash ran a hand over his face.

"Hey," I said. "Cutler is the coolest little dude I've ever met. He's a confident kid. Hell, I didn't have his swagger when I was five years old."

"I don't know… young Romeo was breaking hearts and kicking kids' asses that were twice his size behind the gym at a fairly young age," Hayes said over his laughter. "But I agree. You have nothing to worry about with your boy. He's growing up with a lot of love. And we can't all say that, can we?"

Everyone nodded. We'd all had tough childhoods, each in our own right.

But we'd survived just fine, and it was probably what had led us to one another.

To this friendship.

This brotherhood.

We all wanted things to be easier for Cutler. He may not have a traditional home, but he was surrounded by family, and our love for that little boy was fierce.

"Damn straight. Cutler is more loved than any of your ugly mugs ever were." River pushed to his feet.

My phone vibrated, and I glanced down and groaned.

"What is it?" Kingston asked.

"Mimi wants me to bring her and my mom some sort of pumpkin spice drink from Magnolia Beans one day this week." I rolled my eyes. Anytime something new opened in town, my mom and my grandmother made it a big deal.

"Fuck. I'd say don't do it if it were anyone other than Mimi and your mom asking. I guess we're all drinking Crawford coffee now." River flipped us the bird as he tossed his paper cup into the trash.

"It's not personal. We still hate the Crawfords," Kingston said. "But I do love me a pumpkin chai latte with a foamy heart on top."

More laughter.

We did our usual handshake, and Hayes called out our chant on his way out the door.

"Ride or die. Brothers till the end. Loyalty always. Forever my friend." He held up a peace sign and walked out the door.

And I made my way out to the gym to get back to work.

I had a lot on my mind, and I needed to make a decision on the fight soon.

two

. . .

Demi

THE GRAND OPENING a few days ago had been ridiculously busy. It felt like everyone in town had come by. I was thrilled to finally be open after spending months reno-vating this place and coming up with the menu.

I'd majored in nutrition and minored in business, so my goal was to eventually make Magnolia Beans much more than just a coffee shop. I'd be offering green juice, protein shakes, and a few other healthy options, as well, and I planned to add more to the menu over the next few months.

Things had finally slowed down, and Peyton was in the back cleaning up the kitchen. She and I had grown up together, and she was taking online courses to get her master's in education. She was in need of a part-time job at the moment, so the timing was perfect.

The door swung open, and my eyes widened at the sight of him. He was tall and lean and the best-looking guy I'd ever seen. Wavy hair, longer in the front, dark brown eyes, and bone structure that a *GQ* model would envy.

I'd definitely seen Romeo Knight over the years, and I knew who he was, but we weren't friends, and it had been a long time since I'd crossed paths with him.

But I sure as hell didn't remember him looking like this when we were younger, although I probably wasn't paying much attention at the time.

I was a bit of a late bloomer in that department.

"Hey, it's Romeo, right?" I asked, smiling up at him until I noticed the frown on his face, followed by a glare that made it clear nothing had changed. He'd never been friendly to me, which had always kind of fit with his bad-boy demeanor.

But we were adults now.

"I need two of whatever the hell that pumpkin spice drink is you're selling that my mom and grandmother won't stop nagging me about."

Wow. Not friendly, but okay.

"Yeah. Sure. Two pumpkin chai lattes with a side of cinnamon." I rang up his order in the register before looking back up at him. "If you'd like to add one for yourself, too, it would be on the house."

"Because you think I need your charity?" he said, his voice hard and lacking all humor.

He was actually offended by a free drink?

"No. Because you're my neighbor, and I put a card on all the doors of the businesses on this street, offering one free cup of whatever you choose as a friendly gesture. It's called being neighborly."

"I don't want a drink. I'll pass."

What a dick.

"No problem." I raised a brow and kept my lips in a straight line. *Your loss, asshole.* I'd made an effort, and he'd completely gone out of his way to be a jerk. "Would you like me to apply your free drink to one of these?"

"I'll pay for both drinks."

I rolled my eyes and held my hand out. "That'll be eleven dollars even."

He pulled out the cash and tossed it onto the counter, as if he couldn't even stand the idea of placing the money in my hand.

What the hell was this guy's deal?

This was my first week as a business owner, so I would keep my cool. I tossed the money into the register and moved to make the drinks. I started filling both cups with hot water. I glanced up to see him watching me, and I expected him to turn away, but he didn't. He just stared at me like he couldn't stand the sight of me.

Then why the hell doesn't he look away?

I let out a long breath before looking back down and finishing his drinks in awkward silence.

Saylor Woodson and I had become good friends in college. I knew that her older brother, Hayes, ran in the same circle as Romeo. My brother, Slade, had always told me that group of guys was trouble, and I'd steered clear. I think they'd been busted for stealing and ditching school and things like that when they were young. Not that Slade hadn't caused plenty of trouble all on his own. But two of the guys he'd mentioned, Kingston Pierce and Nash Heart, had both worked on the renovation for the coffee shop, and they'd been very professional. They'd never been super chatty with me, but they were nice enough, and they did good work.

I had no idea why Romeo had such an issue with me. Or maybe he was stressed out that some famous boxer was all over the news, blasting his name to anyone who would listen.

Not that I followed sports.

I didn't.

But everyone was talking about it.

"All cleaned up. I'm going to head out," Peyton said as she stepped in from the kitchen and then halted when she saw Romeo standing there.

"Thanks for cleaning up. I'll see you tomorrow." I glanced over at her, making it clear that I was in the midst of an awkward situation.

She would then try to make it even more awkward. It was kind of her shtick.

Of course, she sauntered over to the register.

"You're Romeo Knight, aren't you?"

His gaze moved to her. "Yes."

"Ah, a man of few words." She chuckled. "Your gym is right next door to us. You two should run some sort of special. You know, all those hot boxers can get a *buy one, get one free deal* over here?" She looked from him to me, and I groaned because Peyton had never been good at reading the room.

"I doubt that's necessary. I think everyone knows you're here. You're a Crawford, after all, right?" He moved closer as I set the two drinks in front of him and glared at him.

"So, you do know who I am." I crossed my arms over my chest.

"I never said I didn't."

He picked up the cups off the counter and turned for the door.

"Well, don't worry about it. I didn't want to do that deal with your gym anyway," I said, internally shaming myself for the weak comeback.

He pushed the door open and glanced at me. "Trust me. No one is going to lose sleep over it."

And he walked right out the door.

My mouth gaped open, and I turned to Peyton and shook my head. "What an asshole."

"Oh my God. He's so freaking hot, though. The face. The hair. The body. It should be illegal to look that good."

"I didn't notice. I was too busy being insulted by him. What in the world did I ever do to that guy? He wouldn't even take the good neighbor discount I'd offered for one free drink. He acted like I'd murdered a family member."

"Yeah, I've seen him around, and he's never been super friendly, but that was next level. I wonder why he hates you."

Oh, wow. I guess I wasn't being paranoid, and even she'd noticed that he despised me.

"I have no idea. I don't even know him."

"Well, your family is like Magnolia Falls royalty, so I think sometimes people get jealous of those who are filthy rich. Lucky for you, you're my bestie and you spoil me, so I don't care." Her head fell back in laughter.

"I've been away at school for four years. I came home and opened a business, one that I'm working at every day. I'm living in a small apartment above the coffeehouse and trying to do things on my own. But I'm hated anyway because my family has money? Romeo Knight can fuck off. I've never judged him. He doesn't have a clue about my life. We've never even spoken before today. He'd made his mind up about me before he walked through the door."

"You are so right. He's an asshole. But damn, he is a good-looking asshole, am I right?"

"I don't care what he looks like. He's a dick. That trumps good looks. Plus, I barely noticed."

I hoped he'd stay away moving forward. I didn't need his negative energy in my coffee shop. I shook it off and turned to face Peyton as she bellowed out in laughter at my comment.

"If I had a blindfold over my eyes and a bag over my head and the world lost all-natural sunlight along with working electricity, I would still know that he was hot."

"Whatever. Let's move on. It was another good day for business. We've been so busy, and I need to place a bunch of orders tonight because we're going through supplies faster than I anticipated."

"Look at you, smarty pants. Your fancy degree is show-ing." She gave me a quick hug and snatched a cookie before waving goodbye.

I finished cleaning up and made my way upstairs. My apartment was a small one-bedroom, but I'd chosen every single finish in both my home and my business, and I loved everything about them both.

My grandfather and my father had always talked about real estate. About working hard and building something from the ground up. My grandfather was in politics, and my father owned an investment company, so a strong work ethic had been ingrained in my head since I was a kid. Yes, I'd been given a break that not everyone had. My trust fund was hefty, and I'd taken a good portion and invested it into buying this building, which would serve as both my work and my home. It was a smart, safe investment. Included in the building was another shop next door, but I hadn't decided what I'd do with that space just yet. Real estate was hot in Magnolia Falls, especially the downtown area. I'd wait to see how things went here and either expand or lease out the space to another business.

My mother was horrified that I was living above the coffee shop, as my parents had offered to purchase me a home as a graduation gift. But I was determined to use the money in my trust and start making it work for me. I had a few girlfriends who'd also come from wealthy families, and they'd spent the months after graduation traveling through Europe, while I'd been here, working on my business plan and renovating the building.

I'd never been that girl. Sure, I liked pretty clothes and nice things, but I'd always worked hard. I had a part-time job in college, and I liked earning my own money. People always thought everything I had was handed to me. When I'd been accepted to one of the most prestigious universities in California, I'd heard endless comments from people saying that they were certain my grandfather had pulled strings to get me in. I knew if I'd countered back and let them know that I'd received a full academic scholarship for all four years, I'd then be labeled a bitch for sounding full of myself. So, I'd bit my tongue. But I'd worked my ass off in high school, and that had continued in college.

I wanted to make a name for myself outside of my family. To prove that I was worthy of the things that I had.

My family had had their fair share of heartache, and I wanted to make them proud.

When I pushed the door to my apartment open, I couldn't help but smile at the place. Rustic plank wood floors ran throughout the apartment. The small white kitchen had a colorful ceramic backsplash, which gave it some character. I'd gotten one of those adorable old-fashioned light-blue refrigerators that had been in the design plan to fit perfectly in the small space. There was a rustic butcher block square island, which was where I ate my meals most of the time, and a white couch with cozy throw pillows and a pink blanket tossed over the arm that sat in the small living room beside the kitchen. I'd added white Roman shades to keep the room bright and light, and my bedroom and bathroom were similar in style. I was calling this vibe: French farmhouse chic.

Even if it was an 800-square-foot apartment with no yard, it was all mine. I fell back on the couch and sighed. I was a country girl at heart. Always had been. And someday, I planned to own a ranch with my own horses, but for the time being, I'd have to go to my parents' or my grandparents' to ride Teacup. For now, the plan was to keep my head down and work hard.

Laughter from the street below wafted into my apartment, and I pushed up on my knees to look outside. Romeo was coming out of his gym with a little kid who looked to be around five or six years old, and they were holding hands. The young boy was wearing a leather coat, and his hair was slicked back as he gazed up at the man beside him. Romeo's smile was wide, and it took my breath away as I watched.

He really is a beautiful man, even if he is a raging asshole.

And he clearly knew how to smile when he didn't hate the

person in his presence. I wondered if this was his kid. I suppose it was possible. I was twenty-two, and I was fairly certain that he was a year or two older than me, so maybe he had a whole family that I didn't know about.

I turned around and fell back against the couch when my phone vibrated and took in the message from my brother.

SLADE

Hey, sis. I miss you. I'm back in town, but let's not tell the parents just yet. Want to have dinner?

My eyes welled as my fingers lingered over the screen. Slade had always been my best friend—until he wasn't. Until he'd completely changed. And I'd missed him terribly. After several stints in rehab, I'd stopped getting my hopes up… or at least I'd tried to. My parents had washed their hands of him after the last incident at our house a year ago. My grandfather continued paying for rehab, and he and I both believed that even if we didn't know what the outcome would be, we'd never stop trying. Because once we all gave up on him, he'd give up on himself.

Hi. Of course. I'd love to see you. Should we meet at the Golden Goose?

The Golden Goose was a diner in town we'd been going to since we were kids. We both loved the milkshakes and french fries.

SLADE

I don't want Mom and Dad to know I'm here. But I want to see your new place. The business and the apartment. That's why I came home for the weekend. I'm proud of you. How about we order takeout?

I swiped at the tear running down my cheek.

Hope was a risky emotion when you were dealing with addiction. I'd grieved the loss of my brother in many ways over the years, but every now and then, I'd get glimpses of him, which I was grateful for.

This felt like a glimpse of him.

> I'd love that. See you soon.

three

. . .

Romeo

"**DAMN**. You're wasting your talent, training and sparring with guys like me, and you know it," Sergio said, as I moved around him, using my hand to encourage him to throw a few more punches. "You belong in the ring with that clown who won't stop babbling about you, Romeo."

"Stay focused," I demanded.

He threw a right hook that I easily dodged, and I jabbed at him a few times, hoping to make him mad enough to light a fire in him. He had a fight in a few weeks, and he was completely slacking.

"I need a break," he said, as he rested his hands on his knees to catch his breath.

"Serg, if you don't start pushing yourself, you're going to be in trouble when you get in that ring."

"I know. Tomorrow, all right?" He guzzled some water before lifting the ropes and exiting the ring.

I shook my head. I knew how to train for a fight. How to prepare and how to win. Sergio was going to get his ass kicked if he didn't start stepping it up.

I spent the next hour breaking up an argument between two boxers, training an up-and-coming fighter, Garcia, and then I made my way to my office to go over some paperwork before I called it a day.

I glanced down to see my phone light up with a ton of messages. That was never a good thing.

> **LINCOLN**
>
> This dude is fucking with the wrong guy. Call me and we can talk it through.

> **TIA**
>
> Just ignore him. He's trying to get under your skin. You don't need to prove anything to anyone.

My younger sister, Tia, hated that I was a boxer. She and my grandmother and my mom had all been thrilled when I'd stepped back from fighting to run the gym.

> **BRINKLEY**
>
> If you decide to fight this guy, I'll write a story that will have everyone in your corner. But I support whatever you want to do.

My brother's wife was a well-known sports reporter, and I knew that she and Lincoln always had my back.

The Ride or Die group chat was an ongoing string of text messages, and of course, they all had something to say.

> **RIVER**
>
> Please beat the fuck out of this asshole.

> **KINGSTON**
>
> Time to glove up, brother. We need to protect your pretty face, so let's start training now.

> **NASH**
>
> This guy could not be a bigger prick if he tried. We've got your back, whatever you decide.

RIVER

This motherfucker doesn't know who he's messing with. I'm ready to get in the ring and kick his ass if you don't.

HAYES

Let's burn that fucker down.

RIVER

I talked to everyone. Nash has Cutler covered. We're meeting at Whiskey Falls at 8:00 p.m. to talk this shit through. We've got you, Golden Boy.

I scrubbed a hand down my face. I didn't know what the fuck had happened in the last few hours, but it was obviously not good.

I opened my social media app to see that I'd been direct messaged by countless strangers. I opened the video of Leo Burns standing in front of the gym where he worked out in New York City, holding a fucking cat in his arms while his entourage surrounded him.

"Hey there. I wanted to introduce my new pet to everyone. This pussy right here is named Romeo. It just seemed fitting to go with that name, right?" He laughed, and his minions followed suit. And then he stared at the camera. *"Stop hiding, young Romeo. Can't use Daddy's death as an excuse forever. Time for a rematch. Or you can always just come out and admit to the world that you're just a big pussy. That works, too. I wonder what your famous brother will think of you being a coward?"* He winked just before the video ended.

Eight hundred and seventy-two thousand views in four hours.

I skimmed through the comments, and the reactions varied. Some people called him out for being an asshole. But some agreed with him that I should stop hiding.

My phone rang, and I saw my brother's name on the screen and answered. "Hey, Linc."

"Are you all right?"

"Yeah. I didn't have my phone on me while I was training, so I'm just seeing it now."

He let out a breath. "He's not going to back down, Romeo. He's got his sights set on you, and he's getting a lot of attention."

"I'm sorry he's dragging you into it."

"I don't give a shit about that. He's trying to get under your skin, and I'm guessing he's doing a good job, because he's getting under mine. I told you before, I'd be happy to go public and defend you. Put the asshole in his place."

"No. Don't do that. That's what he wants. To turn this into a big publicity stunt. They're offering me a lot of money to take the fight. The last offer came in at seven hundred and fifty grand just to show up and fight him. Winner gets two million dollars."

"Don't do it for the money. You know I've got you if you need anything." Lincoln was always offering to do things for me and Tia. Hell, he was covering the cost of our sister's schooling and housing, and I was grateful that he'd given her that opportunity. He wanted to give me money for a down payment on a house, but I was doing just fine on my own. I owned this gym, and it came with a small studio in the back. I appreciated the offer, but I didn't want a handout.

I didn't need it.

"Says the dude worth millions of dollars. It's a lot of money, Linc. I have to consider it when we're talking about that kind of cash. It could be a one-and-done. Use that money to expand the gym, help my mom and grandma out, buy a house on the lake, and tuck the rest away for now."

"The big question is, do you want to fight again?" he asked.

I scrubbed a hand over the back of my neck. "I thought I

was done with it. But I don't know… Maybe one more fight wouldn't be the worst thing. When will I ever have the opportunity to make that kind of money in just a few hours?"

"How long would it take you to prepare for a fight like this? He's been fighting these last few years while you've been out of the game. So he has experience on his side, and he must be decent if he had the belt before Gunner took it from him, right?"

"Yes. He's a cocky son of a bitch, but he's also a beast in the ring. It would take me a couple of months to get where I need to be. I also know that I'd be putting my mom and Mimi through it. And Tia will lose her shit if I agree to fight again."

"Take everyone else out of the equation. What do *you* want to do?"

"I don't want to get punched in the head for the rest of my life," I said, leaning back in the chair.

"Agreed. I don't want that for you either."

"But I wouldn't mind getting in the ring for one more fight, just to shut this fucker up and walk away with a lot of money. I just have to make sure I leave in one piece. If I train right, I think I could withstand his hits. But I'd definitely be taking a beating."

"Romeo, it's Brinkley," my sister-in-law said, as she must have taken the phone from Lincoln, which was not uncommon when we were talking. "I don't particularly like the thought of seeing you get punched in the head either. But if you take this fight as a onetime thing, I will talk to the magazine about doing a whole spread on you. We can make it clear that you are taking this one fight on, and you will be retiring for good afterward, not because you're scared— because you're smart. Let me tell your side of the story and get you some positive press. Hell, with the way you look, you'll probably get a bunch of endorsements out of this."

"It must run in the family, baby," Lincoln said, and I laughed.

"All right. I'll think about it. If I decide to do it, you can break the story, Brinks. Thanks for doing this for me. Let me sleep on it."

"We support you either way. I just want to shut that asshole down either way." Lincoln's voice was hard.

"Yeah. You and me both, brother."

I ended the call and finished up a few things at the gym before looking down to see a new text.

> **MOM**
>
> It's the end of January, and it's still snowing. <eye roll emoji> I'm ready to be done with the cold. Mimi and I want to watch a Hallmark movie and drink pumpkin chai lattes. Can you grab those drinks and drop them off for us?

Jesus. What was the deal with those fucking drinks? I wasn't in any hurry to go back over to the coffee shop after the last time I'd been there. I'd been a complete prick, and I'd like to keep it that way.

The Crawfords had fucked over me and River, and I didn't want anything to do with any of them. Even if Demi most likely didn't know about what happened, it was still her family.

It had surprised me that she'd appeared wounded by how rude I'd been, even if she'd tried to act unaffected. It wasn't like I'd ever been friendly to her or anyone in her family. But I also wasn't dying to go back and be an asshole again.

I groaned because I could never say no to my mom and Mimi.

> Fine. I'll drop them off in a little bit. But you need to buy some pumpkin tea bags, or whatever the hell is in there. I can't be going there every day.

MOM

Stop being a baby. You haven't been there in almost a week. I did give birth to you, remember? That entitles me to a lifetime of pumpkin chai lattes. I swear she puts something special in these drinks. Could you ask her if she adds cinnamon? I could try to make it here if I knew what was in it.

For fuck's sake. That would mean I'd have to speak to her. And I highly doubted she'd have anything to say to me after my last visit anyway.

You do remember that the Crawfords screwed over me and River, right? You're putting me in a bad situation.

MOM

Demi Crawford was young at the time and was not to blame for what happened. I raised you better than that, Romeo. We don't even know if the parents knew what happened. Should you be held accountable for the mistakes that your father made? Go get the pumpkin lattes and stop this nonsense. And find out what kind of magic she's putting in there for me.

I slipped on my coat and walked out to find the gym empty, minus Ray, who was mopping the floors.

"You out of here?" he asked.

"Yep. I'll see you tomorrow."

"Hey, Romeo," he called out.

I turned around to face him. "Yeah?"

"There's only one way to shut down a bully. You know that, right?"

I smirked because I already knew what he was going to say, but I liked to mess with him. "Ignore him?"

He barked out a laugh, and it echoed around the gym. "Nah. Punch him in the fucking face."

I shook my head and held up my hand. "I'll think about it."

I wanted to fight Leo, but I also knew that fighting wasn't my long game anymore. I'd been reading a lot about real estate and investments. A big chunk of money would allow me to fund a business like that, as well as help my family and secure my future. I knew if I trained hard, I could survive the wrath of Leo—at least, I hoped that was true. My height, my agility, and my youth played in my favor. He was a stocky dude, not very technical, but a scrapper with a badass right hook. Leo was a bit of a wild card at times. He was best known for knocking out his opponents quickly, and the dude could take a punch and bounce back, which had always impressed me.

I stepped outside to see there were barely a few flurries falling from the sky. It wasn't even February yet, so my mom knew we'd still see snow for a while longer. She'd lived in Magnolia Falls her entire life. But every year, she did this. Complained about the snow after the holidays passed, as if it hadn't been this way every year since she was a kid.

I walked next door and tugged the door open, seeing that Demi was behind the counter. The place was empty, as it would be closing up in about fifteen minutes. She looked up, and her green gaze locked with mine. She had a little spatter of freckles across her nose, brown hair cut just past her shoulders, and plump lips. She was fucking gorgeous.

Even if she is a Crawford.

She didn't greet me this time. Instead, she just raised a brow, as if she were waiting for me to act like a dick.

I cleared my throat as I stepped up to the counter. "Can I get two pumpkin chai lattes to go?"

She studied me before ringing up the order. "Eleven dollars even."

I set the cash in her hand this time and not on the counter. It had been an asshole move.

She dropped the money into the register and moved to make the drinks. I scrubbed a hand down the back of my neck because I knew she hated me, and she had every right to be giving me the silent treatment.

I actually preferred it, as making small talk with a Crawford was never a good idea.

"Can I ask you what's in the drink?"

"Do you think I'm going to poison you, Romeo?" Her tone was dry, and I kind of liked that she could dish out the attitude.

"I doubt it. I don't think you'd do well in prison, looking like that," I said, and I wanted to kick myself for the lame comeback. Even if it was true.

"Obviously, you're unaware that orange is my favorite color." She smirked, and it was cute as hell. I pushed the thought away.

"No one's favorite color is orange." I leaned over the counter when she turned around to fill the cups with hot water, and my eyes moved down her lean body and soft curves. Her jeans covered her tight little ass perfectly.

Snap the fuck out of it, dickhead.

It had been a while since I'd been laid, and clearly, I needed to find myself a woman. Maybe tonight at the bar I'd make that happen.

She turned around, lips pursed. "Shocker. You're wrong. *My* favorite color is orange. Maybe you shouldn't jump to conclusions about *everything*."

It was a dig. I'm sure she knew that I was being a prick because of who her family was. She probably didn't know the half of it. The real reason.

I didn't hate them because they were rich. I hated them because they were liars and entitled pricks.

It didn't mean that she was—but she was still one of them.

"All right. Your favorite color is orange. I got it. Can you tell me what you put in that drink? My mom is nagging me to find out."

She turned around and set the cups down on the counter in front of me. Her lips turned up in the corners, and her smile reached her eyes. "You want me to tell you all my secrets when you were a complete jerk the last time you came in here?"

"I do."

"Well, at least you aren't denying it."

"I don't lie."

Her gaze narrowed. "Neither do I. But I also don't appreciate someone being an asshole to me for no reason. You don't even know me."

"I know enough."

"Yet you came back a second time." She crossed her arms over her chest, which pushed her tits up the slightest bit. I could make them out perfectly in her white fitted turtleneck, which made it difficult not to stare. They weren't big, but they were perky and proportioned to her petite frame. Her nipples poked against the fabric, and I forced my eyes back up to meet her gaze.

My mouth watered at the thought of using my tongue to flick her hard peaks, and I wondered what her pretty pink nipples would taste like.

For fuck's sake. I'm losing my mind.

This girl's family nearly ruined my life. And it sure as hell caused a lot of heartache for my family.

"I came back a second time because my mother and my grandmother won't stop texting me about it."

"I'll tell you what… Next time you come in here, how about you lose the attitude, and I'll be happy to tell you the secret ingredient in my tea. Or you can have your mama call me here, and I'll tell her directly."

"You're serious?"

"Do I look like a joker to you?" She raised a brow, and her tongue poked against her cheek as she stared at me.

"You're not going to tell me?"

She pinched the tips of her thumb and pointer finger together and slowly ran them along her mouth, acting as if she were zipping her mouth closed.

Her lips were pursed, pink, and plump, and I wondered how they'd look wrapped around my cock.

Hey, I was a horny dude. Apparently, I could dislike someone and still be attracted to them.

I quickly grabbed the two cups off the counter and glared at her.

I was leaving here without the secret ingredient, and now I had a raging boner.

I definitely hated Demi Crawford a little more than I did when I first walked in here a few minutes ago.

"You're ridiculous," I said, turning toward the door.

"That's not the attitude that's going to get the recipe out of me. You better try again next time, Mr. Knight."

"Don't count on it," I grunted as I pushed the door open with my back and stepped outside.

Now, I was in a foul mood.

My mother would have to call to get the recipe because I was not coming back anytime soon.

four

. . .

Demi

I'D JUST LOCKED up for the day, and the business phone rang.

"Magnolia Beans, this is Demi."

"Hi, sweetheart. It's Valentina Knight again," she said with a chuckle.

It had been a few days since her jackass son had asked for the recipe for my pumpkin chai latte. She'd called the very next day, and I'd walked her through how to make it.

"Hey, Valentina. How did it go?"

"Well, it's fine, but it doesn't taste quite as good as yours. I did the cinnamon trick with the magical goodness you dropped off, but I think the latte part is where we failed. Mimi said it's not as frothy as yours."

I hopped up to sit on the counter and chuckled. "Well, I do have the fancy machine here, so that helps."

"Yours is definitely better, but making it here will hold us over between visits. I just wanted to call and thank you so much for dropping those things off for us. It's still delicious. My mom and I are going to bundle up tomorrow and stop by and see you," she said. Romeo's mother was much sweeter than her son. I knew they lived just two blocks away because

I'd taken her a few pumpkin chai tea bags, and I'd poured a little of my specialty cinnamon in a jar for her. She'd been kind on the phone, and I hadn't minded at all.

It was called being neighborly.

Unless your neighbor is a pompous bastard.

"Sounds good. I look forward to seeing you soon."

"Take care, sweetheart. And thanks again."

"Of course. Bye." I hopped down and turned out the lights before heading upstairs. It had been a long day and a long week, if I was being honest. I changed my clothes quickly, as I was going to my parents' house for dinner tonight. Slade had agreed for me to talk to them on his behalf, and I'd broach the conversation carefully. They didn't trust him, that much was clear, and mending this distance between them would not be easy. Somewhere along the way, they'd lost hope in their son. But he needed all of us on his team if he was going to beat this disease.

I pulled my gray sweater over my head and put on my favorite jeans and my tan boots. I slipped my coat on, as I'd definitely be going out to spend some time in the barn with Teacup. I'd taken her for a long ride last weekend, and I was happy to be home, where I could ride often again.

I slipped out the back door, since I didn't use the business entrance when the shop was closed. I cut down the alley and glanced over at Knockout gym, and I wondered if Romeo was still working because I could see the light coming from the windows. I shook it off and climbed into my car to make the short drive to my family's ranch.

We had several acres of land that backed up to the water, and it had always been my favorite place.

It was where I found peace and comfort, even in the darkness. My mom had never gone back on the boat since Slade's accident. She never went near the water, almost like she blamed the lake for everything that had gone wrong after.

But we'd grown up on the water. My brother taught me

every water sport there was. He'd always been so proud that I was a bit of a badass on water skis and a jet ski.

The memories always flooded when I was home, and with Slade showing up for a visit the other night, it felt like maybe things really were getting back on track.

Our family had always been close. My grandparents had a home on the same street. The two properties ran into one another, which meant I could ride for miles between the land shared by the two homes. My grandparents spent more time here now that Gramps had retired from politics. They'd be here tonight, and I was looking forward to seeing everyone. My grandparents were both on the same page as me when it came to Slade. They still had hope. Still wanted to believe he could come back to us. So I was grateful to have them here and hoped they'd back me up when my parents went on the defensive.

I stopped by the barn to check on Teacup and brushed her for a bit before heading out of the barn. I walked toward the house and breathed in the fresh smell of pine and balsam. The sky was starting to darken, and the glimmer of the water in the distance soothed my nerves. When I reached the house, I pulled the front door open.

"Hey, I'm home," I called out, hearing laughter come from the dining room as I kicked off my boots and hung my coat in the mudroom. Our house was large, too large for only two people to be living in, if you asked me. It was grand for a ranch house, as my mother loved interior design, and decorating was her passion. The dark wood floors ran throughout the home, with large beams on the ceiling and white shiplap accents and woodwork that stood out against the dark features. Family photos and endless floral arrangements were placed throughout the house. It took several people to keep this place up and running.

When I got to the kitchen, the smell of garlic and warm bread flooded my system, and I wrapped my arms around

Mariana as she stood at the stove. She'd worked for my family since I was a little girl, and she felt more like family to me than someone who actually worked here. I kissed her cheek, and she turned around and hugged me tight.

"Have I told you how happy I am that you're back home and here to stay?"

"Only a couple dozen times," I said, my voice teasing as I reached over to the counter and popped a cherry tomato into my mouth.

"They're all waiting for you in the dining room. Head on in there. I'll bring dinner in shortly."

"Okay. But I'll eat dessert in here so you can fill me on what Steven and Aubrey are up to." Her kids were a little older than me, and we'd always been close.

"Perfect."

I made my way to the dining room, making my rounds and giving everyone a hug. I settled in the chair beside my grandmother, and they all proceeded to fire off endless questions about the coffee shop. I answered each one and was relieved when Mariana brought dinner in, and the interrogation came to an end.

"I like that you invested in a business for yourself, as well as added an apartment upstairs. That was a smart move from an investment perspective," Gramps said before twirling the spaghetti around his fork and popping it into his mouth.

"Thanks. I think it's going well, so I can't complain."

"I just don't love that you are living above the business. And it's such a small space," Mom said.

"She's young. She doesn't need a lot of space." Grammie winked at me. "And it's so charming. She really put her own touch on it."

"Got that right, Grammie. It's perfect for me. And I love it there." I took a sip of water and then sucked in a breath. "I actually had a visitor the other day."

"It wasn't Ronny, was it?" my father asked, his tone a bit

harsh. Everyone turned to look at him with surprise. I'd confided in my father about what had happened with Ronny Waterstone a few months ago, and he'd asked me to keep it quiet because he'd handled the situation. Our families were very intertwined, as Ronny's father was my dad's business partner, and our grandparents had been friends since they were young. But Ronny knew better than to come near me after what had happened, or the police would definitely be called. If he wanted to keep things quiet, he'd stay away.

"Is something going on with Ronny? You all went to college together. Aren't you two friends? I always thought he was sweet on you," Gramps said.

Nothing about what he did was sweet.

"He's not my type, and we aren't friends." I shrugged. I met my father's gaze and cleared my throat. "Anyway, it wasn't Ronny who came to see me. It was actually Slade. He came to town, and he wanted to see the coffee shop and my apartment."

The table grew silent, and I glanced at Gramps, waiting for him to jump in, but my father reacted first.

"What the hell is he doing here in town? He just got out of rehab, and we paid for an apartment in Boston for him for the next six months. That was the deal. Finish the program and successfully live a clean life for six months, and then we'd talk about bringing him home. But, of course, he broke the agreement." My father reached for the napkin in his lap and wiped his mouth. His jaw ticked, and I noted the way his shoulders tensed at just the mention of Slade.

"He's living across the country, and he misses his family. He just came for the weekend. He has a job back in Boston, and he starts work this week. I'd told him about my opening, and he wanted to surprise me. It was sweet, and he seemed like the old Slade. He wants to come visit again soon, and I said that I'd speak to you about it. I don't think the six-month rule makes any sense. He completed the program. He misses his family. He misses you guys," I said, my eyes bouncing between my mom and my dad. They hadn't visited him once in rehab this last time. They'd shut him out completely, and only my grandfather and I had gone to see Slade during this last stint in Boston.

"Were you alone with him?" Dad's voice was harder than I'd heard it in a very long time.

"Was I alone with my brother in my apartment? Are you serious? Of course, I was. I'm not afraid of Slade, but apparently, you two are." I leaned back in my chair and folded my arms over my chest. I hated that our family was so divided now.

Gramps cleared his throat. "Let's all relax. There are things that have happened that you aren't aware of, Demi. It's not my story to tell, but Slade has caused this family a lot of pain, and he'll need to earn your parents' trust back. I can tell you this… they've been in his corner for a lot longer than many parents would have been. He's depleted his trust fund, and he's hurt his family tremendously over the last several years."

They were all in on some big secret that had gone down while I was away at school. But for whatever reason, they hadn't shared it with me. But something had changed the last time my brother saw my parents.

"And he'll work hard to support himself now. He's an addict. It's not his fault. He's sick," I said, as a lump formed in my throat. I was tired of defending Slade. I wished he'd prove me right one of these times. How many times had I insisted he was better and then he'd be gone just as fast as he'd returned?

"At some point, he has to take responsibility, Demi. He's an addict, and we've put him through rehabilitation eight times. We've paid for the best programs money can buy. But he's done some serious damage to this family, and I'm not quick to believe him anymore." My mom's eyes watered, and I hated that I'd upset her by talking about him. But I needed to try because she missed Slade, too.

We all did.

"I totally agree. But having our support will help with his recovery."

"He has our financial support. He'll have to earn back the rest over time." My father tossed his napkin on the table as if the conversation had completely ruined his appetite. "We've heard you out, and we'll take it into consideration. And now I'm going to ask you for one favor."

"Okay," I said, swallowing past the gigantic lump in my throat.

"I don't want you to meet with Slade alone. It's not safe, regardless of what you believe. If he reaches out, you let us know, and we'll arrange to be there with you."

It wasn't perfect, but it also wasn't the worst answer. He agreed to see Slade at some point. That was progress.

"I can do that. Maybe we can all have dinner when he visits next."

Dad and Mom shared a look again. I couldn't read what was happening there, but my mother's gaze looked almost haunted. I wondered if there'd ever be a time when talking about my brother wasn't so heavy.

"Let's see how he does with his new job and take it from there." Mom sighed. "How about we talk about the white party? The date is on the calendar for the last weekend in May."

"Oh, it's my favorite time of year," Grammie said.

The Magnolia Falls White Party was an event in town hosted by my family, and it had been going on for as long as I could remember. My grandmother and my mother planned the epic spring celebration and charity event, and everyone in town attended. It was something that locals looked forward to all year, and it took place out on our ranch.

My mom spent months preparing, and each year, it grew even larger and grander.

"I'm going to have a few local bands perform this year, which will be fun for all the young people in town." She chuckled.

"I'm happy I'm living here this year so I can help out wherever you need me," I said.

"Absolutely. I'm so glad I'll have you here to help."

"It sure is nice having our girl back in town," Gramps said.

It was great to be back home. Now, I just had to find a way to repair my family.

We spent the next hour talking about the white party, and my dad and my grandfather talked about an investment that Patrick Waterstone had brought to them.

Even the mention of the Waterstones made me cringe.

Patrick was my father's business partner, and his father was a senator for the state of California. He and my grandfather had been political allies for the two terms my grandfather served as governor.

The connection ran deep. Two political families who'd known one another for many years and invested in several businesses together.

The Waterstones had a summer home here, and I hoped like hell that Ronny wouldn't be visiting. He hadn't come here often once we started college, and if he was smart, he'd keep it that way.

I hugged everyone goodbye and let my parents know that I would be coming by early in the morning to ride Teacup before I opened the shop. I made my way outside in the cool, crisp air and glanced down to see a text from my brother.

SLADE

Did you talk to them?

> Yes. It's going to take time, but they miss you. Just work hard and prove you can stay clean for a few weeks, and then we'll see if we can set up a dinner when you come visit next.

SLADE

> Love you, D. I can do that. It's just hard because I'm making shit money right now, and I'm working hard to get back on my feet.

I chewed my thumbnail as I settled into the driver's seat of my car and buckled my seat belt.

> Do you need money?

SLADE

> If you could slip me some cash, just so I can buy some clothes and not feel like a complete loser, that would help. A couple thousand bucks would be amazing.

This was not out of character for Slade. He'd always had rich taste, and we'd joked about his outrageous spending habits for as long as I could remember. But then prescription drugs became his first love. I guess I should be grateful that he was interested in clothes and worrying about how he looked again. But after all he'd gone through, I'd expected him to be a bit humbled. But that wasn't really Slade's style.

> Money is a little tight for me as I've put everything into the business. But I could send you a couple hundred dollars to help you get on your feet. I'm sure Gramps would help you out, too.

SLADE

Gramps said he isn't giving me a dime until I'm clean for six months. Fuck, D. It's hard to fight for something when no one believes in you. You're the only one left in my corner now.

> You know I always will be. What happened the last time you saw Mom and Dad? They seem different now.

SLADE

I was fucked-up, and I guess I scared them because I didn't tell them I was coming over first. I didn't know they needed a warning before getting a visit from their son. It's my own fucking house.

Nothing about it added up. It pissed me off that they were all keeping it from me.

> I know when you're lying, Slade. We both know it was more than that.

SLADE

I can't do this right now. I'm taking it one day at a time, and I don't want to look back. Can we just try to move forward?

> Of course. I want that, too.

SLADE

So, you'll Venmo me the cash so I can get a decent meal instead of eating canned food?

> Yes, Princess. I'll do it as soon as I get home. Give me fifteen minutes.

SLADE

Love you, sis.

Love you.

I started up the car and made my way around the circular driveway before heading toward town. I turned down the alley and parked behind the coffee shop. I pulled out my keys, stepped out of my car, and headed for the back door that led to my apartment. The sound of a door slamming behind me had me turning on my heels. I glanced over to see Romeo Knight locking up the gym. His gaze met mine, and for whatever reason, I held up my hand, waved, and said hello. He shoved his hands into his pockets, and the light above the building shone down, creating a spotlight on him.

He was tall with broad shoulders and muscular arms. His dark, wavy hair fell over his forehead, and his chiseled jaw clenched as he looked at me.

"Are you not going to say hello back? We are neighbors, after all," I huffed as I stared at him.

"Hey," he said, with no emotion in his voice.

"Was that so difficult?" I asked.

"Get inside. You shouldn't be out here alone this late."

"It's nine o'clock at night, and we're in Magnolia Falls. Are you serious?" I laughed.

He glared. "Just get the hell inside and lock up."

My eyes widened, and I wanted to argue, but I was exhausted from a long day of work, attempting to repair my family, and now my rude neighbor thought he could boss me around.

"I'm fairly certain that *you* are the worst person I'll run into out here," I hissed, before pulling the door open and then slamming it closed.

I didn't know why I let him get to me every time I saw him.

But I also didn't know why I was disappointed that I hadn't seen him in a few days.

Nothing about Romeo Knight made sense.

five

. . .

Romeo

IT HAD BEEN A FUCKING WEEK. Leo had upped his game by going on every major network that was willing to allow him to blast his message on every sports program and all over social media. The dude had a wide reach, and I'd heard about it everywhere I went.

My brother, Lincoln, his wife, Brinkley, and River had all met me at the gym today so we could come up with a plan. After a lot of thought, I'd made my decision to take the fight. At the end of the day, it was an opportunity that I couldn't pass up. I'd need someone to negotiate the terms on my behalf and I was thankful that River was an attorney. This wasn't the first time his career choice had come in handy for our group of friends.

But everything about this fight was different.

My past fights weren't for big payouts, or purses in boxer lingo. Hell, this fight probably shouldn't be because I hadn't fought in a few years. But Leo was a big name in the boxing world, and for whatever fucked-up reason, he'd pulled me into this three-ring circus.

River would handle the contract for me, and Brinkley would break the story, as her magazine had agreed to let her interview me. She'd break the news this week and publish her interview with me next month.

This was all really happening.

I still couldn't wrap my head around it.

"You sure you want to do this?" Lincoln asked. "This is your last chance to back out."

"I don't want to be in the middle of this shit show, but I don't see a way out. I'm happy to fight; I would just prefer to fight someone who didn't want the whole world watching."

Lincoln smirked. "You're already in it, brother. I see your face on my screen every time I look at my phone now. This guy is not going away. I don't give a shit about any of the media stuff; I just need to know that you won't get hurt."

"I start training full time this week. I've got a long way to go before I step into that ring."

"We're asking for the fight to be in May. It'll give him three solid months to prepare. Leo is so desperate to fight Romeo that I think we can call the shots. I'm also increasing the terms. I'm asking for a million dollars for showing up. Three million if you beat the fucker. I meet with their legal team in an hour, so we should know by the end of the day if this is happening," River said. I'd intentionally picked early May because I knew that I'd need that long if I wanted to be in top shape. It would mean long days in the gym and grueling workouts. No booze. No partying. A strict diet. The whole nine yards. If I was doing this, I was going all in.

Lincoln would also be in his off-season, and he wanted to be ringside with me. It was important to him that he be there, and it was important to me to have him in my corner.

"You think they'll go for that?" I asked.

"I think they'd do just about anything to get you in the ring at this point. I'll negotiate the contract and make sure it works in your favor, or we walk," he said.

I still couldn't wrap my head around that kind of money. I

was a no-name a few weeks ago, but Leo had put my name in the media, and now it was all anyone was talking about.

"I'll make the announcement as soon as they accept the terms," Brinkley said. "And I'll fly back here next week to shadow you on your workouts and ask you all the burning questions everyone wants to know."

Lincoln barked out a laugh as he elbowed me. "He'll love that."

"Well, he loves me, so he'll deal with it. We need to show the world who Romeo is. They're going to fall in love with you, just like we did."

"Easy now." River quirked a brow. "That's a bit much. I tolerate him at best."

"Yeah, Romeo might need to lose a little of that broody-asshole attitude." Lincoln smirked at me.

"Takes one to know one," Brinkley said as she leaned over and kissed my brother's cheek before turning her attention back to me. "You're fine. Be yourself. When people try to put on a show, it doesn't work. Leo looks like an asshole, so it won't be hard to be the good guy."

"I don't give a shit about being the good guy. I just want to shut this guy up, put my head down, and do the work, then get in the ring and go the distance. And if I can avoid getting my head smashed in, that would be even better."

"You've got this. And we'll all be right there supporting you, all right?" my brother said.

I nodded. Was I actually agreeing to this? To putting my life under a microscope for the next three months? I hadn't told my mother, my grandmother, or my sister that I'd made my decision yet. They were all against it, and this wouldn't go over well. I was waiting to see if Leo's camp would accept the terms first, to get everyone on the same page before I sat down to talk to them.

"I know it." I clapped Lincoln on the shoulder and hugged them both goodbye. They were heading back to Cottonwood

Cove, and I was happy they'd come to talk through all of this with me.

After they left and River went back to his office to make the call, I spent the next few hours watching films of Leo's most recent fights. I took notes on his right hook and the way that he was consistently tired by round eight on the rare fights where he hadn't knocked his opponents out early on. My first step would be not going down in the first three rounds, which was what happened in most of his fights. The longer I stayed on my feet, the better. The fight would be twelve rounds, three minutes each round. Thirty-six minutes of suffering if I could go the distance. Leo could take a hit. The dude wasn't as fast as me, but he was built like a tank, and he could weather a good beating. I had stamina on my side, and if I trained right, I could go twelve rounds in a fight—but I'd never fought anyone of Leo's caliber or strength.

I had a lot of training to do, and I'd be preparing for the fight of my life. Once River negotiated terms with Leo's team, they'd speak to the promoters about the location, the date, and the details.

The negotiations could go on for hours or even days. I found it hard to believe they'd agree to what River was asking for, considering I hadn't fought in a few years. Most people would guess I'd go down in round one, which wouldn't make for a good show. But maybe no one cared about the show.

After all, it was the Leo show when he fought.

No one knew much about me other than I'd fought one professional fight, my father had collapsed ringside at my second fight, and I'd walked away from the sport.

They didn't know that this would become my priority.

My soul purpose.

I couldn't control what Leo did in that ring, but I could control what I did to prepare for it.

And I would go into that fight in the best shape of my life and put up the best fight possible.

That much I was certain of.

My phone rang, and I saw River's face on the screen.

"How'd it go?" I asked.

"They agreed to everything, brother. They'll meet with the promoters tomorrow, but they feel confident they'll go for it. They need someone to have that belt with Gunner being out of the game, and Leo has brought a shit ton of attention to this fight already."

"All right. Looks like we're doing this."

"It sure as fuck does. Buckle up, Golden Boy. Training starts now."

I nodded, even though he couldn't see me. "Yep. I'll talk to you tomorrow."

I ended the call and called Joey, my trainer, and gave him an update. I had things lined up and ready to go so that we could start once this was officially happening.

It was late, and the gym was dark now. I locked up and made my way outside before the sound of shouting had me turning quickly to see a guy run out of the front door of the coffee shop. He had a mask over his face, and I shouted for him to stop, which, of course, he didn't do. He ran down the alley, and I had to make a quick decision if I should follow him or make sure no one inside was hurt.

I knew Demi Crawford lived there, and my instinct had me sprinting toward the entrance of Magnolia Beans. My feet crunched over the glass from where he'd obviously shattered the front door. I heard a whimper from inside but couldn't see anything and climbed through the opening.

"Hello!" I shouted. "Demi, are you in here?"

More whimpering sounded as I reached for the light and flipped the switch, allowing me to see her sitting on the floor with her back against the counter. She was wearing a T-shirt with nothing else, and her bare legs were folded in front of her. Her eyes were puffy, and she quickly swiped away the tears. I bent down to meet her gaze.

"Are you hurt?" I asked, reaching for my phone to call the police.

"I'm not hurt. Please put your phone away." Her voice was quiet, and it was impossible to miss the devastation in her tone.

"We need to call the police. That dude just took off down the alley." I reached for her hand and helped pull her to her feet.

"Romeo. Put your phone away," she commanded, catching me by surprise. Her hand was bleeding, and I set my phone on the counter before turning around to search for a paper towel.

"You're fucking bleeding, and your business just got broken into. Why the fuck are we not calling the police?" I wrapped my hand around her wrist and pulled her over to the sink. Cold water poured over the palm of her hand, and I used my thumb to see how deep the cut was.

"It's just from a piece of glass that made its way over here. No one hurt me."

What the fuck was her deal? She'd just been robbed, and she wasn't pissed or scared? I mean, she acted like her feelings were hurt, but that wasn't a logical reaction after some dude broke into your business and could have done whatever the fuck he wanted to do to her.

I turned off the water and dried off her wound before holding her hand close to me and pulling a sliver of glass out of her palm. She didn't even wince. Hell, when I had to pull a splinter out of Kingston's foot last summer down by the lake, the dude had acted like a theatrical little bitch.

But this girl was stoic as hell.

"You've got two minutes to tell me why we aren't calling the police, or I'm making the call." I looked up to see a first aid box on the wall and pulled it down. I took out the bottle of wound wash and sprayed it over her cut before using the gauze to wrap it up. My gaze met hers, and I raised a brow. "You're down to one minute."

She just stared at me. Eyes hard. I turned and reached for my phone.

"Stop. Please don't call the police. I know who it was."

"You know who robbed you?"

"I do."

"Well, that makes things really easy for the police officers if they know who they're looking for."

A tear ran down her cheek, and for whatever fucking reason, my chest squeezed.

Her eyes were tired, and I could see the sadness there, and it did something to me.

I scrubbed a hand down my face and reached for a tissue and handed it to her.

"I won't tell them who it was, so there's no need to call," she whispered.

This shit was pissing me off. Even if she was trying to pretend that she wasn't hurt or upset, I wasn't okay with letting some fucker get away with shattering her window and breaking into the place.

"Where the fuck is your alarm, anyway? Are you telling me you don't have one, and you live above this fucking coffee shop?"

She glared at me. "I have a fucking alarm, Romeo. I turned it off. I told you that I knew who it was, so I obviously wasn't scared."

"You turned off the alarm?" I repeated her words, my tone dry and laced with irritation.

"Did I stutter?" She pushed her shoulders back and tipped up her chin.

Like I was the fucking enemy.

"I don't know what the fuck is going on here. I'm just the dude who came over here to make sure you weren't beaten up or—" I shook my head with frustration. "Or violated or something."

Her eyes widened. "You thought I was violated?"

"Is this a fucking joke to you? Listen, I have a business next door. I'm not okay with some fucking asshole breaking into buildings on our street and not reporting it. I don't have the kind of money that you have, so I don't have some fancy alarm to warn me that someone is breaking in. And I sure as shit am not okay with the fact that you turned off the alarm and let him run off with God knows how much money, nor do I think any of the businesses on this street will be okay when I let them know what went down here tonight." I crossed my arms over my chest. I had no intention of telling any other business owners, because I wasn't a social guy, and I didn't get involved in other people's business.

But she was pissing me the fuck off.

Her bottom lip trembled, and I had to look away because I preferred when she was holding her own against me, not looking like a damsel in distress with her pouty fucking lips and those sexy-as-shit doe eyes of hers. Of course, my gaze landed on her bare legs that I couldn't seem to turn away from.

"He won't break into any other businesses. Please, don't say anything. Can't we just say that it was a teenager who threw a rock through my door? I'll pay for the glass, and no one needs to know anything more. I wouldn't be okay with it if I thought he'd do this to anyone else. Trust me, he won't. I'm not a monster." She swiped at her tears, and I reached for some more tissue and handed it to her.

Fuck me. I didn't need this shit. Not to mention the fact that she was a fucking Crawford, and now I was mixed up in her shitstorm.

"You have two options, and you aren't going to like either of them."

"You really love this, don't you? Sticking it to me when you don't even know why you hate me."

"Funny you should say that, because right now, I hate you for allowing some fucker to break into your place and letting him get away with it. That's not how this works. So, we either call the police and report this, or you tell me who it was, and I'll decide if we should call the police."

"You're such a power-hungry asshole," she said, as she paced in a little circle in front of me. When she came to a stop and crossed her arms over her chest, her T-shirt pulled up the slightest bit, exposing more of her lean, tanned thighs. I felt like a creep as my eyes climbed her legs once again and moved slowly up her body before her gaze locked with mine.

"Call me what you want. That's the deal."

"And if I don't take either option?"

"Then I call the police, and I tell them that you let the guy run off and refused to report it. You know how the people in Magnolia Falls are when it comes to crime. This will be the talk of the town. No one's coming to get a coffee from a business owner who supports criminal behavior." I was being a dick now, and it was difficult not to laugh at the way she was gaping at me.

She sighed. Her eyes fell to my mouth for a moment before they flickered back up to meet mine. And then she spoke, her voice low. "It was my brother."

"Slade? I thought he was in some fancy rehab somewhere. He's here, in Magnolia Falls?"

"He's not supposed to be. I thought he was in Boston. But he never left after I saw him last week. He's using again," she said, her words shaking as the tears rolled faster down her cheeks. Hell, I knew this kind of pain. I'd grown up with an addict. I'd watched what it did to my mother and my sister. I knew what it was like to love someone who chose addiction over family. "I'm asking you not to report it, Romeo. My family has been through a lot. My parents don't know he's here right now. He said he needed the money to get back to Boston, and he'd go back into the program. He had a relapse."

"You buy that?" I asked. I hated the dude. But I could see that she loved him, because it was impossible to miss the pain written all over her face.

It was a pain that was familiar to me.

"I don't know the answer to that. But the minute I give up on him, he'll have no one. He broke in to steal money because he was too ashamed to tell me that he was using again."

"He had a mask on when he ran down the alley. How do you know it was him?"

"Because he pulled it off and told me to go back upstairs. And when I screamed at him, he admitted he needed the money to get back to rehab. So, I opened the register and threw it at him. He pulled his mask back into place and took off with the money."

I squeezed the back of my neck because I didn't know what the hell to do with this information. River would love it, because he'd love to see that fucker get charged with something after all the shit he'd pulled, and honestly, so would I.

But seeing her so tormented and knowing what that felt like had me wavering.

"All right. I won't say anything. But next time this happens, you'd be wise to stay in your apartment with the door locked and let the alarm go off. If he can't get in and out of here before the cops come, then he's a shit fucking criminal because you know how fucking slow they are," I said. Her lips twitched a bit, and I could tell she was fighting a smile. "Demi, if he's using, he's dangerous. Addiction always wins when it's coursing through someone's veins."

I knew he had an opioid problem. Hell, the whole town knew. The Crawfords did their best to keep the issue hidden, but he'd had a reputation all over town for being high more often than not.

"Thank you. You don't have to stay. I'm fine now." She tugged at the hem of her T-shirt as if she just realized that it was all that she had on.

I nodded. "I'll wait. Are you going to head to your parents' house?"

"No. I'm staying here."

"The fuck you are."

And just like that, we were going at it again.

She may have won the first battle, but she wouldn't win this one.

six

· · ·

Demi

POMPOUS. Arrogant. Self-righteous.

Romeo Knight was an asshole.

And he held all the power right now because all he had to do was open his mouth. Make one call. Tell his friends. And this would be all over town by lunch tomorrow.

I had to put my trust in a guy who couldn't stand me.

"Excuse me? You think you can tell me where I'm sleeping?"

"The front door is smashed in. I agreed to your ridiculous plan of not telling anyone what happened and protecting your scumbag brother. Not because he deserves it, but because you do."

I'm offended and touched at the same time.

I shook my head and moved closer, tipping my chin up to meet his dark, stormy gaze. The man always looked so pissed off at the world, and now he was judging me?

"If I go to my parents' house, they'll find out what happened. Hell, if I go to a hotel or a friend's house, they'll find out. You know how this town is." I shrugged. "I'll wait until morning, and I'll say someone must have thrown a rock through the window. I'll get the glass company out here first thing tomorrow."

"And you think you're going to sleep here, while anyone can just walk in?"

"You seem to have all the answers. What is it that you think I should do, ole wise one?"

"Personally, I think you should report his ass and tell the police. Tell your parents that the fucker robbed you. That's what I think." He held his hands up when I started to speak. "But I know you aren't going to do that. And for whatever fucking reason, I've agreed to go along with your fucked-up plan. But you're not sleeping here."

Loud laughter escaped my lips. I was on edge. My brother had, in truth, scared the hell out of me. His eyes were wild, and he looked at me like he didn't know me. It had been terrifying. But tomorrow, I'd find him, call the program, and help get him back to Boston. The whole thing had been a bit more dramatic than I'd let on. But Romeo was acting like a righteous prick at the moment, so I was trying to keep things as tame as possible.

"And where, exactly, do you think I'm sleeping?"

He glanced around, taking in all the broken glass, and he cursed under his breath. "You can sleep at my place. It's just behind the gym."

Well, this is unexpected.

"You want me to sleep at your place? You better not get any creepy ideas. I'm not sleeping with you to keep my secret." I raised a brow, my chest rising and falling faster now. He may be an arrogant prick, but he was the best-looking guy I'd ever laid eyes on.

A wicked grin spread across his face. "Don't get excited, Princess. You're the last girl I'd sleep with. You're a Crawford, after all."

I didn't want to sleep with him.

I had no interest in him.

So what if he was ridiculously good-looking?

I couldn't stand the guy.

But hearing those words hit me hard.

Being hated for your last name. Being called *Princess* because you have a wealthy family was *old fucking news*. I'd worked hard my entire life, but people made judgments about me before they even knew me, and I was sick of it.

And saying that I was the last girl he'd ever want to sleep with?

That was low, even for him.

But I was too tired to be hurt or angry or strong at the moment.

Everything was hitting me all at once, and before I knew what was happening, my hands covered my face and hysteria left my lips.

I am ugly crying in front of the sexiest guy in town—who I also despise.

And I couldn't stop if I wanted to.

Two strong arms wrapped around me, and I wailed and cried against Romeo's chest.

I didn't care how weak I looked at that moment. I'd get my mojo back tomorrow. But tonight, I'd had enough.

And he just held me there.

I wanted to hate him, but this was the first time since that alarm went off that I actually felt safe.

I cried for what felt like hours but was probably more like ten minutes. Which was a pretty damn long time to cry in the arms of your nemesis.

My tears slowed. The lump in my throat eased.

I was taking deep breaths to calm myself, and I tipped my head back to look at him.

"Sorry about that. It's just been a bad night." I could hear the exhaustion in my voice.

"I was being a dick," he said, the corners of his lips turning up the slightest bit. "You're not the last girl I'd sleep with. I mean, Midge Longhorn scares the shit out of me. She's definitely at the top of the *no-fuck zone*."

Midge owned the Golden Goose and was a terrifying woman who also happened to be in her mid-sixties. She'd snap at customers and had the worst case of resting bitch face I'd ever seen. She'd gone through three divorces, and she didn't hide her disdain for people well.

"I'm flattered. Don't worry, Romeo. No one wants to sleep with you here. If you were the last guy on Earth, I'd take a vow of celibacy." It was the best I could do in my current state.

My wittiness wasn't on par. I'd just survived a devastating encounter with my brother, I'd had to put my trust in a person who despised me, and I was standing barefoot in a T-shirt that barely covered my ass.

Witty comebacks were low on the priority list at the moment.

But his tongue swiped out and ran along his bottom lip, and I squeezed my thighs together as hard as I could, because I was suddenly remembering that it had been a long time since I'd had sex.

Which should be the last thing I was thinking about right now.

"A vow of celibacy, huh?"

"What can I say? You're not my type."

He smirked. The cocky bastard. "Go get dressed. We're not walking out the door with you in only a T-shirt."

"Such a gentleman." I backed away from him, careful not to step on any glass, and ran upstairs to throw on some sweats and slip on my tennis shoes. I pulled my coat on because it was freezing outside and came down the steps to find Romeo duct-taping black trash bags over the shattered door. All the glass had been swept into a pile in the corner.

He looked up, eyes perusing me from head to toe, just like he'd done earlier. For a man who claimed he wasn't interested, he sure didn't look at me like I was the last woman on Earth that he was attracted to.

But that didn't matter at the moment.

He'd agreed to keep my secret, and he'd offered me a place to stay.

"Can you lock your apartment so that if anyone gets in here, they can't break into your place?"

"Yeah. It's double bolted."

"Do you have any money in the register or in a safe?"

"No. He took everything from the register, and I did a bank run earlier today, so there's nothing here." There was that lump again. I'd have to go to the bank first thing in the morning and pull out some cash to have in the register tomorrow. On top of the cost of the door, it was going to be a bad hit.

We'd just opened, so I'd invested a lot into the kitchen appliances and stocking up on supplies. Money was lean at the moment.

Obviously, I had a safety net. My family would always help me.

But I was not going to tell them that I'd been robbed. My father would know immediately that it was Slade.

I now felt pretty confident about what had happened with my brother and my parents. If Slade had behaved that night at the house the way he had here tonight, I understood why they were cautious.

Fearful, even.

So, I clearly couldn't tell them what happened, or I'd never repair my family.

A teenager throwing a rock through the window was an easier sell.

"Before you freak out, I called my buddy, Brett Rogers." He held his hands up to stop me from losing my shit, because Brett Rogers was a cop. "Relax. He's a friend. It will look more suspicious that you didn't call the cops when it happened. I told him that I was walking home right as the alarm had gone off, so that way, he can write it up, and there won't be any questions tomorrow. He'll be here in five minutes, and then you can deal with the door in the morning."

"Good thinking. Of course, I'd call if the door got smashed by teenagers. Thank you."

Brett Rogers arrived and wrote up a quick police report. Romeo surprised me when he told him that he'd come out of the gym just as a couple of teenagers ran off, laughing down the alley.

The officer didn't question anything about our stories, and he told me it wasn't safe to stay here tonight. I'd made it clear that I would not be staying here, but thankfully, he didn't question where I was going.

I'd come back in the morning to deal with this mess.

We said goodnight after he ran caution tape all over the front door and said he'd have a car parked out front so we wouldn't risk anyone else vandalizing the place tonight.

"Ready?" Romeo said, and his hand found the small of my back while we stepped out the back door. I bolted all three locks, which made him laugh, considering the front door was covered with a plastic bag.

"Thanks for that," I said, keeping my voice low. "And for letting me stay at your place."

"What am I going to do? Let you sleep in the alley? I'm not a complete dick."

"Is that your story?" I said, my voice all tease.

We walked a few paces across the alley to his house, which sat right behind the gym. He pushed the door open, and I took in the space. It was small but very cool. The ceilings were vaulted, with raw wood beams forming a peak at the top. Cement floors ran throughout the studio space. There was a modern kitchen in the center, with a couch on one side and a bed on the other. It reminded me of a loft that a friend of mine had in the city.

"I can sleep on the couch," I said, clearing my throat, because we were in a very small space now. I'd always had a keen sense of smell, and suddenly, the scent of cedar and sage was flooding my senses. Like he'd bottled up manly swagger and doused himself in it.

He chuckled. "You can take the bed. I've got a rollaway that I keep here."

He moved across the room, opened the double doors of what appeared to be a closet, and pulled out a twin-size bed, which was on wheels and standing straight up. He moved it near the couch and away from his bed. Thank freaking God for small blessings because sleeping near this man was going to be torture.

Even if I claimed I'd choose celibacy over a night with him, I was fully just trying to save my dignity when I said that.

I imagined sex with Romeo Knight was probably like the kind of sex I read about in romance books. I was an avid reader, and I lived vicariously through the many heroines' sex lives I'd read about over the years. I'd personally never found sex to be all that memorable. But I would bet my life that this man knew how to please a woman.

He dropped the bed down and then went to the closet and pulled out some sheets and a blanket and pillow, as if this was something he did all the time. I moved closer and took one end of the sheet, helping him make up the bed.

"I'll take the cot because I don't think you'd fit on it anyway," I said, trying to hide my smile. "Do you have a lot of visitors who sleep in their own beds?"

"One of my best friends, Nash, has a little boy named Cutler, and he likes to have a sleepover here once a month, sometimes more if Nash needs a break. He's raising him by himself."

"I know Nash. He and Kingston worked on my renovation. They're both nice."

He raised a brow as he shook the blanket out and tucked it beneath the mattress. He was full of surprises. I wouldn't have guessed him to be such a proper bedmaker. "I don't know that anyone would describe them as nice."

"Well, they were nice to me."

"That means they were probably hitting on you, the dickheads." He tossed a pillow at the head of the bed.

"It happens occasionally. Even if I'm the last person you'd be attracted to, not everyone finds me to be hideous."

He stared at me for the longest time. "I don't think anyone could find you hideous, Demi. Your looks have nothing to do with why someone wouldn't be hitting on you, but you know that, don't you?"

My cheeks heated at the intensity of his stare. "I don't know another reason someone would feel that way."

"You're a smart girl. I'm sure you can figure it out." He turned away, pointing toward a door. "Bathroom's in there. If you're hungry, I've got some leftover pizza in the fridge."

"Thank you. I'm okay. I'll just go to sleep if that's fine with you."

"Yeah. It's late. I'm ready to crash, too." He moved toward his bed and tugged the sweater over his head, and my mouth went dry. His back was chiseled perfection. Damn, was this what boxers looked like? Cut and toned, almost like someone had sculpted him from stone. All hard edges and defined lines. Before I could even process what was happening, he kicked off his shoes and dropped his jeans to the floor, standing there in a pair of black fitted boxer briefs.

Holy freaking hotness.

Strong thighs, a lean, tapered waist, and a perfectly hard ass. I hadn't seen the other side of him yet, but I couldn't look away. When he turned around slowly, I had no shame in my game as my eyes perused down his entire body. Dark ink on his right arm and his left thigh had his last name written across it. A six-pack that looked like something you'd see photoshopped in a sports magazine. He had a deep V that led down to a light layering of hair, and I stood stunned when I realized I was staring at the outline of his erection. When I finally forced myself to look up, I met his dark gaze, watching me with a sexy smirk on his face.

"Is this the first time you've seen a man in his boxers?" His voice was low and deep and sexy.

"Those aren't boxers. Those are briefs."

"I guess you'd know since you've been staring at my dick for a ridiculously long time."

"I have not!" I hissed, before quickly whipping around and kicking off my shoes. I climbed beneath the blanket, fully clothed and completely mortified.

And awkwardly turned on.

Because he was right—I was staring at his package.

He just chuckled before the lights were turned off and the room was dark.

seven

. . .

Romeo

NOW I COULDN'T FUCKING sleep because the smell of strawberries and coconut was wafting around my room, and after having her stare at my dick for a good thirty seconds, I was hard as a rock. And it wasn't like I could relieve myself with her sleeping ten feet away from me.

A fucking Crawford was sleeping in my house.

The guys were going to shit themselves when they found out.

But what was I going to do? Leave her in that place with a broken door? I'm not a complete asshole.

I tossed and turned multiple times, unable to get comfortable because my dick had a mind of his own, and he was literally begging me to wrap my hand around him and release this tension that was bordering on painful.

"Romeo," she whispered, catching me off guard.

"Yeah?"

"Are you having a hard time sleeping?"

"I guess. I've got a lot on my mind." It was true, but the main reason I couldn't sleep was because she was here.

"Is it about the fight with that Leo guy?"

I reached for a second pillow and propped it behind my head so I could sit up a bit. "That's part of it."

"Are you going to fight him?"

I liked the sound of her voice. It was smooth and sort of sultry, but effortless at the same time.

"I haven't announced it yet." I cleared my throat. "But yes, I am."

"Well, we're even. You kept my secret, and I'll keep yours."

"Mine is going to be public record tomorrow or the next day, so you won't need to keep it in the vault for that long." I chuckled.

"Are you nervous about it?"

I could feel the corners of my lips turn up at the question. Demi Crawford could hold her own when I was being a dick, but there was a sweetness there that I wasn't used to. The last girl I dated sliced my tires with a razor blade, and the one before that fucked a guy at my gym because I went out with my boys one night when she wanted me to come over.

Sweet wasn't something I'd ever been drawn to.

Not that I was drawn to Demi. She just happened to be here.

"I'm not necessarily nervous. I'm dreading telling my mom, my grandmother, and Tia. They won't be happy. And I'm not looking forward to this being such a public fight. But I know that I'll put in the work, and I'll show up in the best shape of my life, and that's all I can do, right?"

"Well, just for the record, the *Rocky* movies are my favorite. Will you train like that? Drink raw eggs and chase chickens around a coop?" I could hear the humor in her voice.

"I guess. It'll take me about three months of training all day, every day, between work. Luckily, my business is a gym, so that works in my favor. And I'll need to change the way I eat so I can have the stamina to work out that hard. But I don't think I need to drink raw eggs. I'm guessing I'll cook them first."

"Ahhh… you could be my guinea pig," she said.

"I don't think pumpkin chai lattes are on the menu for a boxer."

"Don't offend me. I know what kind of food is required when you train like that. I was a nutrition major. That's my goal for the coffee shop, to incorporate juices and protein drinks into the menu. There's a green drink I've been working on that would be perfect for you. It's loaded with protein and packed with supplements that will help with energy and muscle repair. Protein shakes would be beneficial between meals, as well. While you're building muscle and training hard, you need to meet the needs of your body."

"You worried about my body, Demi?" My voice was gruff.

Jesus, we were talking about green drinks and protein shakes, and I was making it sexual.

She's a fucking Crawford, dickhead. You won't speak to her after tonight.

"Sure. I think it will help you to stay healthy. How about you let me try out some of my recipes on you, free of charge? If you like them, you can just tell people about them. It will be an advertisement for me."

"I can pay for my own drinks," I said, and it came out much harsher than I meant it to.

"What is your deal with that? I'm not offering you cans of food. We're neighbors. I offered every business on the street one free cup of coffee. It's called marketing, not charity. You were the only one who didn't take me up on the offer."

"My deal is that I don't like handouts from rich people, Princess."

She sighed loud enough for me to know she was annoyed. "I fucking hate being called Princess."

"Why? If the shoe fits…"

She sat forward, and I could make out her form with the

little bit of moonlight coming through the opening beside the window shades. Her back was straight, her shoulders back, and it looked like her hands were in little fists. "The shoe doesn't fit, genius. Do you see me working every day? I lug in my own deliveries from the alley. I oversaw the renovation and even saved money by helping with the demolition where I could. I work long freaking hours every day. It's not really princess behavior, is it? You seem to hate being judged about money, yet you're judging me for the same thing without even knowing me."

She fell back down, lying on her back, and I knew her rant was done.

"Fair enough. I won't call you princess again."

"Wow. He does know how to concede," she said, her tone lighter now.

We weren't friends, so I didn't know why I wanted to keep talking to her. I should end this now and go to sleep. But I didn't want to.

"I'll try your green drink, and if it's good, I'll mention it at the gym."

"Thank you, neighbor. That's the normal response. Was that so difficult?" she asked.

"It was fine." I pretended to be annoyed, but I was fairly certain she knew I wasn't. "Why'd you name the place Magnolia Beans if you want it to be more than just a coffee shop?"

She was silent for a long pause. "If I tell you, you can't tell anyone."

"I can't wait to hear the dark and devious secret behind the name Magnolia Beans," I said dryly, but I couldn't wipe the smile from my face.

"So, when I was in middle school, everyone called my brother *Slade the Blade*. It's a cool nickname, right?"

For a dickhead named Slade. But I wouldn't say that to her.

"Not really my style, but okay."

"Well, my cousins all had nicknames, too. You probably know them, although they're a few years older than us and live on the East Coast now. Elliott and Dalton Clark. They're on my mom's side of the family."

"I've heard of them," I said.

"Everyone called Elliott, E-Money. And they called Dalton, D-Dog."

I barked out a laugh. "E-Money works, but D-Dog is kind of stupid. Why not just Dog?"

"Hey, I didn't make up the name. But they were all older than me, and I was the only girl, so I wanted a nickname, too."

"Is there a point to this story?" I asked, my voice light.

"I came up with Beans. You know, like cool beans."

Now I was laughing hard. "Beans was the coolest name you could come up with?"

"I was twelve or thirteen years old. Beans sounded a whole lot cooler than Demi."

"So, did your cool sibling and cousins call you Beans?" I asked, and fuck, she was cute the way she just shared her ridiculous shit with me. That was very unexpected.

"Nope. Not a soul called me Beans. I asked my friends, my parents, my cousins, my brother. No one remembered to do it more than once. Slade said I wasn't really the type to pull off a nickname. So, I've always just been Demi."

That dick.

Why the fuck didn't he let her use the stupid name if she wanted it?

"Your brother sounds like an asshole."

"You don't even know him."

Oh, but I do.

"I know that he didn't use the nickname that you asked him to use. I know that he broke into your business tonight and robbed you. That's kind of enough to label him an asshole."

And I know that he let me and my best friend take the rap for something that he did.

But the more I knew of her, the less I thought she probably knew about it.

"Fair enough. How about you? Do you have a nickname? Or a handle, like the 'Italian Stallion' when you fight?"

I fucking loved that she kept quoting *Rocky*. They were my favorite movies, as well, but I hadn't expected them to be hers. 1970s films about a boxer weren't exactly as popular these days.

"Golden Boy. My friends sort of started it when I'd get into fights when we were young, and it stuck in my boxing career, I guess."

"Romeo 'Golden Boy' Knight. It works. Very cool."

"Says the girl who thought Beans was a cool name," I said with a chuckle as I heard her yawn.

What the fuck were we doing talking like this?

I needed to end it.

"You haven't fought in a long time?"

"Not in a few years."

"How come?"

"That's a story for another time." One I didn't plan on ever telling her. "Let's try to get at least a few hours of sleep."

"Fine. Thanks for letting me stay here tonight. Good night."

"Good night, Beans," I teased. I lay my head back down on the bed and closed my eyes as she chuckled.

And I let sleep take me.

———

RIVER

Big news, boys. Our Golden Boy just agreed to fight that fucker, and Brinkley broke the news about three minutes ago, so get ready for this to be blasted all over town. Let the training begin.

KINGSTON

Let's go! I'm ready to see you wipe the mat with his annoying ass.

NASH

Dude, you've got this. Looks like we're all going to Vegas in May, yeah?

HAYES

Fuck, yeah. If you need to use anything at the firehouse for your training, just let me know.

RIVER

What's he going to do? Climb a ladder and dive into a burning building? Seems a little risky when preparing for a fight.

HAYES

<middle finger emoji> We've got equipment he can use, asshole.

I officially start training tomorrow. Working on a training plan right now with Joey.

Joey was Rocco's son, and he'd trained several professional fighters over the years, as well as being the heavyweight champion forty-some years ago himself. He'd retired a few years ago from training fighters but was coming out to officially train me for this fight. He was family, and I was lucky to have his experience on my team. He and I had spent the last two hours working on a plan for how I'd train. He was old-school, gritty, and he'd get me in the best shape of my life, no doubt. Joey had trained me for the fight against Gunner when I'd earned professional status. I knew he was exactly what I needed. He was scribbling in a notebook and organizing things by the week.

My phone vibrated, and I glanced down to see the group chat still going off.

KINGSTON

I'm glad he agreed to train you. The dude is going to torture you, though.

That's what I need.

KINGSTON

Think of the ladies that we're going to pull with our boy being all over the media.

HAYES

Don't be a dick. He's training for the fight of his life. This is not about how it benefits us.

KINGSTON

Obviously, we're there for Romeo. But if we happen to get laid a lot in the process, I'm happy to take one for the team, yeah?

Happy to help you out, old-timers.

NASH

Isn't there some rule about no sex while you're training?

KINGSTON

Mick said that women make the legs weak.

RIVER

Are we talking about Mick, the fictional character who trained Rocky in the movies?

HAYES

For fuck's sake. <eye roll emoji>

KINGSTON

Do not hate on Mick. He's the best trainer to ever live.

HAYES

That's offensive to trainers that have actually trained fighters in real life.

KINGSTON

I said what I said.

> I'm fairly certain the no-sex thing is a myth.

RIVER

I heard you shouldn't have sex for six weeks before a fight. Ask Joey what he thinks.

"Hey, the guys and I have a question for you," I said, and he kept writing, but he nodded for me to go ahead.

"Let's hear it."

"Is sex bad for training? Isn't that something someone just made up?"

He set the pen down and looked up at me. Joey was in his mid-sixties. He was a big dude, bald, and covered in tats. No one messed with him.

"I went home with the championship belt after having sex with Myrna the night before, though I don't know that I'd recommend doing that. It was a risky move, but you know I can't keep my hands off my woman." He reached for his water and took a sip. "I think the rule is that you shouldn't be out chasing women and boozing it up when you're training. You need to follow a strict diet and start eating right as of today. No booze. No partying. No fast food. You've got three months to show the world who you are, Romeo. The man I know you are. The man your father, God rest his soul, knows you are. It's game time, son."

I knew diet was going to be important in my training, and I thought of Demi and her offer about health drinks. I figured it would be easier to drink some of my nutrients each day because I wasn't much of a cook.

"Got it. Thanks, Joey."

"I'll meet you here after your morning run tomorrow. Six miles. I don't care if it's snowing. None of this high-class treadmill shit either. You get outside in the cold and the wind, and you run hard. Don't stop until you're puking." He clapped me on the shoulder and left the gym.

I picked my phone back up.

> Joey said sex is fine. No more drinking for me for a couple of months.

KINGSTON

Thank Christ. I couldn't go three months without sex.

HAYES

You're so fucking soft sometimes, King.

KINGSTON

Nothing soft about me. Ask the ladies.
<winky face emoji> <eggplant emoji>

RIVER

Well, you may not be soft, because we share the same genes, so I'm guessing you're right. But you're definitely too fucking full of yourself. I'd like to see you get into the ring and go a few rounds with Romeo.

KINGSTON

I'm a lover, not a fighter.

> Anyone want to run six miles in the morning with me?

RIVER

Fuck no.

KINGSTON

It's Saturday. I plan on sleeping in, Golden Boy. You're on your own for the running side of things. But I'll come by the gym after I wake up and cheer you on.

NASH

Interesting, because we have a job this weekend, and we're meeting at the Wallen Ranch at 7 a.m. tomorrow, asshole. You aren't sleeping in. River, you're still good to hang with Cutler for a few hours tomorrow?

RIVER

Yep. I'll take him to breakfast, and we'll go check on Uncle Ro at the gym afterward.

NASH

Romeo, did you hear anything about a broken window last night? Someone shattered the front door at Magnolia Beans. We had to do a rush order and get someone out there to repair the glass for her this morning.

I'd never lied to these guys, and I wouldn't start now. But I also wouldn't offer more than I had to in a text.

> Yeah. I'll fill you in when I see you tomorrow. But I don't think it's anything to worry about.

KINGSTON

Such a shady answer, Golden Boy. There's a
story there, isn't there?

RIVER

I'll see you tomorrow, and you can fill me in.

He wouldn't drop it. None of them would. But I'd just helped out a girl who was in a bad situation.

They'd do the same thing.

It didn't mean anything.

When I left the gym and locked up, I noticed the glass on her coffee shop's front door had been replaced. I paused for a minute and thought about checking on her, but instead, I turned down the alley and made my way home.

I had no business getting involved with Demi Crawford.

eight

. . .

Demi

IT HAD BEEN a week since I'd last seen my brother. I'd spoken to the program director and was relieved that Slade had been readmitted for a temporary stay. Apparently, they'd reached out to my grandfather, and he'd covered the bill. He hadn't said anything to me, and I was starting to realize that my entire family functioned around endless secrets. It was hard to keep track of who knew what anymore.

My parents hadn't said a word about Slade, so I figured they didn't know about what had happened. Although, I hadn't said a word either, and I knew exactly what had happened.

Of course, my parents freaked out about the front door. My mom was worried about me living downtown and about my safety. She'd always been a worrier. My father, on the other hand, had all sorts of theories regarding the break-in, and most of them included pointing the finger at the gym next door to me.

I'd seen Romeo run past Magnolia Beans through the large window every morning for the last week, and he hadn't stopped in to say hello since the night I'd slept at his house. He'd been cold the following morning when we both woke up, and he'd barely said two words to me before I'd made my way back home.

I hadn't told a soul what happened, and no one had asked where I'd slept.

"That was quite the rush today," Peyton said, fanning her face even though it was cold as hell outside. "I swear, we just keep getting busier."

"I know, and then we've got all the nosy people that can't stop talking about the break in. How does everyone find out everything in this town?"

"I know! Our town slogan should be *Magnolia Falls, where everyone knows your name and your business*."

We laughed as the door swung open, and my mom and dad stepped inside with Benjamin Lowden and his crew right behind them. They wanted to up the security system at the coffee shop, along with adding extra security to my apartment upstairs. I'd agreed because otherwise, my mother had threatened to start sleeping here with me.

"Hey there. I'm going to start in the kitchen. Feel free to spoil us with those famous lattes everyone's talking about," Benjamin said, as he and his guys moved to the kitchen.

I chuckled, and Peyton got to work making their drinks.

"I just saw some guy covered in tattoos going into the gym next door. Are we sure it was teenagers who broke the glass on the door? What if it was a strung-out gym rat who was looking for cash and got scared when the alarm went off?" my father said, and I rolled my eyes.

If he only knew it was his own son who'd been the one to break in and rob the place.

"Strung out? Seriously, Dad. They're professional fighters who work out in the gym. Working out and drugs don't usually go together. I know the owner, and he's definitely not breaking into businesses for cash."

"That Knight kid took over the place, right?" my father asked, crossing his arms over his chest. The way he referred to Romeo pissed me off. "His dad was a train wreck. Spent some time in prison, if memory serves. And his kid and his friends were always trouble."

My mother shook her head. "They were kids. Our own son has made his fair share of mistakes. We don't like when people judge him, do we?"

"Well, even Slade said they were trouble back in the day, so there you go." Dad shrugged.

Slade, his son, who he wasn't even speaking to? The guy who'd just robbed his own sister? He was our moral compass now?

"Well, by all means, he's a great judge of character." I made no effort to hide my sarcasm. The way he spoke about Romeo and his friends bothered me. Romeo was an asshole most of the time, but he wasn't a bad guy. He was moody, and he didn't seem to like me for reasons I couldn't wrap my head around. But if this was the way my father had behaved around him, it was likely that he'd been rude to him and his friends over the years.

"He warned us about those guys long before his boating accident, Demi. He wasn't on drugs back then. Trust me. These are not people you need to be talking to," my father added.

"Jack, stop this nonsense right now." My mother gaped at my father.

"Are you for real? Nash and Kingston did the renovation on this place. They were great to work with and very professional. Romeo owns the gym next door. He's been in a few times, and they're all nice guys. Romeo was the one who called the police the night of the break in. I hardly think he'd be calling the cops on himself."

"They did do a great job on this place, and I'm grateful that Romeo called the police on your behalf." My mother smiled before raising an eyebrow at my father.

He could be very judgmental at times, but I'd never noticed it as much as right now.

He pinched the bridge of his nose. "We can agree to disagree."

"Okay," Mom said. "Let's focus on the security system. I'd like to discuss the idea of getting a wooden door for your entrance so that it's not glass and wouldn't be so easy to break into."

"It's a coffee shop. I can't hide it behind a large wooden door. Anyway, there's a window beside the door. They could just break that."

"Your mother would like that window removed, too." Dad covered his mouth with his hand to keep from laughing.

"What? Mom, you are overreacting. It was teenagers. It happens. But with the cameras you're having installed, I don't see it happening again any time soon."

"Fine. We'll start with the cameras and the added security. My concern is your safety, sweetheart. I'm hoping it was just a bunch of teenagers getting into trouble."

"You both already know my thoughts on the matter." He held his hands up to stop us both from arguing. "I guess time will tell."

It took everything I had not to throw Slade under the bus. I'd always protected my brother, but I was not okay with my father blaming innocent people for something their son did. I bit my tongue.

"Anyway, I heard the Knight kid is going to fight some famous boxer. I can't understand why anyone would want to get their head bashed in for a couple of bucks," Dad said.

"It's hardly a couple of bucks if you've been paying attention at all to the news. He's fighting a contender for the belt. It's a big deal. And he happens to be a professional boxer. He's an athlete. This is his sport."

"Since when did you get so defensive? Don't we deal with enough stress from your brother? I hope you're not going to start giving us trouble now, too."

Was he serious? He was comparing my sharing my

opinion to the hell that Slade had put them through, all because I didn't agree with what he was saying about Romeo and his friends?

"Jack, that's not fair." My mom tucked my hair behind my ear, and her smile reached her eyes. "He's just worried about you, sweetheart. Let's focus on getting the cameras installed and doubling up the security."

"Your apartment door will have three dead bolt locks and a camera of its own outside the door." My father walked around, inspecting the walls as if he were seeing if he could add security behind the drywall.

I loved my parents so much, but they could be over-bearing at times. I think the trauma they'd been through with Slade had made them even more controlling when it came to me. I hadn't felt it to this extent over the last few years because I'd been away at school. But now that I was here, it was definitely more extreme than ever.

My mom excused herself to use the restroom, and my father pulled up a chair and motioned for me to sit across from him.

"Your mom is worried about you. She doesn't like you living above the coffee shop."

"*She* doesn't, or *you* don't?" I quirked a brow.

"You know what a worrier she is. You live downtown, you're next door to a gym full of random guys, and everyone in town knows who you are. Who we are. It's no secret that we have money. I don't like you living here."

"That's incredibly judgmental. Not everyone cares about money, Dad. The guys at the gym are the least of my worries. And I'm almost twenty-three years old. I'm an adult, and I'm also quite capable of taking care of myself."

"We're your parents, and we love you. It's not judgmental; it's the truth."

"Well, Ronny has money, and he's more frightening than anyone I've ever dealt with before," I whisper-hissed.

And that included my addict brother, who'd broken into my place of business wearing a face mask.

He leaned forward as he glanced around to make sure no one was listening. "I handled things with Ronny, and you know that. He got the message loud and clear. You don't need to worry about him anymore. Subject closed."

God, he could be so stubborn. "I'm just saying… No one at the gym has been inappropriate in any way. It's the people *we* know that are more alarming." I raised a brow. Dad could think what he wanted, but it was the truth.

"Point taken, Demi. Just do me a favor. Keep your head up, and be aware of your surroundings."

I didn't have time to argue because my mom came out of the restroom, and we got busy following Benjamin around and making sure he turned my cute coffee shop into a damn fortress.

The rest of the day went by in a blur, and Peyton convinced me to go to Whiskey Falls bar tonight. I hadn't spent much time in Magnolia Falls since I'd turned twenty-one because I'd been away at school. It was fun that I could get into bars now without worrying about fake IDs, which never worked well in small towns. Everyone knew your name and your age.

I slipped into my fitted white bodysuit, a distressed, short jean skirt, and my favorite cowboy boots. Country music, cold beer, and cute boys were the plan tonight. I hadn't dated anyone in months, as I'd sworn off the opposite sex after what happened with Ronny right before I'd graduated.

Not that I'd ever considered dating him. We'd been friends leading up to that night. But the experience completely freaked me out, and afterward, I'd thrown myself into the renovations at the coffee shop and focused on starting my own business. I had no desire to date.

But I was ready to get my flirt game on. I added some waves to my hair and dabbed on some lip gloss and a few coats of mascara. It had been a while since I'd taken the time to get ready.

Peyton and I walked the short distance to Whiskey Falls, where we were meeting up with a few friends from high school. Thankfully, it was no longer snowing outside, which made wearing this jean skirt a lot more tolerable.

"Roxy and Taylor are meeting us there," Peyton said, handing me her pink rhinestone flask. I took a sip and coughed as the cool liquid moved down my throat.

"Is that whiskey?" I gasped at how strong it was.

"The Daily Market's finest," she said with a chuckle when I handed it back. "Oscar is such a grump. He carded me like he didn't know my age. It's so annoying."

Oscar Daily was her dad's best friend, and he owned the grocery store in town. The man had a way of making you feel like you were breaking the law when you bought booze, even if you were legal.

"He stopped into the coffee shop the other day when you were off, and he told me he didn't think this town was going to buy coffee at my prices. Meanwhile, he was cashing in on his free cup and complaining about the price."

We both laughed as she pulled the door to the bar open, and the sound of Zach Bryan's sexy voice had us swaying our hips from the moment we stepped inside. Roxy and Taylor waved us over to a large table they were at, and I groaned because Blane, Scotty, and Brayden were sitting beside them. I dated Blane Johnson for a few months during my senior year of high school. He'd cheated on me at our senior prom when he'd gotten wasted, and I walked in on him balls-deep in Sabrina Marsh in a coat closet.

Good times.

I'd broken up with him immediately. We hadn't been all that serious anyway, but it wasn't exactly the way I'd planned on spending my last prom. But he'd taken the breakup hard and acted like the victim during the whole thing. He'd blamed me because I hadn't slept with him, and apparently, he had a bad case of blue balls, so he had no choice but to bang Sabrina while I was only a few feet away at the after-party.

I can't make this shit up. That was his defense.

After he'd chased after me, I'd kicked him in the balls and told him to lose my number.

He'd called every day for the next six months, long after I'd left for college, and I'd ignored him. He'd finally given up, but now, every time I ran into him, he acted like I'd broken his heart.

"Mr. Blue Balls is here," Peyton whispered against my ear as the smell of whiskey wafted around me.

"Well, looky here," Blane said as he pushed to his feet. "The girl who got away in the very flesh." His words slurred as he wrapped his arms around me, and I rolled my eyes, even though he couldn't see me.

"Hey, Blane. Good to see you."

"Yeah. I'm just in town for the weekend. It's my grand-mother's ninetieth birthday. I was going to come by the coffee shop tomorrow. I heard you're killing it."

"I don't know about that, but it's going well so far," I said, as I pulled away and made my way around the group, giving everyone a hug and trying to put some distance between me and Blane. I sat on one of the chairs across from him and made small talk with everyone.

Of course, Blane shoved Scotty out of his chair and settled right beside me. His best friend, Brayden, gave me an apologetic look. Blane was clearly heavily intoxicated. We ordered a round of shots and beers, and I tipped my head back after we all clinked our glasses together. I could feel the booze as it hit my system. I reached for my beer and felt some sort of pull. My head turned to see Romeo Knight holding what looked like a glass of water, surrounded by his best friends and a bunch of women I didn't recognize.

Dark eyes locked with mine as his tongue slipped out and ran along his bottom lip. I smiled, and he looked away when someone beside him laughed. I forced my attention back to the table as Scotty told us that he was going to propose to Brynn next weekend. They'd dated all through high school, and I was surprised he hadn't already done it.

Peyton shouted when our favorite song by the Zach Brown Band, "Chicken Fried," started playing through the speakers, and most of the bar moved to their feet. I hurried out to the dance floor with the girls, raised my hands over my head, and swayed my hips. We were singing along to the lyrics when Blane stumbled out to the dance floor. He was harmless but a little annoying in the way he kept leaning in to talk to me and spitting all over me.

I pressed my hands against his shoulders to push him back a little, just as Romeo appeared out of nowhere. He wasn't dancing. He wasn't singing.

He looked pissed off, per usual.

He twisted Blane's arm behind his back as he leaned down and whispered something in his ear, and my ex-boyfriend winced. Before I knew it, Scotty and Brayden were helping Blane off the dance floor. When I turned around, Romeo was gone.

"Looks like you've got yourself a sexy protector!" Peyton shouted in my ear as she continued jumping up and down and having a good time.

I watched as Blane left the bar with his friends, and my eyes locked with Romeo's again. He hadn't left. He was back in his seat, and no one there seemed aware of what he'd just done. His eyes were hard, and he looked pissed.

What the hell is his problem?

I tried to shake it off and danced to a few more songs before returning to our table to sip my beer. My phone vibrated, and I looked down to see a text that had my shoulders stiffening and my back going ramrod straight.

UNKNOWN NUMBER

Hey, D. Long time no chat. I was hoping we could talk sometime soon. Clear up this misunderstanding.

I got these random texts every once in a while, from unknown numbers, and I knew exactly who it was. I'd blocked Ronny's number when I'd gotten the restraining order against him. I blocked the number before tucking my phone into my back pocket and pushing to my feet.

Nothing would sober you up quicker than a text message from a guy who scared the shit out of you.

I leaned into the table where my girlfriends were taking another shot. "I'm going to head home. I've got to be up early."

"What?" Peyton whined. "We got you another shot."

"You drink it." I kissed her cheek. "I had a lot of fun."

"I'll be coming in for a nice, hot latte in the morning," Roxy said as she wrapped her arms around me. "I'm so glad you're living back home now."

"Me, too."

"I'll come see you tomorrow," Taylor said, as she reached for my shot glass and tipped her head back, downing the liquid. "I have a hunch we'll all need one of those special concoctions you keep telling us about."

"Yes! We love the magic hangover juice," Peyton said. "Are you fine walking home alone?"

"Of course. It's less than two blocks away, and we're in Magnolia Falls." I gave them each a hug goodbye before heading for the door.

The temperature had dropped, and I definitely regretted wearing my short skirt now. A sound behind me had my head whipping around.

Romeo.

My stomach dipped with excitement, but I raised a brow

and feigned irritation. This man was so hot and cold. I couldn't read him at all. "Are you following me?"

"Well, we do live next door to one another, Beans." His voice was all tease as he moved in stride beside me.

My cheeks heated that he'd used the nickname.

I still couldn't believe I'd shared that story with him.

If I'm being honest, I couldn't believe he'd actually remembered the name.

"The timing seems strange, though, right?" I chuckled. "You happened to be heading home at the exact same time that I am?"

"Don't read into it. I'm leaving. You're leaving. Don't you keep reminding me that we're neighbors when you push those endless free drinks at me?"

Romeo Knight has a sense of humor. Who knew?

"The one free drink you passed on?"

"Maybe I'll cash in on it someday." He shoved his hands into his pockets and kept his eyes in front of him.

"You also managed to run Blane Johnson off, too. Were you just being neighborly?"

"Blane is an asshole. He was hanging all over you, and I could tell you didn't like it. If that makes me neighborly, so fucking be it."

He paused when we turned down the alley, and I stopped to fish my keys out of my purse. "I've seen you running every morning. Looks like you're training hard already."

He nodded, and his eyes settled on my mouth before they snapped back up to meet my gaze. "Get inside. It's cold."

Like I said. The guy was giving me a bad case of whiplash.

I rolled my eyes and put the key into the door and stepped inside without another word.

nine

. . .

Romeo

"YOU LOOK WORN OUT," River said, as he tossed me a sub sandwich before passing Kingston and Hayes theirs.

"Thanks, *Dad*." I made no attempt to hide my sarcasm. Obviously, I was tired. I was two weeks into a grueling training routine, and I had a long way to go.

Kingston fell back against the couch in laughter. "Nothing like training season to put Romeo in a foul-ass mood."

"He's puking more than he's keeping down; that's why he feels like shit." Hayes shrugged as if he were a fucking doctor. "You're pushing too hard, brother."

"No shit. That's what happens when you train for a fight."

"Maybe you're going a little too hard right out of the gate. You're not going to make it if you're depleted nutritionally."

"What the fuck are you talking about? It's the biggest fight of my life. There's no backing down. My body will adjust to the training," I said, leaning back against the couch and chewing slowly.

I didn't miss the look that passed between them, but I didn't have the energy to dissect it. I had a second workout with Joey in an hour and a half, so I'd need to rally.

The door swung open, and in walked Nash, with Cutler a few steps ahead of him.

"Hey, Cutler. Give me some." River held his hand up, and Cutler jumped up and slapped it hard.

Little Dude was a badass, and he wasn't even six years old yet.

"My name's not Cutler anymore." He paused, looking between each of us, and his gaze stopped on me. "Why does Uncle Ro look like that?"

Jesus. Even Cutler is on my ass now?

"Uncle Romeo is stubborn, and he's running himself into the ground, but he doesn't want to listen to anyone. Apparently, he prefers to suffer," Kingston said over a mouthful of food. "Tell us what you decided your name should be."

Nash groaned and shook his head, and I leaned forward because, for the first time today, I was looking forward to something other than puking in the back alley after my run.

The little dude had been claiming for months that he didn't think his name should be Cutler. He'd run all sorts of names by us, and then he'd follow it up by saying that none of them were quite right.

But he looked really happy with himself, and I was here for it. The fact that Nash looked tortured by the choice made it even better.

"Let's hear it," I said.

He wore a white tee, a pair of dark jeans, and a black leather coat. The kid had more swagger than all of us put together. He crossed his arms over his chest and smiled. "From now on, you can call me Beefcake."

Kingston spewed the soda that he'd just swigged across the coffee table. Hayes had an unusually wide grin on his face for a guy who rarely smiled, and River looked between Cutler and his dad with a wicked smirk on his face.

"Yes. I think Beefcake works." River held his hand up again and high-fived Little Dude again.

"You guys are not helping," Nash said, as he took the last two sandwiches on the table and motioned for his son to take a seat on the stool that we kept in my office for him.

"Beefcake is cool, Little Dude. I like it." Kingston smirked.

"What do you think, Uncle Ro? Beefcake sounds like a fighter's name, right?"

I ran my hand over the top of his hair and tried not to chuckle because the kid had so much gel in his slicked-back hair that I was afraid it would break in half if I pressed too hard.

"I like it, buddy. Or should I say, *Beefcake*? It's a cool name, and you're definitely the best fighter I know." I'd been training him a little bit. He wanted to know how to punch a bag, and he liked to get into the ring and dance around.

I'd never thought about having kids or a family of my own, but Cutler was the kind of kid you'd change your ways for. There wasn't anything I wouldn't do for him.

"See, Pops? The guys love it."

I raised a brow at the new term of endearment he was calling Nash, and everyone tried to hide their smiles.

"Yeah. I'm 'Pops' now. Apparently, the name 'Dad' isn't cool enough." Nash rolled his eyes before taking a bite of his sandwich.

"Pops has an attitude. Am I right, Beefcake?" Kingston said, and Nash flipped him the bird when Cutler turned his attention to the door that had just swung open.

"Hey, Romeo. You've got a visitor, and I didn't want to send her away because she brought you something," Pinky said.

I sat forward and set my sandwich down, just as Demi Crawford stepped through the door with a bag in her hand. My shoulders stiffened because she was walking into a rough crowd, and I had no idea what she was doing here. Yes, I'd filled the guys in on what had happened that night I'd found her with her door shattered after her brother had broken in.

We didn't have secrets and they hadn't pressed when I'd told them I had to offer her a place to stay.

They'd all have done the same thing, aside from River who said she had enough money to go to a hotel.

"Hey," she said, not hiding her discomfort when she realized I wasn't alone. I glanced over at River, wondering if he'd be a dick and I'd have to step in. But he just sat there, staring at her like the rest of them did. "I'm sorry. I didn't mean to interrupt. I just, um, I wanted to run something by you."

"Wow. You're really pretty. What's your name?" Cutler pushed to his feet and walked over to her.

This fucking kid.

Like I said, the little dude had more swagger than all of us put together.

She smiled down at him. "My name is Demi. What's your name?"

"You can call me Beefcake."

"For fuck's sake," Nash said under his breath, but I heard him.

She didn't even flinch. "Nice to meet you, Beefcake."

"You want to share my sandwich with me?" Cutler asked as he gaped at her.

I pushed to my feet because I could feel her discomfort, and everyone was just staring at her and wondering what the fuck she was doing there.

"That's so sweet of you, but I'm okay. I need to get back to the coffee shop."

"Oh, Pops worked on the coffee shop with Uncle King. That was for you?" Cutler asked. The kid didn't miss a beat.

"Yeah. That was for me." Her green gaze searched mine, and I could tell she was anxious to get out of there. She held her hand up and waved uncomfortably as they all continued to stare.

"What did you need?" I asked, glancing over my shoulder

to see River looking between us. Nash called Cutler over to finish eating, and I turned my back to the guys.

"I, um, I noticed you were getting sick again in the alley when I took out the trash this morning, and I just thought I'd drop these off."

"What are they?" River asked, and I closed my eyes for a second because he'd think there was more going on here than there was. I'd avoided her since seeing her at Whiskey Falls bar when I'd wanted to beat the shit out of Blane Johnson.

"They're protein shakes. When you're training hard, it helps to supplement in between your actual food meals. So, you can incorporate post-workout protein supplements," she said, before clearing her throat.

"That was nice of you, Demi," Kingston said from behind me. "Our boy isn't keeping much down with these workouts he's doing."

"I'm fine. I'll try them," I grumped. I didn't want her here, knowing how River felt about her. How we all felt about her last name. Her family.

But I'd come to realize that I didn't hate Demi Crawford the way I pretended I did. Hell, I'd gotten off to her in the shower too many times to count, and this morning was no different. So, I'd been keeping my distance for a reason. I'd never act on this attraction, but it didn't mean I didn't want to.

It didn't mean it didn't exist.

Because it did.

But it couldn't go anywhere.

But if River was a dick to her, I wouldn't allow it. And I didn't feel like getting into a fight with him at the moment. "How much do I owe you?"

"I was actually going to see if we could work out a trade." She shrugged, and my gaze ran down the length of her, taking in her black leggings and fitted sweater. Her body was tight and lean, her tits small and perky, and my mouth watered at the thought of tasting her.

Good Christ.

I was clearly over-training because I'd been exhausted two minutes ago, and now here I was, finally hungry for something.

Something that I couldn't have.

There were lines you didn't cross.

Loyalties you stayed true to.

These guys were my family.

Ride or die.

Helping her out when she was in trouble that night was one thing. But anything more than that would never work.

She was a fucking Crawford.

Magnolia Falls royalty.

I was getting ready to get into the ring so that another idiot and I could bash one another's heads in.

Demi and I were from two different worlds, and we needed to keep it that way.

"Like I told you, I don't need charity. I'm happy to pay for them."

I saw River move in my peripheral vision, and he walked over to stand beside me. "Don't be rude, Romeo. Hear her out. What's the trade?"

Her gaze bounced between us, and she did that thing I'd noticed her do every time I was around her. She pushed her shoulders back, lifted her chin up, and locked her gaze with his. Almost like she'd practiced standing up for herself so many times and had to consciously remind herself not to back down.

"I'd like to take some self-defense lessons. I wanted to see if you had anyone here at the gym who could train me?"

"Did someone fucking touch you?" The words were out of my mouth before I could stop them, and River raised a brow as he looked at me.

I was clearly concerned about her, and I'd just shown my hand.

"What? No. I just think with the gym being next door, it wouldn't hurt to know how to fight if I needed to."

"Do Crawfords ever get their fucking hands dirty?" River asked, and I shifted forward the slightest bit, because if he said anything more to her, I'd end the conversation right there.

He had his reasons for being angry. We both did. But they had nothing to do with her.

She didn't even flinch. "Hmmm… let's see. I helped with the demo at the coffee shop, and I chopped a whole lot of vegetables to make these shakes, so I'd say yes. This Crawford gets her hands fucking dirty when she needs to."

A whistle came from behind me, and I turned around to see Kingston falling back on the couch in a fit of laughter. Nash was smiling at her with his hands over Cutler's ears, and Hayes was just taking it all in.

"All right, then. Sounds like this girl needs some boxing lessons, Romeo." River extended his hand to her. "Maybe you can get this guy in shape for the fight."

She smiled as she shook his hand, and then she handed me the bag. "Drink one now before your next workout, and then drink one right after your afternoon workout."

"All right. I'll see if Pinky can train you," I said as I took the bag from her hand, and my fingers grazed hers. And fuck me if I didn't get hard just from the slight contact. Having an erection would not help my afternoon workout, so I needed her to leave. "I'll let you know. Thanks for the drinks."

"Yeah, sure." She took a step back, her gaze moving to River, who was still watching her. "See you guys later."

"Goodbye, Demi." Cutler jumped up and hurried over to the door to open it for her.

This fucking kid was out of control, and I wouldn't change a goddamn thing.

"Bye, Beefcake. I hope I see you again soon." She smiled so wide that my fucking chest squeezed. Damn, maybe I was getting sick. Maybe the guys were right, and I was training too hard and not eating enough to support it. But I just stood there, staring at her.

"Oh, you will see me again," Cutler said as she stepped out the door, and he closed it behind her. "I think I'm going to marry her someday."

Everyone laughed, aside from River, who was watching me now. "I think you might have to get in line to do that, Little Dude."

I flipped him the bird and set the bag down before pulling out one of the drinks she'd made and walking back to the couch.

I unscrewed the top off the plastic bottle and took a long pull. It didn't taste great, but I downed the whole thing in two sips and then rested back against the cushion.

"What's the story there?" Hayes asked.

"No story." I closed my eyes because I was fucking tired.

"Earmuffs, Beefcake," River said, which was code for Cutler to cover his ears. "Open your goddamn eyes and stop being a pussy."

I opened my eyes and raised a brow. "Dude, I don't have the energy to do this with you. Nothing is going on."

"Listen, she's not like the rest of her family. I can see that. But you don't need to lie to me either. These two fuckers had no problem working for her and telling me how nice she was. Why are you being so weird about it?" He smirked.

Yeah, that's because they weren't thinking about the same shit that I was thinking about when it came to Demi.

"I think we all know why," Kingston said. "You like her."

"At least Beefcake has the balls to admit it," River said over his laughter.

"She's fine. I don't even know her that well. Nothing's going on, if that's what you think."

"I think we all noticed the way you looked at her the other night at the bar. I saw the way you ran out of there right after she'd left. And let's not forget the night you rescued her after her break-in and let her sleep at your place," River said.

"She slept on Cutler's bed."

"Hey. It's Beefcake," Cutler said, looking at me like I'd just shot him in the heart.

"Sorry. Won't happen again."

"Do you have a problem with it?" Hayes asked, directing his question toward River.

"Listen, that family is toxic in my eyes. They had no problem doing what they did to me and Romeo. But I agree; she doesn't seem like the rest of them. She probably doesn't even know what happened back then."

"But…" Hayes said, raising a brow because we all knew it was coming.

"But I'm telling you, her parents won't be cool with her dating anyone that isn't rich like them. So, if you want to go for it, that's your choice. They fucked you over once, and they'll do it again. But I'll be there when they try to run you off because I've got your back. Got it?"

I shook my head. "Nothing. Is. Going. On."

"But you want it to be, don't you?" Kingston teased.

I flipped him the bird just as Cutler spoke up.

"I call first dibs on the girl."

And the room erupted into laughter.

But my gaze locked with River, and he knew exactly how I felt.

But acting on it was a whole different story.

Because he was right. Her world and my world didn't mix.

And right now, I needed to focus on my fight.

There was no room for distractions.

And Demi Crawford was one big distraction.

ten

· · ·

Demi

I'D BEEN COMING to the gym every night this week after work, training with Doug, who everyone called Pinky. Apparently, having the last name Pinkerton was a real pain in the ass for him as a boxer. He wanted to be called Doug, Slug 'Em, or Pinkerton, but everyone called him Pinky.

I understood it because I hadn't been able to pull off the nickname that I'd wanted either. Of course, Romeo told Pinky to call me Beans and said it was my boxing handle.

Romeo had come by the coffee shop the day after I'd given him the shakes I'd made for him and said he'd had two great workouts in a row after adding the drinks to his diet.

It felt good to put my degree to use.

I knew he was depleted just by the way he'd looked after his runs. His body would shut down on him if he couldn't get the nutrients he needed.

"So, what's a girl like you doing boxing in a gym on Valentine's Day?" Pinky asked as I danced around him, holding my hands up defensively, waiting for him to swing at me.

"I could ask you the same thing, Casanova."

I heard a low chuckle, and my eyes darted over to see Romeo watching me. He did that sometimes. Hell, he did it all the time. I did, too. I was always watching him through the window at the coffee shop when he'd come back from his run.

But I didn't miss the way he'd passed me off to Pinky the minute I'd asked for a trainer. I knew Romeo trained people, but he clearly didn't want to train me.

"I told you that I've got a girl. I'm taking her to dinner in an hour," Pinky said, and he took the moment my gaze moved back to Romeo to jab at me.

I lunged forward because I'd prepared for it, and that was when he moved quickly, causing me to fall back against the ropes as he put his two hands on each side of me and caged me in.

"This is why you can't get distracted in the ring, Beans. I have you cornered right here, and I could throw so many punches you wouldn't be able to see them coming."

But his words were jumbled, and I started breathing heavily at the feel of his body holding me in place.

Trapped.

Powerless.

I was frozen, and I couldn't move as my breaths came faster, and everything went black.

When I opened my eyes, I was lying flat on the mat, which had my arms swinging up in panic, as both Pinky and Romeo hovered over me. Romeo was staring at me with concern, and he gently touched my shoulders and asked if I was all right. I pushed to sit up before moving to my feet as his arms helped steady me.

"Take a breath, Demi. You're okay. You passed out." The empathy in his gaze relaxed me in the strangest way.

Pinky was standing behind him, looking like he'd committed a crime. "I didn't mean to scare you or hurt you, Beans."

It was coming back to me. The way I'd felt trapped. But he hadn't done anything wrong.

"It wasn't your fault. I just got a little claustrophobic."

"Have you fainted like that before?" Romeo asked as he helped me step out of the ring.

"No. It's a newer problem, I guess."

Pinky hurried over to the cooler and brought me over a bottle of water. "I'm really sorry about that. I was just giving you a hard time. I wanted you to know how easy it is to give your opponent an opening."

"We won't be teaching life lessons in the ring next time," Romeo hissed at him, and Pinky looked wounded.

"It was not your fault. That was all on me. Now, go get your girl and take her out for Valentine's Day. I'll get out of your hair." I took a swig of water and went to grab my purse, but Romeo stopped me. He gently placed a hand on my shoulder as if I were too fragile to touch now.

Although, the man avoided touching me at all costs anyway.

"Just sit here and finish your water. Pinky, you can take off. I'll stay here with her." He walked me over to the bench, and I dropped down like a rag doll. Wow, I really did freak myself out, I guess.

"All right, boss. I'll see you tomorrow afternoon. We still good to spar tomorrow, Beans?"

"I wouldn't miss it," I said, wanting desperately to make him feel better.

This had nothing to do with Pinky and everything to do with me.

Everything to do with the reason that I was taking boxing lessons.

He waved and left the gym, leaving just me and Romeo in here now. I was usually the last one here with Pinky because I came after work.

I knew he had a date tonight, so I'd tried to get here a little early.

It was Valentine's Day, after all.

"You don't have to sit with me. I can drink water in my apartment. I'm sure you have plans tonight," I said, because I was dying to know. I wondered if he had a girlfriend. I hadn't seen him with anyone, but there were a lot of women hanging out at the gym now because Romeo had become a local celebrity due to all the press he was getting about his upcoming fight.

And I wanted to claw every single one of their eyes out, and that alone was mortifying. I had no claim over this man.

We weren't even really friends.

"Is that your way of asking if I'm going out for Valentine's Day?"

His voice was so sexy; it was difficult to breathe around him sometimes. His dark gaze did something to me every time it locked with mine.

"No. Why would I care what you do for Valentine's Day? I just didn't want to hold you up."

"What about you? Don't you have plans tonight? Let me guess, you're probably dating some rich dude who wears polo shirts and drives a small-dick sports car."

I tried not to smile, but I couldn't help it. "Wrong. But is that *your* way of asking if I'm going out for Valentine's Day?"

"It is." His voice was hard. Firm.

Did it just get hot in here? I took another gulp of water. Sometimes it felt like he was flirting with me, and other times it felt like he couldn't stand the sight of me.

My heart raced at the way he'd just admitted that he wanted to know.

"Let me guess, you're asking for a friend?" I smirked.

His tongue dipped out and moved slowly back and forth across his bottom lip, and I squeezed my thighs together, shifting the slightest bit before letting out a breath.

I was so freaking frustrated.

Romeo Knight was wreaking havoc on my hormones.

"Well, Beefcake called dibs on you. So, I've got to make sure no one snags his girl when he isn't looking."

My head fell back in laughter because Cutler Heart was the cutest kid I'd ever met. I knew Nash had a son, but I'd been away at school for a few years, and I'd never met him.

"I wouldn't dream of cheating on Beefcake. I know a good thing when I've got it."

"I bet you do. So, how about you tell me why you fainted?" His eyes darkened as he studied me.

"I told you that I'm a little claustrophobic."

"Don't bullshit me, Demi. I know fear when I see it. I was already jumping in the ring right before you dropped. I saw the look on your face. Pinky just isn't good at reading signals. But you were fucking scared. Terrified is probably more fitting."

I looked away. How the hell did he see all that while I was several feet away from him?

"You're misreading the situation."

"I don't think so. Why won't you just tell me?"

"Tell you what?"

"Who did this to you? Who made you feel like you need to protect yourself? Is it your brother?"

That pissed me off. Yes, he had every right to suspect it was Slade. Sure, he was a drug addict who'd robbed me, but he'd never lay a hand on me. "Of course, you think it's Slade."

"He's the most likely suspect."

"I told you before that I'm not afraid of my brother. He'd never hurt me."

"He could have hurt you when he broke into your place. If memory serves, the glass cut your hand," he said, his gaze dropping to my hand as he reached for it, settling it in his large hand. He turned it over to inspect my palm and traced his finger over the long cut that was still healing.

I sighed and leaned back against the bench, not pulling my hand away. I liked the way he held it. The way he seemed to want to protect me. I didn't let my guard down easily, but for whatever reason, I trusted Romeo Knight. He hadn't told anyone about my brother, as far as I knew.

"I'm not taking boxing lessons because I'm afraid of Slade," I whispered.

"But you're afraid of someone?"

"I'm not afraid of anyone, but I'm aware that there are people who are stronger than me, and I want to be prepared for them."

"Are you preparing for someone you know? Someone who's scared you before?"

I wanted to push to my feet and walk out the door because I didn't want to talk about this. But the way his fingers were stroking the inside of my palm was so soothing, I had no desire to move at the moment. Even if the conversation was heavy.

"Fine. Yes. I've been in a situation that I don't want to be in again."

His gaze softened. His wavy dark hair was tussled on his head, his sharp jaw peppered in just a bit of scruff, and his eyes felt like they were looking straight into my soul.

"Is the person who put you in that situation here in town?"

My teeth sank into my bottom lip, and I smiled. "What are you going to do, Romeo? Beat up anyone who scares me?"

"Yes. I'd be fine with that. It would be good for my training anyway."

God, he is gorgeous.

"He's not here in town. And he won't be. Let's just say, he's not allowed within one hundred yards of me. But no one knows this, aside from my father, and I'd like to keep it that way."

"Your father knows someone scared you, and the guy is still breathing?" he asked, his jaw clenching as he thought about it.

"Not everyone handles everything with violence. He's the son of a powerful man. It would be—complicated for my family if anyone found out."

"Did he put his fucking hands on you?" His words were so fueled with anger that chills ran down my back.

"He tried, but he failed. He would not be breathing or walking if he'd done that." I'd wondered a million times what would have happened if I hadn't gotten out of there when I did.

His eyes searched mine. "Well, he did something to you."

"You do know it's Valentine's Day, right? This is not what I want to be talking about right now."

He raised a brow, and I realized the way it sounded.

"Not that I think this is a date. Oh my gosh. No." I covered my face with my free hand; my other hand was still resting in his large palm. "I just meant that this is a little heavy for gym talk."

He nodded. "Sometimes talking about things helps."

"Fine. You want to know what happened? Tell me why you're so hot and cold with me. Why do you seem to hate my family so much? That's how this works," I said, motioning my hand between us.

"This? What is this?"

"Well, I'm making you protein shakes to help with your training. You're providing me with boxing lessons and sitting on a bench with me on Valentine's Day. I'd say this makes us friends."

"I've never been friends with a woman. And I don't know that I could be friends with you, if I'm being honest."

It felt like a slap in the face. Like he still had this weird hatred for me. I tugged my hand away and pushed to my feet.

"Fine. Then let's call this done." I stormed toward the door, and he caught my wrist. It didn't scare me when Romeo touched me. I whipped around, my chest slamming into his.

"I didn't mean it the way you think I did," he said, his gaze searching mine.

"You've had this anger toward me since the first day you walked into the coffee shop. That's exactly how you meant it," I huffed.

He remained completely calm. "I said I didn't think I could be friends with you because that's not the way I think about you."

I cleared my throat. "How, exactly, do you think about me? As your enemy?"

He sighed like he was completely frustrated that I was making him spell it out for me. "Most of the time, I think about you naked. I think about the way you'd taste. The way you'd respond when I touched you. The way your lips would feel against mine. The way you'd look when you came for me."

Hello, Romeo Knight.

The Golden Boy had entered the arena.

And I…

Was.

Here for it.

My breaths were coming fast now.

"So, why don't you kiss me and find out?" I whispered.

"Because I don't take things that aren't mine, Demi."

So earnest and proud.

"Your morals are exhausting," I groaned.

He barked out a laugh that echoed around the large gym with the high ceilings and cement floors.

Don't ask me how, but standing in this cold space where most of the people who worked out here smelled like dirty socks and were covered in sweat still somehow managed to be the most romantic moment I'd ever experienced.

Because I felt a connection to him that was foreign to me.

Something I'd never felt before.

And just hearing that he was struggling the same way that I was, made me want him even more.

"I've never been accused of being too moral. Don't give me credit that I don't deserve."

"Heaven forbid anyone give you undeserving praise, Romeo. I have a hunch that you don't take praise easily."

His eyes settled on my mouth. "Maybe I'm just good at giving praise to the few people that I like."

Please. Give it to me right now.

"You like me, don't you, Golden Boy?"

He nodded. "Liking you is one thing. Acting on it is another."

"Because you hate my family?" I rolled my eyes. "This is so ridiculous."

"We're from two different worlds, Demi. I doubt your parents would appreciate you hooking up with Keith Knight's kid."

"My parents don't tell me who to date."

"You can't even tell your parents that your brother is in town, and he's their son. You wouldn't be able to sell this to them, and you know it. I think you've got a lot of answers, but I don't think you're thinking it out."

"And I think you've got a lot of excuses," I said. The urge to kiss him was so strong that it was painful. My hands fisted in his T-shirt.

"I just speak the truth." His thumb stroked across my bottom lip.

"Tell me why you hate them so much," I whispered.

"Tell me who scared you so badly that you just fainted in the ring."

I raised a brow. "So, when I tell you that, you'll tell me what I want to know?"

"Something like that."

But I wasn't ready to tell anyone else the details about what had happened with Ronny. What if Romeo told his friends? My father would never forgive me if word got out about his business partner's son.

"And if I don't tell you?" I asked.

"Well, then, it looks like I'm having dinner with my first female friend. I'm starving. Friends eat together, right?" He smirked.

"They do. But it's Valentine's Day, so I don't think we'll have any luck going anywhere, aside from The Golden Goose Diner."

"Sounds like we're having grilled cheese and tomato soup, Beans. I'm sure this will go down as the best Valentine's Day you've ever had." His voice was all tease.

But I couldn't think of a Valentine's Day that could even compete with this one.

I didn't know what was happening between me and Romeo, but I liked it.

I liked it a lot.

eleven

. . .

Romeo

RIVER

Guess where I am right now?

KINGSTON

Well, you're sitting next to me and Nash, so we already know the answer to that.

HAYES

Some of us are at actual work right now. Are you going to tell us or just fuck around?

> I just ran seven miles, and I'm fucking exhausted. Let's hear it.

KINGSTON

Are you exhausted from the run or from something else?

NASH

Romeo, he's fucking with you. We're at The Golden Goose. You can take it from there.

HAYES

What am I missing?

RIVER

Our Golden Boy has been here several times over the last few weeks with a certain lady friend, with whom he continually says that nothing is going on with.

KINGSTON

Midge said you two were here on Valentine's Day. And several times since. It's becoming a habit, apparently. <winky face emoji>

NASH

And your name is Romeo, lover boy.

HAYES

Listen, if he doesn't hold what her family did against her, neither should we.

RIVER

Did someone steal your phone, Hayes? Since when are you the voice of reason?

KINGSTON

I think Hayes must have gotten laid last night.

HAYES

None of your business. I don't have to get laid to call shit as I see it.

NASH

I think Cupid shot his fucking arrow right through Romeo's heart.

HAYES

Give him a break. He's working his ass off. If he likes the girl, let him be.

RIVER

So, what's the story? We don't keep things from one another. Why are you keeping this from us?

> Something happened at the gym a few weeks ago. She got spooked and fainted. We went to get grilled cheese sandwiches after. That. Was. It. We're friends, I guess.

RIVER

What spooked her?

I KNEW he'd react this way. Beneath his asshole exterior was a big heart. He just didn't like anyone to know it.

> She won't tell me. Something that happened with some dude, I guess.

My blood still boiled every time I thought about it. And I wanted to fucking know—*needed* to fucking know what happened to her. I'd tried over the last few weeks. We hung out a lot. More than I was telling them. I always stuck around when she trained with Pinky to make sure she was okay. I walked her home after she worked out at the gym every night. Sometimes, we grabbed a bite to eat. Nothing had happened beyond that, but I'd never spent this much time with a woman. Not even one that I was dating. I liked being around her. Craved it most days.

KINGSTON

Enough to make her faint? That means some shit went down with her. Do you think it was Slade?

> She's adamant that it wasn't him.

NASH

Maybe she's afraid of her father. He's an asshole, too.

> Yeah, maybe. She wants to know why I hate her family so much.

RIVER

Did you ever think about telling her? It's not really a fucking secret at this point. Maybe she should know who they are. See what she thinks of it. If she makes excuses, you'll have your answer.

I scrubbed a hand down my face as I chugged one of the shakes Demi made for me. They were making a huge difference in my training, and Joey was impressed with how well I was holding up now.

> I don't like dredging that shit up. We both survived, right? But I'll think about it. How about you dickheads eat your breakfast and stop gossiping with the locals.

RIVER

Don't shoot the messenger. It's the first time I've seen Midge Longhorn seem excited about anything. She asked if we knew who you were out with.

KINGSTON

She actually smiled. I had no idea that Midge had teeth.

NASH

Stop with the fucking teeth talk. They were stained yellow from years of smoking, and I think she should go back to her standard resting bitch face. It's not good for business.

RIVER

Yet you ate four pancakes.

NASH

What can I say? Buttermilk pancakes are my weakness. Don't tell Beefcake we came here. He'll be pissed that he's at school while I'm eating fucking pancakes between jobs.

HAYES

I'd be more worried about Beefcake finding out that Uncle Ro is spending a lot of time with his girl. <head exploding emoji>

KINGSTON

You better watch your back, Romeo. He's got his mind set on your woman.

She's not my woman, you fucker. Don't you have work to do?

RIVER

I love it when you deflect, brother. The writing is on the wall. Just be prepared for the wrath of her family when they find out. But you know we have your back, so stop being a pussy with this girl.

HAYES

I think that's River's way of saying you have his blessing. <praying hands emoji>

KINGSTON

Hayes is going biblical this morning. Can I get an amen?

NASH

You can get a shut the fuck up. Romeo, stop holding back. We know you like the girl. King and I liked her when we worked with her. She's good people. Just don't tell River that I said that.

RIVER

You're hilarious. <middle finger emoji>

Can we stop talking about this? Some of us have to get back to work now. Thanks for this enlightening conversation.

RIVER

We can stop talking about it if you stop hiding this shit from us. We've got your back. You know that.

HAYES

Yep. Ride or die. Brothers till the end. Loyalty always. Forever my friend.

KINGSTON

There he goes again. Hayes definitely got laid last night.

HAYES

<middle finger emoji>

I laughed and set my phone down on my desk. I'd spend the next few hours working at the gym before I'd have to suit up for my afternoon workout. Brinkley had sent me a text reminding me that the article she'd written about me was in every store today, as if I could forget when she'd reminded me multiple times. She'd come to town a few weeks ago and followed me everywhere that day, and the article was now out in the world.

There was a knock on my office door, and I shouted for them to come in.

Demi peeked her head in and then held up the magazine that had me on the cover and waggled her brows.

"The Golden Boy is preparing for the fight of his life," she said, as she closed the door and hurried over to the couch to sit beside me. "You didn't tell me this was coming out today."

I groaned. "I didn't know if they'd carry it here."

"Are you kidding? The Daily Market has a line out the door. Peyton ran and got us a couple of copies."

"Great." I leaned back before glancing over at her. She wore a cream sweater that hung off of one shoulder, a pair of faded jeans, and her favorite cowboy boots.

"Let's read it together," she said, turning to face me. The urge to touch her was overwhelming lately. I liked just sitting with her sometimes, memorizing every line and curve on her face. The way her tongue dipped out in the corner of her mouth when she was concentrating. The light spatter of freckles on her nose was cute as hell.

"All right, I'll read it to you," she said when I didn't respond.

"I've read it," I grumped. Brinkley had sent me the final article over a week ago.

"Well, I haven't. And you haven't heard me read it aloud. So, consider yourself lucky. Sit back and enjoy the moment. You're on the cover of *Strive Forward* magazine. That's a big freaking deal."

I closed my eyes and listened to the sound of her voice. I fucking loved the sound of her voice. It was sweet and sexy all at the same time.

Had I ever noticed a woman's voice before?

A woman's freckles?

"Romeo Knight is set to take the boxing world by storm in just a couple of months. When Leo 'The Flamethrower' Burns set his sights on Magnolia Falls' small-town Golden Boy, Romeo was left

with no choice but to agree to the challenge. After months of what many would consider online bullying, through social media posts and interviews with any sports network who would listen, Burns was relentless in his pursuit. Demi paused, and I opened one eye and looked at her.

"What?"

"I really hate Leo. I hope you kick his ass." She smiled, and my fucking chest squeezed. My hand was resting right beside hers on the couch, and I wrapped my pinky finger around hers playfully. She didn't pull away. She liked it.

We both did.

This pull was so fucking strong I didn't know how to fight it anymore.

"I'm just hoping to leave that ring in one piece. If I can kick his ass in the process, that would be a huge bonus." I chuckled.

The concern in her eyes was cute as hell, but she forced a smile and continued reading. The article went on about my intense training and about how the last fight I'd participated in was the fight where my father had dropped to the mat and was rushed to the hospital. Demi paused after she read the line about him not coming home that day.

"Is it hard for you to be training for a fight now? You know, is it bringing up memories about losing your dad?"

This girl, man.

So fucking sweet.

"I'd be lying if I said I didn't miss him. It's hard for people to understand. He wasn't perfect. He made a lot of mistakes. But he was still my dad, and boxing was something that we shared."

Her brows pinched together. "It doesn't really matter what anyone else thinks. When you love someone, you love all of them. That's how I feel about Slade. His addiction doesn't make me love him less. It makes me sad that he is struggling, but I don't weaponize love."

"What does that mean?" I asked, as I turned her small hand over in mine and traced the scar that had faded on her palm.

"It means that I don't hold love over people's heads. I'm careful about who I love, and when I love someone, it's forever. I can't just turn it on and off, and I don't think you can either."

"I guess we have more in common than we thought," I said, my voice quiet.

"Because we both love fiercely?"

"I was thinking more that we both have fucked-up family members, but your answer sounds better," I said, teasing.

She burst out in laughter, putting her attention back on the article to read the ending.

"Romeo is training hard every day. He's running until he pukes, boxing until his arms are so sore he can barely lift them the next day, and putting his body through every imaginable form of training to prepare for this fight. I think it's fair to say that we're all going to be in for a good showing in Las Vegas come May. I'll be there. Will you?"

She glanced at the photos that Brinkley's photographer had taken.

"I look so shiny." I laughed.

"You look really good."

"Yeah? Should you be saying that to a friend, Beans?"

"Should you be stroking my palm like some kind of sex god, Golden Boy?"

Goddamn, she was funny.

And cute.

And honest.

And kind.

And sexy.

I was so fucked. The guys knew it. And I knew it, too.

"Some kind of sex god, huh?"

"I don't know. You're just looking at me with those

bedroom eyes, and your warm finger is tracing over my palm in a way that's got me all… flustered."

There was a knock on the door, and I pulled my hand away from hers, and we both straightened.

"Yeah, come in," I called out.

It was Pinky, and he looked between us curiously. "Hey. Joey called and said he'd be here in twenty minutes and that you should prepare for a beating today."

"Great," I groaned. "I'll be ready."

"Is it all right if I'm training Demi in the other ring?"

"Yeah. Of course. She can get some inspiration." I waggled my brows.

Her teeth sank into her bottom lip, and she smiled. Pinky looked between us and cleared his throat. "Great. I'll see you in an hour. I've got a client now."

"Perfect." She pushed to her feet. "I've got to place a few supply orders and change my clothes, and I'll be back."

"See you soon." Pinky stepped away.

"Oh, I almost forgot. I wanted to tell you about some research that I did. I found some recipes that I think would be good for you. I was going to make one tonight if you want to come over and try it."

"Are you asking me out?" I smirked.

"I'm asking you to try some salmon. I've already told you, I'm not going out with you until you tell me why you hate my family."

"Well, I'm not going out with you until you tell me why you fainted that day in my gym."

What the fuck was I doing?

"Then I guess we're having salmon, friend."

"I guess we are." I pushed to my feet. "My workout will last several hours, so I'll just come by when I'm done?"

"Yeah. And if you need a sparring partner, just holler."

I rolled my eyes. "Take it down a notch, Champ. I won't be getting into the ring with you."

"I think you're a little scared of me, Romeo."

She didn't have a fucking clue.

She terrified me.

The way she made me feel.

The way I wanted her.

All of it.

She walked out of the office, and my phone rang. My sister Tia's name lit up my screen.

"Hey, T," I said, as I walked toward the locker room so I could change back into my workout clothes. My sister and I were close, and we talked a couple of times a week. My family had taken the news of the fight better than I'd expected, aside from my mom blinking back the tears as she listened. We'd talked it out over dinner and then I'd Face-Timed Tia and gone through it all over again. But they understood my decision and even if they weren't thrilled about it, they would support me.

"Hi! I just bought five copies of the magazine. My God, Ro, you're on the cover of a freaking magazine. My roommates are all starstruck," she said with a chuckle.

"Well, let's see how starstruck they are after the fight."

"You're Romeo 'Golden Boy' Knight! No one works harder than you."

"That's all I can do, right?" I pulled my gym bag out of my locker and set it on the bench.

"Well, Brinks killed it on the article. It's so good. I'm proud of you."

"Thanks. How are classes going? Is chemistry still a fucking nightmare?" I asked, because she'd called crying about how challenging it was a few nights ago.

"Yes. I hate it. But school's great. I can't wait for you to come visit again."

"Yeah. I'll come after the fight. Right now, I need to focus on doing the work."

"Agreed. Anything else you want to tell me?"

"About?"

"Mom thinks there's something going on with you and Demi Crawford."

I clearly wasn't doing a good job of keeping this quiet.

And nothing had even fucking happened.

I knew I could say anything to Tia because she was like my mother, and they didn't judge. Even if they'd hated the women I'd dated in the past, they were always supportive. And Demi was different, so I wasn't surprised that they'd both push for something there. They'd like her. What wasn't to like? Aside from her family and her shitbag brother.

Hell, everybody liked her.

"There's nothing going on," I said, but there was no conviction behind my words.

She squealed, and I held the phone away from my ear.

"But… you want there to be."

"I don't know about that. It would be pretty awkward if I was at one of her family dinners, right? After what they did?"

"That was all Slade. And he's a weasel. But that doesn't mean Demi's not great. I've always liked her. And her mom is really sweet, too."

"The timing isn't right anyway. I've got to focus on this fight. I don't need any distractions."

"Well, you can't always pick and choose when someone walks into your life and knocks you on your ass."

"No one has been knocked on their ass."

But even I didn't believe the words coming out of my mouth.

Because Demi Crawford had definitely knocked me on my ass.

twelve

. . .

Demi

I'D FINISHED my workout at the gym, and I'd found it difficult to keep my eyes on Pinky and not keep looking over at Romeo. He looked so damn good when he was training. I mean, he looked good when he wasn't training, too, but seeing the way his muscles flexed in his biceps every time he hit the bag… The way the sweat dripped down his chiseled abdomen…

My mouth watered at the thought.

I was trying to focus on the positive things, and Romeo was at the top of that list. I'd gotten another cryptic text this afternoon, and I knew it was from Ronny. He asked if we could talk, but he'd sent the messages from yet another unidentified number, so I couldn't prove it was him or that he'd violated the restraining order.

I'd asked my father what to do, and he'd just said that he would handle it. He said Ronny wasn't stupid enough to try anything when he wasn't allowed to come near me. I hoped like hell that he was right.

I'd spent the last hour cooking while Romeo finished his workout. I'd researched the hell out of diets for boxers.

Because when I wasn't with Romeo, I was thinking about him.

I knew that he didn't cook, so the shakes could make up for some of his needed caloric intake, and he'd already said that they were making a huge difference. But he needed actual food, as well. A balance of carbs, proteins, and fats if he expected his body to perform efficiently.

He'd texted a half hour ago to say he'd finished his workout and was heading home to take a quick shower, and he'd be right over. I finished up the salad and paced around the apartment.

Why was I nervous?

We'd been spending a lot of time together. Never at one another's homes, though, so maybe that had me on edge.

Maybe it was the way we were openly flirting now. Talking about dating one another and teasing each other about it every chance we got.

I walked over to the window just as Romeo walked out his front door with some voluptuous blonde stepping out behind him. My mouth fell open, and I squinted when they turned around.

"Ugh," I groaned once I realized it was Monica Vain.

Her name was very fitting. She was a stuck-up drama queen. She'd made endless fun of me one day when I'd been out at the lake with a group of friends in high school. She'd called me "string bean" as if that was some original, brilliant insult. I couldn't stand the girl.

If you looked up *mean girl* in the dictionary, there'd be a photograph of her. She liked to break down other girls and women and thought it elevated her.

I'd never been impressed by her.

And what were they even doing? Sneaking in a quickie before he came over to my house for dinner?

How shady is that?

I was seething. He could go back to eating his lame-ass diet for all I cared.

But of course, I couldn't look away. He had his arms folded over his chest, and she kept touching his shoulder, which infuriated me even more.

What right did I have to be this pissed off?

We weren't together.

We'd never even kissed. What was wrong with me?

But I was so freaking pissed off I couldn't see straight.

As if he could feel my anger, his head snapped up, and his gaze locked with mine. I jumped back and tried to hide behind the curtain.

Shit.

I'd just been caught snooping on a guy I wasn't even dating.

I hurried over to the kitchen and pulled dinner out of the oven and sipped my water as I tried to tamp down my irrational anger.

I quickly dialed Peyton.

"Hey, girl. I texted you to come meet me and the girls at Whiskey Falls."

"I can't tonight. But I have a quick question."

"Let's hear it," she said.

"Is it normal to be jealous over a guy that you aren't even dating?"

"Hell yes. Totally normal. Let me guess… your non-boyfriend, who you spend endless time with, who happens to be a *Greek freaking god* and is ridiculously protective over you, is the one we're talking about?"

"Yes. He's coming over to eat," I said, but she interrupted me.

"Eat what? You?" she said, her voice laced with humor.

"Oh my God," I groaned. "Stop acting crazy. Salmon."

"Bummer. Okay, so what's the problem?"

"He ran home to shower after his workout, and then I

looked out the window and saw Monica Vain leaving his house. And she keeps touching him. I have a crazy urge to claw her eyes out."

She was laughing hysterically now. "You're jealous, babe. You like him. Just admit it and then tell him and claim your man."

"What if he just slept with her?"

"Please. He doesn't strike me as a man who would do the deed quickly. He seems like the kind of lover who takes his time. You know, worships every inch of your body."

"You are not helping," I said, just as the bell rang from the back door downstairs. "Damn it. He's here. I'll call you after."

"Tell him how you feel, and stop being a baby. And then offer yourself up for dessert!" she shouted.

I ended the call and stormed down the stairs because I was pissed. Regardless if we were nothing, he'd agreed to come to dinner, and then he'd squeezed in time with another woman before he came over here? Who does that?

I pulled the door open and glared at him. "Thanks for gracing me with your presence, Lord Romeo."

He chuckled, and I turned around and stomped up the stairs to my apartment as he followed me inside.

"Wow. This is nice."

I'd almost forgotten he'd never been here.

I moved to the kitchen and started scooping the pasta aggressively onto his plate. I didn't reply, and I could feel him moving closer. He stood right behind me, his chest pressed to my back. His warm breath tickled my ear, and I snapped the ladle against his plate and added more pasta.

"You mad, Beans?" he whispered.

"Why would I be mad?"

"I don't know. I saw you looking out the window, and it seems like you're taking your aggression out on that pasta."

I dropped the ladle to rest in the bowl and set the plate

down because it was hard to breathe with him this close to me.

Cedar and sage were flooding my senses.

But it was more than that. It was just Romeo. His whole essence was overpowering.

All-consuming.

My heart was beating loudly in my ears.

"Did you sleep with her?" I had no right to ask, but I wanted to know.

He chuckled before leaning closer and nipping at the lobe of my ear. He turned me around so we were facing one another. "Are you serious right now? You think I finished that grueling workout and then had a quickie with Monica before coming over here?"

"How would I know what you do?"

"Would it matter to you if I slept with her?" he asked, his fingers moving to my jaw and his thumb tracing along my bottom lip.

It was hard to think straight. "I don't want to make you dinner if you just fucked my teenage bully."

"I love when you say fuck." His lips turned up in the corners. "What did she do to you?"

"She always made fun of me for being too skinny in high school. She had it out for me."

"Because she was clearly jealous. You're gorgeous, and she's insecure. And the answer to your question is, no. I didn't fuck her tonight—haven't been with her in over a year. I used to date her, and it was a volatile relationship. She slashed my tires when I ended things with her. I wanted away from that shit."

"So why was she there?"

"She showed up at my door and asked if I could sign her younger brother's boxing gloves. He used to train with me, and he's away at school now. She wanted to send them to him because she said he's excited about the fight."

"Oh."

"Oh," he said, his tongue shifting back and forth across his bottom lip.

"You done being jealous?"

"I was never jealous." I tried not to smile.

"Sure, you weren't. So, are you going to feed me now?"

I studied his features, and for the first time, I saw how tired he looked. He'd worked out for hours today, with not one but two intense workouts. The poor guy was probably ready to fall over, and here I was, acting completely irrationally.

But he was still standing so close to me. I put my hands on his hard chest.

"I'm sorry," I whispered.

"For what?"

"You're going to make me say it, aren't you?"

"You just stormed up the stairs and beat the shit out of that wooden spoon, so yeah, I'm going to make you say it."

I tipped my shoulders back, and my gaze locked with his. "I was jealous. Is that what you want to hear?"

A wide grin spread across his handsome face. "Yeah. That's what I want to hear."

"Why are you so happy about it?" I groaned.

He pulled back, and his mouth collided with mine. His hands cradled the sides of my face as if he wanted to hold me there forever. My fingers moved beneath his hoodie, desperate to feel his skin. His tongue slipped into my mouth, and he turned my face to get better access.

There was a desperation. A need so strong, that before I knew what was happening, his hands moved to my ass, and he lifted me onto the counter as he stood between my thighs. The spoon rattled to the floor, and the plates clanked against one another, but I didn't care.

We tasted and explored and kissed until my lips ached. He pulled back, eyes wild as they took me in. My chest was rising and falling, and I missed him the minute his lips weren't on mine.

"You're fucking beautiful, you know that, right?" he whispered. "I can't stop thinking about you. Wanting you. Even though I know I shouldn't."

My hands were still tracing the muscles on his abdomen. "Why shouldn't you want me?"

He looked so tortured by the question.

"Like I said, I don't take things that aren't mine."

His stomach rumbled beneath my fingers, and we both laughed. "All right. Let's leave it right here. That was some kiss. And now I'm going to feed you, and you can tell me all the reasons why we shouldn't kiss again."

He grabbed me by the waist and set me on the floor. I laughed when I saw the spoon on the floor and the pasta from one of the plates had spilled all over the stovetop.

He helped me clean up the mess, and we both washed our hands. I loaded him up with salmon and explained the reasons why he needs extra protein right now. We sat at the little table for two in the kitchen, and I placed the fresh salad between us.

He listened intently as I explained the benefits of carbs and protein and fat while he was training. He groaned when he took the first bite of the pasta.

"It's homemade pesto. You can take a jar home with you. It's made with fresh basil, garlic, and pine nuts. You can add it to your protein or your grains."

"Were you always interested in this stuff?" he asked as his eyes widened when he popped a bite of the salmon into his mouth. "Holy shit, this is good."

I couldn't stop smiling. "Thank you. I got really into nutrition after Slade had his boating accident. He was in a lot of pain and wouldn't eat. I was convinced good food could cure him. But I hadn't been prepared for him to get addicted to opioids, and no amount of nutrition could overcome what he was dealing with."

He chewed, and his gaze watched me intently as he listened. We talked for hours, and he told me about his father's battle with drugs and alcohol after we'd cleared the table and moved to the couch.

"It was a lot of responsibility when he was gone during those years, serving time for his third DUI." He shook his head. "But it was also the reason he finally got sober, and he came home a different man. I'm grateful for the years we had together after that."

"I love that he got clean and sober. It's not easy, and my biggest fear is that Slade will never get to the other side of this."

"Opioids are brutal. He got hooked after the boating accident?" Romeo asked.

"Yeah. It's not fair, you know? He was in this horrible accident, and the doctor prescribed a medication that was supposed to help him, not derail his whole life."

His mouth opened, and he looked like he had something to say, but he stopped himself.

"What? You can tell me. Nothing will shock me about my brother at this point."

"No, it's nothing. I just didn't know that he didn't have a drug problem before the opioids. I thought it started earlier," he said, his voice low as he ran his fingers up and down my forearm.

"Not that I'm aware of. It all started with his accident. With that medication they gave him."

He nodded and leaned back against the couch, his eyes heavy with exhaustion.

"I should probably get going. I've got to be up early to run. Joey is going to ride an electric bike next to me tomorrow to push my ass even harder."

"You're already pushing so hard as it is. You don't want to run yourself into the ground."

He reached for my hand and intertwined our fingers. God, I even loved his hands. His fingers were long and lean and engulfed mine.

"You worried about me?"

"What if I am?"

"You don't need to worry. I've got a lot more in the tank than this. Yes, I'm tired, but I'm ready to do this. To see how far I can push myself. I look forward to waking up and getting after it."

"Hey, I have an idea. You could come run at my house. I mean, my parents' house. We've got several acres that we share with my grandparents. There's lots of wide-open space, and I could ride Teacup, and push you out there, too. She's an older horse, but she can go for several miles. We've got trails, and there's the area down by the water that would be good for training."

He studied me like the offer was completely ludicrous. "I don't think that would go over well."

"For them or for you?"

"For either."

I shook my head. "What the hell is your problem with my family? Yes, my father can be judgey, and they're a bit much sometimes, but if they got to know you, and you got to know them, this would be something we'd laugh at later."

"Let's do this another night. I need to get home." He pushed to his feet.

"I'm not kissing you again until you tell me why you hate them."

He tugged me to my feet. "You ready to tell me about the dude who scared the shit out of you?"

"Another night, Golden Boy." I echoed his words.

He nipped at my bottom lip, and I groaned. I wanted to

get lost in this man. To wrap my arms around his neck and keep him here.

"Thanks for dinner."

"Thanks for the hot kiss." I followed him down the stairs so I could lock up.

He walked backward after he stepped outside. His eyes moved to my mouth, and he shook his head before holding his hand up and jogging to his place.

And I missed him the minute he was gone.

thirteen

. . .

Romeo

ANOTHER WEEK HAD PASSED, and I'd buried myself in my workouts because kissing her had been a huge fuckup. I couldn't stop thinking about it. About her.

I knew going there was a bad idea because one taste wasn't enough.

There was too much shit between us.

And she was naïve enough to think I would go train at her parents' house? On their property? She didn't have a fucking clue how deep this ran for me.

But hearing her talk about her brother and how much she loved him—I hated the dude. He'd fucked me and River over.

Caused my family a shit ton of unnecessary pain.

I couldn't tell her that and devastate her. This shit had gotten complicated quickly. She'd dropped off a bunch of shakes, and I'd been working out with Joey when she came to train with Pinky after work. She'd texted a few times, and I hadn't responded.

What was the point?

If I was with her and told her the truth, she'd end up blaming me and hating me for it.

And if I didn't tell her the truth, there'd be this big lie between us, and she'd hate me anyway.

The guys all thought I was being a pussy and should just tell her. Let her decide.

I was at my mom's house for dinner, and Mimi had made her famous lasagna.

"You look really tired, honey," my mom said, as she sat beside me on the couch.

"That's a good thing. I need to end my days exhausted. I pushed an enormous tire up and down a hill this morning after my run. Joey doesn't mess around."

"I'm proud of you for working this hard." She smiled as Mimi came to sit in the chair across from us.

"I want to hear about the girl," my grandmother said.

My mom chuckled. "You haven't talked much about Demi this week."

"Yeah. I'm putting some space there."

She raised a brow. "She scares you, doesn't she?"

"I'm not scared of her, Mom."

"You're scared of how you feel about her. I saw the way you were with her when we stopped in her shop last week, and you just happened to be there."

"I was picking up my protein shakes. Her business is next door to mine." I really didn't want to get into this with them tonight, or any night, for that matter.

"You're reading into it." I pushed to my feet. "I need to get some sleep. Thanks for dinner."

I kissed each of them on the cheek and slipped on my coat.

"Love you," they both said at the same time.

"Love you."

I made my way home, and just as I was putting the key in the door, the sound of gravel beneath someone's feet had me turning.

Demi was storming toward me. A ball of fire.

She slammed me in the chest with the bag in her hand. "Here are your shakes for the next few days."

And then she turned on her heels and started marching across the alley.

"Hey." I chased after her because avoiding her was one thing, but seeing her and staying away was a completely different thing.

I couldn't.

I wrapped my arm around her wrist, and she shook me off. "Leave me alone, Romeo."

"Stop."

She whipped around, and there were tears streaming down her face. My chest was so tight that it was painful. I reached forward to wipe the tears from her cheeks with the pad of my thumb, and she slapped my hand away.

"I can't figure you out. You spend all this time with me and then you kiss me, and what? You didn't like it, so you just decided that you won't talk to me again? You avoid me at your gym, and you won't make eye contact with me." Her lip quivered, and the need to pull her against me was strong, but I crossed my arms over my chest to stop myself.

"That's what you think? Come on, Demi. You're smarter than that."

"So, tell me what it is. Tell me why you hate my family. Why are you punishing me for something that I'm unaware of? Because all I think about is you, and now you're shutting me out!"

"I think about you every fucking second of the day. That's the problem!" I was shouting now, and I set the shakes on the ground and threw my hands in the air. How could she not know this?

"So do something about it. Don't run from it." She shook her head. "I didn't take you for a coward."

"I'm not a coward. It's not me that I'm protecting. It's you."

"Tell me what it is, then. Let's figure it out," she said, as she swiped at the tears that continued to fall.

"The way that you told me what scared you enough that you actually fainted at my gym? Trust works both ways. And the difference here is that you're protecting someone else by not telling me what happened. I'm protecting *you* by not telling you what happened. There's a difference."

"Okay. You want to know so badly? My dad's business partner and our good family friends have a son, Ronny Waterstone. We grew up together. We went to college together." She let out a long breath. "We never dated. It was never, ever romantic. At least not on my side. But right before my college graduation a few months ago, he showed up drunk at my house on campus. My roommates weren't home. He said that he'd had too much to drink and needed a place to crash."

My hands fisted, and I could feel the rage coursing through my veins. "What the fuck did he do to you?"

"I gave him a pillow and blanket and said that he could sleep on the couch, and I went to sleep. I've known him my whole life." Her voice trembled. "But he wandered into my room an hour later while I was sleeping, and he climbed on top of me in my bed. He was so heavy, and it was terrifying. I tried to scream because I knew my roommates had most likely come home, but he pressed his forearm against my throat, making it hard for me to breathe. His eyes were— empty. Like he was a complete stranger. He tried to force himself on me, and I knew if I didn't do something, he'd kill me because he was pressing so hard against my throat. I don't know how I did it, but my leg broke free, and I kneed him hard enough in the balls that he fell off the bed and onto the floor. Then I hit him with a lamp before my roommate, Liz, came running into the bedroom. He acted like it was all a big misunderstanding. He told Liz that he'd walked in his sleep into my room by mistake. But that's not what happened."

"Did you call the police?"

She shook her head. "I called my dad."

"What the fuck did he do about it?"

"He was really mad. He told me not to call the police. Ronny had run out of our place and apologized on his way out the door."

"And your father just let him get away with this?"

"No. Not at all. He was furious. He didn't want me to go to the police because Ronny's family was in politics, and this would make the news. He didn't want to have me dragged through the mud, so he thought we should keep it quiet."

"Why the fuck would *you* be dragged through the mud? That dude is a psychopath."

"Because I'd agreed to let him sleep on the couch? I don't know," she said, as she cried harder. "My dad filed a restraining order for me and requested that it stay private, and he called Ronny and let him know that he would make it all public if he came near me ever again. He insisted that Ronny get help, and apparently, he's seeing a therapist weekly to deal with his issues."

This was not adding up to me.

A private restraining order and she wasn't involved in the process?

Her dad had handled it?

I'd bet a lot of fucking money he didn't do jack shit.

How the hell was he making sure this asshole was in therapy? It was a load of bullshit from where I was standing.

Her father wasn't worried about her being dragged through the mud; he was worried about his business relationship.

I pulled her close and wrapped my arms around her, kissing the top of her head.

"I'm so fucking sorry that happened to you. If I see this dude, I will put my fist through his face."

She stayed right there, little whimpers escaping her lips, and I just held her until her breathing calmed.

She tipped her head back, her eyes puffy under the moonlight. She was the most beautiful fucking woman I'd ever laid eyes on.

"Romeo, I'm trusting you with this. If you tell your friends, or you tell anyone at all, it will cause a lot of trouble for my family. It's very messy, and as long as he stays away and gets help, that's all I can ask for. You can't go after him or do anything—promise me."

I nodded. "As long as he doesn't come near you, I won't do anything. Has he contacted you at all?"

Her eyes darted away from me, and I fucking knew the answer to my question before she even spoke.

"Tell me." My voice was hard because this rich prick didn't live by the same rules as everyone else.

"I don't know for sure if it's him. I've gotten some texts from unknown numbers, asking if we can talk, and he calls me *D* in the texts, which is what Ronny always called me. My gut tells me that they're from him."

"Do you respond?"

"No. I block the number after he texts. I told my dad, and he said he'd handle it."

The fuck he would. He was handling the whole situation in a way that behooved him.

"Let's get you inside." I grabbed the shakes and walked her back to my place and pushed the door open. This was foreign territory for me. Sure, I'd dated my fair share, but never someone like Demi.

Sweet and genuine and good.

With a complicated fucking family that I'd have to navigate, because she loved them, and I saw them for who they were.

I kicked the door closed and led her to the couch before pulling her onto my lap. She unzipped her jacket and dropped it onto the couch, burying her head beneath my neck.

"Thank you for telling me what happened."

"I trust you, and I hope you trust me and will tell me what your hang-up is with my family. I can take it. I've dealt with my fair share of shit, too. Just because my family has money does not mean our lives are perfect." She pushed up to meet my gaze. "My brother broke into the coffee shop and is a drug addict. My parents aren't speaking to him. I've got a family friend who attacked me in the middle of the night. I'm not made of porcelain. I'm tougher than I look."

I nodded because she was right. And she'd trusted me with her fucked-up secret, so I'd tell her mine.

I tugged her back down and settled her head beneath my chin so I could tell her this without looking at her. Because if she looked upset, I wouldn't go through with it. This was the only way I could get through this.

Hurting Demi Crawford was not something that I was looking forward to doing.

"Tell me," she whispered. "We can't move forward until we get it all out there."

"Do you remember years ago when River and I got into trouble at The Daily Market?" Small-town gossip was real, and two local kids getting busted didn't go unnoticed by many.

"I remember hearing something about it, but I was young, so I don't know the story."

"My dad had just gone to prison, and I was angry and nervous for my mom and my sister. Wondering how we were going to survive. It had been a long road with my father, so I was dealing with a lot of shit back then."

"I'm sure that must have been really hard. Seeing someone you love battle addiction is emotionally exhausting."

I took my time. Reliving that day was not something I did often. "I was fourteen years old, and I'd ditched school because I was too pissed off at the world for my own good.

And River, he was seventeen years old at the time. And the five of us, you know, we're more like brothers— but with River being the oldest, he almost took on a paternal role in my life back then."

"I can see how close you all are."

I nodded, wrapping my arms around her, keeping her close. "He left school and came and found me hiding out at the park. We talked for a while, and he told me they'd all have my back and my family would be fine. Then we went over to The Daily Market to get some junk food."

"I'm glad he was there for you," she whispered.

"Your brother was there with another kid. He wasn't from here, and I don't know who he was. Your brother was River's age, so older than me. And they were fucked up."

She sat up to look at me. "Slade was drunk?"

I raised a brow. "I think he was drunk and high. It was no secret back then that your brother was partying hard, Demi."

Her gaze searched mine, and I motioned for her to lean back because I couldn't do this if she kept looking at me with that sadness in her eyes. She rested her head on my chest, and I stroked her hair.

"I didn't think he did any of that until after the boating accident."

"Well, I've had my fair share of experience with people who mess with drugs and booze, and your brother was doing both back then." I cleared my throat. "Oscar wasn't working that day. He was home sick, apparently. It was a guy who worked part-time at the store covering him, Walt Salden. And he didn't know how to handle your brother and his friend, because they started pushing things off the shelves and breaking shit."

"Oh my God," she whispered. "What did you do?"

"River gave me a look like we needed to get the fuck out of there. And then your brother shoved a bottle of booze down his pants, and Walt came running around the counter to stop him."

"I never heard anything about this."

I wasn't surprised. They'd brushed it under the rug.

"Walt started shouting, and your brother got in his face. There was a lot of shoving and yelling going on. River and I made a run for it. We wanted to get the hell out of there."

"And did you?"

"We ran out the door, but we turned back just as Slade shoved Walt hard enough that the dude fell into a display of booze, which tipped over and shattered. The old guy went down hard on his head, and your brother and his friend took off, laughing and running."

"Oh my God," she said, and I could hear the pain in her voice. "What did you do?"

"River and I… we were fucking young, you know? I was scared, and he wouldn't admit it, but I know he was, too. We ran back inside, and Walt was unconscious. We called 9-1-1 and got him help. We stayed with him until they got there."

"Was he okay?"

"He had bleeding on the brain from hitting his head and was in the hospital for a week."

"How do I not know about this? Slade must have gotten in trouble for this. And who was the other kid?"

"He didn't, and I never knew who the other kid was because your brother denied even being there. The surveillance cameras miraculously didn't work that day, according to the police report. River and I were blamed for what happened. We'd been on the scene when the ambulance arrived. We'd explained what happened to the police officers assigned to the case, and they'd claimed that your brother wasn't at the store, and neither was his friend. Slade had a watertight alibi that he was fishing with your dad. Your father had visited Walt at the hospital, from what River and I later found out, and once Walt was up for talking, he'd corroborated the story. And they'd come down hard on me and River because we'd been skipping school, and we'd been blamed for the damage at the shop and for shoving Walt so hard that he'd been hospitalized."

She pushed up now, looking me right in the eyes as tears streamed down her face. "What happened after that?"

"We were sent to juvenile detention. They'd said we were violent and dangerous. Neither of us had families who could protect us at that point. My mom was in way over her head, and all she could do was cry. My father had just gone to prison, so no one thought it was a stretch that I'd have done this. And River and King were being raised by their elderly grandparents, who weren't equipped to go to bat for us either. Slade had found the perfect scapegoats."

And I'd hated them every day since.

fourteen

. . .

Demi

MY EARS WERE RINGING, and my head was spinning as I listened with horror to what had happened to Romeo and River.

The injustice.

All at the hands of my brother, and possibly my father.

I couldn't wrap my head around any of it.

My dad was a good man. He worked hard for our family. His investment company gave back to the community. I couldn't fathom him going along with this.

I remember hearing bits and pieces about Romeo and River, but I hadn't known the half of it.

"You were fourteen years old, and they sent you away?" I croaked, and now I needed to look at him. To feel all the things that he went through at the expense of my family. I needed to understand it and apologize and try to make this right in any way that I could.

"Yes. Originally, we were told that I'd be staying for six months, and River would be staying for a year, which was the appropriate time based on our age, apparently. We'd been presented to the judge like the scum of the earth. Two kids who ditched school and vandalized their neighborhood. One who had a dad who was serving time, and the other who didn't even have parents who cared enough to stick around. So, they'd given us the worst. For a crime we hadn't committed."

"Did you tell the judge?"

"We told anyone who would listen, but after a while, we stopped telling our side of the story because our free legal representation said we were making things worse. They said we should apologize and take what they gave us."

"Did you?"

"Fuck no. Neither of us was going to apologize for something that we didn't do. But we stopped telling our side of the story when we realized no one wanted to hear it. Hell, Walt sat in that courtroom and couldn't even look at us. He knew. He fucking knew. He claimed he had no memory, but I saw the guilt there. Hell, I still see it when I run into the asshole in town. I think Oscar figured it out, too, but your father made sure that none of this came down on your brother and whoever else was there with him."

I shook my head frantically. "I can't fathom that my father would send innocent kids away for a crime they didn't commit." But as the words left my mouth, I couldn't help but wonder what he could, or would, do. I was questioning everything now. Things with my brother and everything that had gone down with Ronny. I knew image was important to my father, but this was unfathomable.

His gaze softened, as if he'd expected me to say that. "I know you love him, but your father and your brother both know what happened, Demi. I want you to really think about something, okay?"

"Okay." I nodded, swiping at the falling tears.

"If your father had to choose between your brother getting into trouble or me and River, do you really think he'd do the right thing when his back was against the wall? Look at how he's handled your situation with Ronny."

A lump formed in my throat, and my voice wobbled. "What do you mean?"

I knew what he meant, didn't I?

But admitting it would mean that I didn't know my father at all.

"Come on. You're a college graduate. A smart business-woman. Do you really think there's a situation where a father can go and get a restraining order for his adult daughter, where she doesn't have to tell the police what happened? Where she doesn't sign anything? A restraining order that's sealed and kept private? What fucking good would that do? The whole point of a restraining order is to make sure everyone knows that the fucker needs to stay away. Why would it be a secret?"

His words were swirling in my head. None of it had made sense to me, but I trusted my father. Of course, I did.

I'd found the whole thing to be odd. He'd asked me to keep my mother out of it.

A restraining order that I'd never seen.

And now, hearing what had happened to Romeo and River…

That my father had been behind it. Slade was a kid. He couldn't have pulled this off by himself.

"Did you end up staying there for six months, and River for a year?"

His hands settled on each side of my face, his thumbs swiping the liquid falling from my eyes. "No. My mother went to anyone who would listen. She found someone to look at our case pro bono, and he got us out of there sooner. We never knew exactly what happened, but I served three months, and River served eight months."

"I'm so sorry," I croaked, my words barely audible. "You must have been so scared."

"Listen, Demi." His voice was calm and even, and he waited for me to meet his gaze. "I'm not going to sugarcoat it. It sucked. There was some dark shit going on in that place, but we survived it. River went on to become a lawyer because of it. And I became an even better fighter. I learned at a young age to defend myself, and my three months in that hellhole made me tougher."

I lunged forward, my arms wrapping around his neck. I hugged him so tight it took the air from my lungs. All these feelings, all these emotions.

"I'm sorry that happened to you. I'm sorry that my family did this. They robbed you of your childhood," I said, still trying to wrap my head around it.

He pulled back so he could look at me. "No. No one took shit from either one of us. We made it out of there in one piece, and we're stronger for it. And your brother got into that boating accident a few months later, and they covered that shit up, too."

I could feel my head spinning. "What do you mean? He lost control of the boat. It was an accident."

"Everyone in town knows that he was drunk and high, Demi. Boomer Wilkes was hospitalized for a month after that accident. But he, too, was silenced by your father back then, or at least that's the story. There were four people on that boat, and none of them spoke about it again. They were most likely threatened or bribed. I don't know what it was, but they were scared and didn't say anything. I'm guessing your brother wasn't hanging out with those friends after the accident, was he? Because they knew the truth."

I rubbed my temples as I processed his words. I remembered the accident. The hysteria in my house when the call came late at night. I was in middle school then, and I just remember a lot of crying and panic.

"They said the boat malfunctioned," I whispered. "And

Slade was hurt, too, and that's when he was prescribed opioids."

"Your brother was an addict before that boating accident, Demi. Maybe it wasn't that bad before the accident, but he was partying hard, and everyone knew it. They just covered everything up because they had the money to do it, and everyone around him was just collateral damage."

"Do you think my mother knew about this?" I shook my head rapidly. "My mom is such a good person, Romeo. She would never be okay with this."

But I thought the same thing about my father and my brother.

My head was spinning with thoughts.

"I don't know. I know that your father went to see Walt at the hospital, and that's when everything turned in our direction."

"You believe that I didn't know anything about this, right? I need to know that you don't think I'd ever be okay with any of this."

His forehead rested against mine. "I know who you are, Demi Crawford. And that's why I didn't want to go here with you. But I can't seem to stay the fuck away from you, no matter how hard I try."

"Why wouldn't you want to go here with me? Because you think I'd blame you for what my family did to you?"

"At first, I thought you'd side with them. Hell, the guys and I never knew if you were aware of it before now—before I got to know you. I figured out pretty quickly that you didn't know anything about it."

"How?"

"Because your heart is too goddamn big. You're so busy protecting everyone around you that you don't realize that no one is protecting you." He stroked my cheek, and I leaned into his touch.

"You going to protect me from all the bad guys, Romeo?"

I'm not sure why I asked. I mean, why would he want to protect me when my family did him so much harm?

"I will if you let me."

I'd never felt this connected to another person, yet at the same time, it felt like the world I'd known was crumbling around me.

"I don't know why you want to be with me after what my family has done to you and River, and God knows who else," I said, unable to hide the devastation from my voice as my words broke on a sob.

"Because you deserve better than the shit you've been dealt. I know you love your family, and a part of me has an easier time rectifying what your brother did than what your father did."

"Why?" I asked, because they'd both been evil to do what they'd done to them.

"Because your brother was young and stupid and an addict. But your father knew exactly what he was doing, and he never owned it. My guess is that he'd been doing what he wanted for so long that he justified it. Probably thought it was for the greater good."

"I don't know what to do with this information now. I mean, I have to confront them. You know that, right?"

"I only kept it a secret because I didn't want to hurt you. River and I are honest about what happened to anyone who asks. And do you know what the consensus in this town was when we told our story to the few that actually cared to hear it?"

"What?"

"They weren't shocked, Demi. But they warned us to be careful who we told. So, I don't think it's the first or the last time your father has manipulated the system in his favor. People don't respect your father; they fear him."

"I need to talk to them. Find out what my mom knows. My mom…" I placed my hand on my heart. "She's a good woman, Romeo. I just can't fathom that she'd be all right with this. And her parents, Gramps and Grammie, they would not be okay with any of this. My grandfather is my idol. He's honest and caring and—he's really good, Romeo. I look up to him so much, and I can't be that wrong about everyone in my life."

"Hey, this isn't on you. It's not your job to find out who's lying and who's evil. That's why I hesitated to tell you at all. Because I don't want you to see the world the way I see it. To know that evil exists and that life isn't all sunshine and rainbows." He smirked. "I like that you see the good in everyone. That you defended your asshole brother after he fucking robbed you. The world needs more Demi Crawfords in it."

"And what do you need?"

"I need more Demi Crawford, too."

"So, we're doing this?" I asked, my fingers intertwining with his.

"Yeah, Beans. We're doing this."

My mouth crashed into his, and before I knew what was happening, he pushed to his feet. Our mouths never lost contact as he carried me across the room. When he pulled away, he set me on the bed, like I was something breakable.

Precious.

He pulled off my shoes and tossed them on the floor, and then he tugged his sweater over his head and climbed in beside me.

I ran my fingers over his chest, taking my time to trace every single defined muscle.

"Thank you for telling me the truth," I said, feeling a heaviness on my shoulders and my heart and my entire being.

I believed Romeo, and I trusted him. Deep down, I always wondered about Slade's accident. I was aware that he'd caused trouble in town, not just that one incident. It hurt that

I might not know the people in my life. The people that I loved fiercely. The people that I trusted.

How could they do this?

"No more secrets, all right?" he said. His hand settled on my waist, and I squirmed the slightest bit. Desperate for his touch.

To feel something other than sadness.

He leaned over and kissed me before pulling back. "I want you so fucking bad, but tonight is not the night."

I nodded in understanding and tried to make light of it. "I'm fine."

"You're not. And this was a lot. But I'm not going anywhere, so we can take our time, okay? And if you need to cry, I want you to cry. I don't think you're being disloyal to me by being upset after hearing that your family might not be who you think they are. That shit hurts. I know you feel bad about what happened to me, but I'm fine, Demi. River is fine. Right now, you're hurting, and I want you to deal with that and not bottle it up, because it'll fester and eat you alive."

There was a lump so thick in my throat now that it was difficult to breathe. And I just let it all out. I lay in his arms as sobs wracked my body.

I cried, and I sobbed.

And I let go.

The sadness that my dad was not who I thought he was.

The fact that my brother's struggles started long before I knew they did.

The truth that regardless of who in our home knew what, we were all living a lie. And I was done with it.

After my breathing settled, he continued running his hands through my hair and holding me close when I needed it most.

I listened to the sound of his heart, and it soothed me.

"You okay?" he whispered.

"I will be."

"I don't doubt that for a minute."

I snuggled closer and tried to push away thoughts of a young Romeo living away from his family and being mistreated and scared, and I couldn't get close enough to him.

One thing I knew for damn certain, I'd be getting Romeo and River an apology if it was the last thing I did.

fifteen

. . .

Romeo

> I talked to Demi about her family. She knows everything.

RIVER

How'd she take it?

> The way you'd expect someone who's been lied to for a long time to take it. She was devastated. Shocked. But she didn't doubt me or think I was lying.

KINGSTON

Told you. She's a good one. And I thought we decided a long time ago that we don't judge others by their family members, right? We should have included her in that.

NASH

That was deep, King. You must have gotten laid last night. I'm glad you told her, Romeo. It's nice to see your grumpy ass happy for once.

HAYES

So, what happens from here? Will she confront them?

She wants to. I don't blame her. I'd want to know who knew what and how involved they were.

KINGSTON

Agreed. You think her dad will come after you?

RIVER

I fucking dare him. He can't intimidate anyone anymore. We're all grown up.

Fuck, yeah. She did share something with me. The son of a family friend of her parents tried to force himself on her several months ago. She fought like hell, and he ran off. Her dad claims he got a restraining order, and I'm not buying it. I don't think he's going away. Can you look into it, River? See if there's a restraining order in the system for this guy?

RIVER

Of course. What's his name?

Ronny Waterstone.

HAYES

As in, the grandson of the senator of California?

NASH

Isn't his father, Patrick, business partners with Demi's father?

Yes, to both.

KINGSTON

I get the feeling Jack Crawford didn't file shit
on his daughter's behalf.

RIVER

I'll do some digging and let you know what I
find out.

> Thanks. I need to go for a run. I'll catch you
> boys later.

HAYES

Proud of you, brother.

KINGSTON

You're training out in the elements and
puking and sore, and Leo is posting endless
shit on his social media about his fancy gym
and the slew of women who hang out during
his workouts. He's such a cheesedick.

RIVER

Why the fuck are you following him on social
media?

KINGSTON

Didn't anyone ever tell you that you should
keep your enemies close?

NASH

Is that why you went home with Shana
Richards last night? I thought you hated her...

KINGSTON

Listen, Looselips... Shana and I are friends. I
am all about forgiveness.

RIVER

Are you fucking her again? Didn't she shave your eyebrows when you were sleeping once?

> I thought she shaved your balls?

KINGSTON

Hell no. She squeezed my balls once when I tried to break up with her. And she's got those long, scary nails. It hurt like hell. She shaved that mustache I was trying to grow in my sleep last year. I'm smarter now. I walked her home, and when she tried to kiss me, I said that it took us a long time to become friends again, and I didn't want to cross that line.

HAYES

How'd that go over?

KINGSTON

She dug her nails into my chest and stabbed my nipple. She practically pierced it. You guys know I have sensitive nipples.

> <laughing face emoji>

NASH

Well, you and your nipples better get your ass to work in twenty minutes, because we've got a shit ton to do today.

RIVER

Toughen up, little brother. Let's meet at the gym later today, and you can update us on what Demi decides to do with this information.

"YOU READY?" Joey asked as I dropped my phone onto my desk.

He had the electric bike, and he'd be pushing me today. We made our way outside, and he handed me a backpack.

"Jesus. Did you load it with bricks?" I pulled it over my shoulders, and he chuckled.

"Yeah. You're getting too fast. We need to make these runs more challenging."

"Me puking at the end of every run isn't enough?" I rolled my eyes and glanced over at the coffee shop as I stretched my legs and adjusted to the weight on my back.

I'd spent the night with Demi, and the talk had been very heavy. But she hadn't run or shouted or blamed me for what happened.

She'd listened.

"Stop gaping over there at your girl. You look like a moron," Joey grumped, which made me laugh.

"I'm not a moron. Just making sure she's okay."

"Well, you didn't deny she was your girl, so I guess you're growing up, Romeo." He climbed onto the bike, looking ridiculous with all his tattoos and his giant body hovering over the handlebars. "Now, get your ass moving. No time for chitchat."

And I took off on the same path I'd been running. He moved ahead of me, shouting and yelling all sorts of insults. That was Joey's style, and it worked well for me; however, it was pouring rain now. I had a forty-pound backpack on my shoulders, and I was running six-minute miles. So, I tuned his mean ass out, and I focused on the fight.

On Leo fucking Burns, who wouldn't shut up about me on social media.

On Demi's family, who had fucked over me and River all those years ago.

On my father's battle with addiction and all the shit we

went through to get to the other side of things, only to have him pass away at a young age.

I thought about my life.

About surviving and fighting and never giving up.

And then I thought about Demi.

How maybe all the shit I'd gone through was supposed to lead me here.

"Pump those motherfucking arms, you big pussy!" Joey shouted, and I pushed harder just to shut him the fuck up.

Faster.

Stronger.

I left it all out there.

Everything I had in me.

I came to a stop in front of the gym and moved to the bushes, where I proceeded to vomit, and then I wiped my mouth with the back of my hand.

"Fuck, that was tough," I said. I pulled the backpack off my shoulders and dropped it onto the ground. The rain was easing up.

"You know what's tough, Romeo? You're fucking tough. Go take a shower and get some food in your belly. I'll meet you back here for your afternoon workout." He glanced over at the two women who pulled the door open and walked inside the gym. "It's getting too distracting in there with all this attention. It's not a goddamn circus. We may need to find another place to work out in the afternoons."

I nodded. "You want me to keep the backpack?"

"Hell yeah. That's your new best friend. And I'm bringing Butch this afternoon to beat the shit out of you, so be ready."

"Always am." I held my hand up and walked toward the back door of the coffee shop. I heard Joey laughing, and I flipped him the bird.

"She's making me some new shakes!" I shouted.

"I'm sure she is, Golden Boy."

I couldn't get that kiss out of my head, and my dick had

been on high alert because she'd spent the night in my bed. But I was dog-tired now, and the truth was, I just wanted to see her face.

I pulled the back door open, and Peyton raised a brow. "Hey there, superstar. We just had two women in here who were wearing T-shirts that said, *Just here for the Magnolia Falls Golden Boy.*"

I rolled my eyes. A lot of locals were cashing in on the upcoming fight. They were making shit and selling it. I didn't care. If it could make people a couple of bucks, I was fine with it.

"It'll blow over. Where's Demi?"

"You two sure are spending a lot of time together." She waggled her brows. "I think something's going on."

Demi walked into the kitchen, holding a bag of what I assumed was protein shakes, and as soon as her eyes met mine, her teeth sank into her juicy bottom lip.

"Trust your gut on that, Peyton." I winked, and she let out a too-high-pitched squeal in celebration. I turned my attention to Demi. "Can you take a break for a little bit?"

"Yeah. The breakfast rush is over. You got things covered, Peyt?" she asked.

"Abso-freaking-lutely. Take your time." She waggled her brows.

I chuckled and took the bag from Demi, and she glanced at the backpack as I pushed the door open.

"What's with the backpack? It looks heavy."

"Joey is the devil." We stepped outside into the rain, and I reached for her hand as we ran across the alley to my place.

Once we were inside, I dropped her hand and moved to the kitchen area, pulling out a shake and offering her one.

She smiled. "Those are for you. I had a muffin for breakfast. You just ran with that heavy pack on your back. You should get that drink down and then have a good breakfast, as well."

I dropped the heavy backpack onto the floor, unscrewed the lid, and guzzled the shake. "Damn, that's good."

"You'll be feeling revived in twenty minutes," she said.

I studied her. My gaze moved down her pretty face to the tan hooded sweater she was wearing. It was damp from the rain and sticking to her perfect tits, and my mouth watered at the sight.

I dropped the bottle into the recycle bin and turned around to see Demi with her arms wrapped around herself, trying to get warm.

"You cold?" I moved closer.

"I'm wet," she said, and I raised a brow and chuckled. "From the rain, amongst other things."

"Yeah?" I ran the pad of my thumb over her bottom lip. This fucking mouth would be the death of me. I couldn't get that kiss out of my mind.

"Yeah."

"I'm going to catch a shower. You want to join me?"

Her heated gaze moved back up to meet mine. "Hmmm... I'm already wet, and I'm freezing, so a hot shower sounds pretty good."

"Let me warm you up, then." My voice was gruff. We'd been holding back for weeks. Kissing her just wasn't enough. We'd said all that needed to be said last night, and we were doing this, so I was done holding back.

It didn't mean we needed to rush things, but I wanted to make her feel good.

She took my hand, and I led her the short distance to the bathroom. We were both wet, and I reached for the hem of her sweater, tugging it up and over her head. She wore a pretty pink bra underneath, and my fingers traced over the hard peaks poking through the lace.

She sucked in a breath, and I dropped to my knees and lifted her leg to pull off her tennis shoes. I tossed them to the side and reached for the hem of her leggings before slowly pulling them down her lean, tanned legs. Goose bumps covered her skin, and I chucked them near her shoes. I glanced up at her, and her gaze met mine.

I turned my attention back to the pink lace panties that matched her bra, and my fingers moved beneath the band as I leaned forward and kissed her right over the fabric. I breathed her in.

"Fuck, Demi. You're so beautiful."

I tugged her panties down her legs and kissed her thighs and her knees and her ankles. I wanted to worship every inch of her gorgeous body. I pushed to my feet, my hands moving behind her back and unsnapping her bra, as the last bit of fabric covering her fell to the floor.

Fuck me.

She was perfect.

Made for me.

I'd never wanted anyone more.

Her trembling hand moved to my hoodie, and she did her best to push it over my head, but with me being much taller, I helped get her there. She smiled up at me before mimicking what I'd done to her. She moved to her knees and helped me out of my shoes before reaching for the band of my gray joggers and pulling them down my legs. She set them beside her, and then her eyes widened at my dick bulging through the black briefs I was wearing.

"I've been hard since last night. Having you in my bed, being wrapped around you, it's doing crazy shit to me."

"I like doing crazy shit to you." She tugged my briefs down my legs, leaned forward, and kissed the tip of my dick before swirling her tongue around it. I sucked in a breath and reached for her, pulling her to her feet.

"Things will end very quickly if you start there." My laugh was strained. "I want to make you feel good."

I opened the glass door and turned on the hot water before reaching for her hand. She was still trembling.

"Are you cold or nervous?"

I needed to know.

"Probably both. I've never showered with a man." She shrugged.

My eyes widened in question.

"I'm not a virgin. I've just never showered with someone."

Goddamn, I was crazy about this girl.

"I like being your first anything," I said, leading her into the water.

"I like it, too."

The hot water sprayed down on us, and I handed her the body wash. We both filled our palms with soap and took our time washing one another. My hands trailed over her gorgeous tits, her flat stomach, and her neck as her head fell back in the most erotic way. I soaped up the curve of her gorgeous ass and then turned her around so I could wash her hair. I'd never done anything like this with a woman before. Sure, I'd fucked in the shower.

This was different.

Intimate.

This connection was so strong that I wanted to do everything with her.

She turned around and faced me, water drops falling down her pretty face. "My turn."

She took her time, running those hands into my hair as I bent down so she could reach the top of my head. Once I was standing fully upright, she took her time running her palms over my shoulders, her body moving easily around me as she washed my back, my arms, and even my hands and fingers when she came back around to stand in front of me. It was sexy and soothing all at the same time. And then she poured more soap into her palm and made her way down my abdomen. Every inch of my body ached, but it came alive beneath her touch. She ran her hands up and down my shaft slowly, and I was so fucking turned on I couldn't see straight.

My hands moved to each side of her face as she gripped my dick harder, and my mouth crashed into hers.

I tilted her head to the side so I could kiss her deeper. One hand moved over her hip and around the curve of her narrow waist before sliding up her rib cage until I covered her breast. My thumb circled her nipple as our tongues swirled. I fucking loved kissing this woman. I loved her mouth and the little sounds she made. I moved to her other breast and took turns tweaking her hard peaks. She arched her back, trying to get closer as she continued sliding her hand up and down my shaft.

My hand moved down her flat stomach, our mouths never losing contact. I traced along the outside of her hip and down the inside of her thigh before sliding up and grazing her pussy with the tips of my fingers.

"Please," she whisper-groaned into my mouth, and it was the sexiest fucking thing I'd ever heard. I pulled back long enough to meet her gaze and make sure she was okay. Her green eyes were half-mast, cheeks flushed, and lips red and swollen from where I'd kissed her. She gave me the slightest nod, and I slipped a finger inside.

Jesus.

She was so tight. I wasn't sure how my dick would ever fit, but I didn't give a shit right now. Her hand felt like fucking heaven as she continued to work her magic on my cock. Her lips parted the slightest bit, and her breaths came faster as her back pressed against the shower wall. She rocked her hips as I pulled my finger in and out of her faster now, before adding a second digit. She gasped the slightest bit as I fucked her hand, and my mouth crashed into hers once again. Her hips bucked in motion with my hand, and my dick was on the verge of exploding. My thumb moved to her clit, making little circles and knowing just what she needed, as I thrust forward, faster and faster, into her hand.

Loud moans flooded the shower, and she cried out my

name as her walls tightened around my fingers in sharp pulses. And that was all it took. I thrust one more time as bright lights exploded behind my eyes, and I came so hard I couldn't see straight. I continued fucking her with my fingers as her head fell back against the wall, and she stayed right there with me. Her hand glided up and down my shaft.

And I was done for.

This girl owned me.

sixteen

. . .

Demi

ROMEO FOUND a blow dryer for me beneath his vanity, and I dried my hair quickly, still coming down from the sexiest shower time I'd ever experienced. He was sitting on the counter in the bathroom, watching me dry my hair.

He was all long legs and big muscles and sexy smirks.

I turned it off and used his brush to make myself presentable before I hurried back to work.

"Is it obvious?" I asked, looking in the mirror.

"Is what obvious?"

"I feel like I'm having my sexual awakening at twenty-two years old."

He chuckled, and it was this sexy, gruff sound that had butterflies swirling in my belly.

"We haven't even had sex yet."

"Oh, I know. But that was my first shower experience, and my first—" My teeth sank into my bottom lip, and I felt my cheeks heat.

"Your first what?" He tugged me over to him, and I settled between his legs.

"My first orgasm with a man."

This sexy grin spread across his face. "Yeah? And that was

just my fingers. Wait till you see what I can do with my mouth and my dick."

Oh. My. God.

I squeezed my thighs together and covered my face with my hands.

"You don't need to be shy with me. You've obviously had shitty partners." His fingers circled my wrist, and he pulled my hands away so he could look at me.

"I've only been with one guy. My college boyfriend. He was two years older than me. He's actually a really good guy," I said.

Romeo growled, which made me laugh. "Fuck him. I hate him already."

"Stop. We're still friends."

"Why'd you break up, then? Because he sucked in the sack?" He tugged me closer and buried his face in my neck. His scruff grazed my skin, and I groaned.

"No," I said over my laughter. "Maybe I suck in the sack."

"Trust me. You don't. How long were you with him?"

"Three years. We lasted a year after he graduated, and it just wasn't the same after he started working full time. He wanted marriage and kids and all of that, and I was twenty years old at the time. I just didn't see a future with him that way."

He nodded. "And not one orgasm in three years? How is that possible?"

"He was the quarterback for our college football team. He worked out hard, and he'd be pretty worn out most of the time. So, it was usually pretty quick but always sweet."

"I just ran seven miles with a forty-pound backpack on my shoulders, and I made you come with just my fingers. Trust me. Working out has nothing to do with it."

"Apparently not. So, what's your longest relationship?"

"A year. But I've always had volatile partners, if I'm being honest. Lots of drama and breakups and fighting. This feels different." His hands were on each side of my face, his eyes staring at my mouth like he couldn't wait to kiss me again.

"It does feel different." I sighed. "Well, you're clearly more experienced than me. I'm curious—what's your favorite sexual position?"

He smiled, and my stomach did these little flips. "This really is your sexual awakening, isn't it?"

"Are you avoiding the question?"

"No. You can ask me anything. Sex is my favorite topic. Before now, my favorite position was doggy style. But I don't see myself doing that with you. Not unless we're standing in front of a mirror and I'm behind you."

My mouth fell open. "Why not?"

"Because I love your face. I loved watching you come apart for me. You're so fucking pretty. I want to be looking at you all the time. At those soulful eyes of yours. Those plump lips and your cute-ass nose with that perfect little sprinkle of freckles."

"That was a really good answer." I stepped forward and wrapped my arms around his neck. "You're definitely going to get lucky soon, Golden Boy. But I need to go deal with the lunch rush and then get this conversation with my parents over with."

"All right. I'm going to eat some breakfast and get to the gym. Call me if you need me, okay?"

"Yep. I'll see you later?"

I started to walk away, and he caught my hand and turned me back toward him. His mouth was on mine, his tongue slipping inside.

When he pulled back, I was breathless. He jumped down off the counter and led me to the door. I expected him to say goodbye, but instead, he linked hands with mine and walked me across the alley.

It had finally stopped raining, and I chuckled. "It's a

twenty-foot walk at most across the alley. You didn't need to escort me."

"What can I say? I can't get enough of you, Beans." He smacked my ass and jogged back to his house.

And I stood there gaping at him before heading back to work. The next few hours went by quickly, and Peyton agreed to stay while I went over to my parents' house. I'd called my grandfather and asked him to meet me there, as well. I needed to know who was involved in all of this.

My stomach twisted as I made my way to the home I'd grown up in. The rain had started falling again, and I watched the road through my windshield wipers as they moved back and forth. I pulled up the long driveway and saw Gramps's car parked there.

I stepped inside, and Mariana was the first to greet me. "Hey there, sweetness. I just brought some tea into the living room. I figured you'd want something warm with all this rain today."

"Thank you," I said. The nerves were there now because I knew this was going to be a very heavy conversation. I wanted there to be an explanation that would make everything okay, but I couldn't think of one that would even be a possibility. How could what they did ever be explained?

"You all right?" she asked.

"Yeah, I'm good."

"Is Peyton covering Magnolia Beans for you?" She walked beside me as I made my way to the living room.

"She is. She's got it down. And I'll get back there in time to close up for the day."

"Sounds good." She squeezed my hand as she continued on to the kitchen, and I turned into the living room area where we liked to hang out and chat or play board games.

"Hey," my mom said, with a big smile on her face. "I'm so happy you were able to sneak away from work. But we were surprised you wanted Gramps here, too, so we're hoping everything's okay."

"I told you that our girl is a brilliant businesswoman. She's always thinking of new ideas." Gramps sipped his tea.

My father looked up at me with all the pride in the world. Not a clue about the bomb I was about to drop. I poured myself a cup of tea and sat in the chair across from them, as they were all three sitting on the couch.

"It's not about work, actually. It's about something that is pretty upsetting, and I'm hoping we can make sense of it and figure out how to move forward."

My mother's eyes widened. "Are you sick?"

"No. I'm not sick, Mom. But what I've learned has made me feel pretty horrible, if I'm being honest." My gaze locked with my father's, and I saw something there. Fear, maybe?

"What is it?" Gramps asked.

"Do you remember years ago, before Slade's boating accident, there was a situation at The Daily Market? Two teenagers apparently stole something and then shoved Walt down, and they were sent to a juvenile detention center for the crime."

"Yes. That young man who owns the gym, the boxer, he was involved. And his father had just gone to jail, as well. It's all everyone was talking about back then. And his friend was there, as well. He was a few years older. The whole thing was very sad." My mom set her teacup down on the table.

"I remember this," Gramps said, as he ran a hand over his jaw. "They could have killed Walt. He hit his head and was hospitalized for some time."

I turned my attention back to my father. "Do you remember this, Dad? I believe you went to see Walt in the hospital."

"Why are you dredging this up? This has nothing to do with you," he said, pushing to his feet and walking to the window to look out at the gray skies as the rain continued to fall.

"I'm bringing it up because I just learned about it. That boxer, the one you are so quick to label as trouble or a bad kid —he had nothing to do with what happened. The irony of this whole situation is unbelievable. And I just want to know who was involved in this. I know that you were," I said, waiting for my father to turn around and look at me.

He finally did, and he glanced over at my mother before his gaze moved back to mine. "I did what needed to be done. For this family." He wasn't even going to try and deny it. I should be glad that this lie was finally going to be out in the open, but knowing Dad had done what he'd done made me look at him differently.

"I don't know what we're talking about," my mother said. I didn't miss the slightest tremble in her voice.

Gramps looked between me and my father, as if he were trying to figure out what was going on.

"Romeo and River were not the people who stole anything that day, nor were they the ones who pushed Walt over. They were just two teenagers who were in the wrong place at the wrong time. And you let them take the blame for something that Slade did." The tears were falling now, because even saying the words aloud made me sick to my stomach.

"What? Is this true, Jack?" Gramps asked, and his hands were fisted at his sides.

I knew in this moment that my father was the only one involved in this whole mess. And as devastated as I was that he'd done this, I was relieved that my entire family hadn't taken part.

"It's not as devious as you're making it out to be." Dad shoved his hands into his pockets. "I found out that Slade and Ronny were there. Ronny had been in town with his father, and apparently, he'd convinced Slade to skip school that day. They'd stolen a bottle of whiskey. He'd told me that they ran out and that the other two boys had been there, as well. I thought they were all in on it. I just did my part to keep Slade and Ronny out of it."

My heart raced at learning that Ronny had been the other person there that day.

"How, exactly, did you keep him out of it, if they'd been at that store?" Gramps's voice was ice cold now.

"I just said that Slade and Ronny had been with me fishing. There weren't witnesses at the store, aside from the other two teenage boys, who, by the way, had been ditching school, as well."

"Ditching school is different than robbing a store and violently attacking the man who worked there!" I shouted, because his casual demeanor was pissing me off. "They'd cut school because Romeo's father had just been sent to prison. He was devastated and a little lost. They were there buying candy, Dad. They got out of there when your drunk son and his disgusting friend started vandalizing the place. And they left. But they turned around and saw Slade push Walt into the liquor counter and run out the door, laughing. They went back inside to help him." My hand was on my chest as tears ran down my face, and I tried to speak through my hysteria.

"I didn't know that at the time."

"You didn't ask. And you went to the hospital and got Walt to say what you wanted him to say, didn't you? It seems awfully convenient that the surveillance cameras weren't working that day." I made no effort to hide my disgust.

"I can't believe this," my mother whispered, and I looked up to see tears running down her face, as well.

"This is appalling, Jack. Even for you." Gramps was on his feet now, and the vein on the side of his neck bulged. There'd never been a whole lot of love between him and my father, but they'd tolerated one another.

"You had just been reelected governor. Are you telling me you would have been okay with having your grandson's name splattered all over the news? Please. I did what I had to do. I didn't know the other boys weren't involved. I just asked Walt to leave Slade and Ronny's name out of it. Hell, Ronny didn't live here, so that was easy enough. And Slade wasn't himself that day. It was a mistake, and I did what I needed to do to make it disappear."

"You sent two innocent kids away, Dad. They spent months in that hellhole. You put them and their families through hell!" I shouted.

"They would have been there twice as long if I hadn't gotten involved. So be careful who you're accusing of being the bad guy. Slade derailed after everything happened. Maybe it was the guilt—hell, I don't know. But he came to me and told me the other two boys hadn't been with him and Ronny, and the guilt was eating him alive. I hired someone to get their time shortened. Did he mention that? That he stayed for three months instead of six? And the other kid got his time shortened from a year down to eight months."

"Oh my God. Do you hear yourself? You didn't do them any favors. You put them in there. They didn't commit the crime. You used your money and power to put two innocent people away for something they didn't do. And you want fucking credit for getting them out early?"

"Don't you use that language in this house." My father stormed toward me, face bright red.

Zero guilt in his eyes.

"Her language is the least of my concerns right now," my mother said, as she moved to stand beside me. "I am disgusted that you would do this, Jack. And you need to apologize to them at the very least and spend the rest of your days trying to make it up to them."

Dad looked completely stunned by what she'd said. "I got them out early. Everyone has moved on. I protected *our son*. Are you telling me you wouldn't have wanted me to protect Slade? Come on, Rose. You were not handling the things that were going on. He was partying and out of control, and you were a mess. I carried this secret with me so that you wouldn't have to."

"Don't you dare try to act like you did this for me. Yes, I would always want you to protect our children, but not at the expense of innocent kids. We could have hired the best attorney—that's how you protect your child. You don't lie and cheat to keep him out of trouble. What sort of example does that set for anyone?"

"So, you would have been fine with him being sent to that hellhole for a year? Because that's what would have happened, Rose. He had drugs in his system. He would have gotten his ass served to him for what he did."

"And maybe he wouldn't have been drunk and high on that boat when he nearly killed his friends and himself in that accident. Maybe if he'd been held accountable, none of that would have happened," Gramps said, his voice remaining completely calm because he never lost his temper.

Romeo was right. Slade had been using drugs much earlier than I'd realized. It had nothing to do with the accident and him getting hooked on opioids.

"You two didn't mind covering up that particular incident, did you?" my father hissed.

"There was no cover-up, Jack." Gramps went on, "Everyone knew he was drunk and high on that boat. We hired an attorney, and he found a loophole that allowed Slade to go to rehab instead of prison. We acknowledged that he had a problem, and we sure as shit didn't frame innocent children for what Slade had done. There's a big difference, and if you don't see that, then you're dumber than I thought you were."

"Yet you still support him, don't you?" My father glared at my grandfather.

"And I will continue to provide help to my grandson. I have the resources to get him the best help, and I will do it until the day I die. But I will not lie for him or let him off the hook for his actions. What you did is very different. Shame on you." Gramps pointed his finger in my father's face.

"I tried to make things right by getting them out early. I thought they were involved," Dad repeated, like that made things all better.

"You need to apologize to them, Dad. They were terrified and young and stuck in an awful place because of what you did."

"Because of what Slade did. I didn't rob that store. I didn't push Walt into a goddamn display shelf and nearly kill the man!" he yelled, as he paced around the room in little circles. "And I carried it all on my shoulders to keep you from being heartbroken," he said, turning to face my mother. "You would have been a mess if he'd been sent away."

"I'm sure Romeo's and River's mothers were a mess," my mom whispered. "I never asked you to lie to me, Jack. What else have you kept from me?"

The devastation on my mother's face nearly brought me to my knees. I hated that I'd come over here and turned their world upside down. But it needed to happen.

"I think it's time we stop with the secrets. I need to ask you something else, Dad."

"You don't think you've done enough for today, Demi?" He glared at me, and for the first time in my life, I did not see love in my father's eyes when he looked at me. I saw pure disdain.

My chest squeezed. Even with all I'd just found out about him, I still loved him. He was my dad. He'd always been someone that I'd looked up to.

Gramps quickly came to my defense. "Don't you put this on her. She did the right thing by telling us. It's what you should have done years ago when it happened. I'm just grateful your moral compass didn't rub off on my granddaughter. She's always been wiser than you, though, hasn't she?"

"You're loving this, aren't you? You've just been waiting for me to mess up all these years." My dad and my grandfather were standing close now, and I wondered if this was going to turn physical.

My mother moved between them, and her gaze locked with mine. "What else did you need to ask your father, Demi?"

"Did you file that restraining order against Ronny Waterstone? Or did you lie about that, too?"

He let his eyes fall closed, and he didn't respond.

That told me all I needed to know.

I filled my mom and Gramps in on what had happened, and my mother cried harder as Gramps wrapped his arms around me and apologized over and over to me.

My father admitted that he'd handled it by directly speaking to Ronny. He'd called him and told him to stay away from me and threatened to go to his father and tell him what happened if he came near me.

There was no restraining order filed.

Business had taken priority over my safety.

All of it hurt, but I was glad there were no more secrets.

When I left the house, my father was upstairs, packing his bags. He'd be staying at our condo in the city while my mother worked through all of this.

I felt a weird mix of guilt and relief.

Logically, I knew this wasn't my fault.

But it didn't stop the heaviness settling in my chest.

The feeling that life as I knew it was never going to be the same.

seventeen

· · ·

Romeo

THE LAST THREE hours had been excruciating. Butch was known for bringing the heat, and he and Joey had definitely been putting me through it. I hadn't heard from Demi yet, which made it tough to focus on this workout, but every time, Butch slapped me harder in the stomach when I sat forward on the endless sit-ups, it forced me to get my head in the game. We'd roped off a corner of the gym where I could work out, because more and more people were working out here now, which was good for business, but not great for work-outs, as they were gaping over at me while I trained. A group of women had started coming in to hang out and watch boxers train, me in particular.

"Faster, Romeo!" Butch shouted, and the sweat pouring down my face made it tough to see. My chin grazed my thighs each time I came up, and he'd slap me right across my middle.

And I pushed harder.

"Last ten," Joey called out. "Nine. Eight. Seven. Six. Five. Four. Three. Two. Done." I fell back on a gasp and let out a few sharp breaths.

"Good Christ, did you have to hit me so hard?" I hissed at Butch, and he chuckled.

He had a few titles under his belt, and having him on my team was a huge asset. But it didn't mean I had to enjoy the beating.

"Trust me. That asshole Leo is going to hit a hell of a lot harder than that."

"Thanks for the reminder." I took his hand when he offered it, and he pulled me to my feet.

"Can I get a picture, Romeo?" a woman called out, and I glanced over to see her standing next to Pinky's girlfriend, batting her lashes at me.

"For fuck's sake. If you aren't boxing, you have no business being here. This isn't a goddamn show. You want a show? Buy your ticket to the fight in Vegas, sweetheart," Joey grumped, as Pinky hustled over and ushered her away.

I guzzled my water, and Butch studied me. "You're looking good, kid. Couple more weeks of this, and you'll be ready. But we may need to find somewhere else to train in the afternoons. Having all these people filming you and sharing it on social media is just going to let Leo know how hard you're working."

I nodded. "All right. I can try to find a place."

I wiped my face off with a towel just as Demi walked into the gym. Her eyes were puffy, and when her gaze met mine, I could tell her smile was forced. She held up a bag, asking if it was an okay time to give it to me.

This girl.

My girl.

She was always bringing shakes and food over.

Joey motioned for her to come over before leaning close to me. "I like this one for you."

"Yeah? Me, too."

"Hey," she said, as she moved under the roped-off area that Joey had put up for me to use. "I made a bunch of chicken and salmon and thought you might want some post-workout protein."

I didn't give a shit about the protein. I was worried about her.

"That's exactly what he needs," Butch said as he winked at Demi. "This one's a keeper, Romeo. I think I heard Pinky call you Beans. Is that your handle?"

She chuckled, but her smile didn't reach her eyes. "I mean, only the people here call me that, but it works for me."

I took the bag from her hand and linked our fingers with my free hand. I wasn't hiding a damn thing anymore, and I wanted everyone to know that she was mine.

That we were together.

A flash went off, and Joey whipped around to see someone taking pictures again. "Get the hell out of here and give the man some privacy!" he shouted.

"We need to find somewhere else to train, Romeo. This isn't working, and I know it's a business and it's money in the bank to have all these people paying to be here. But we need another location for when we don't want people watching you."

"I'll call around and see what I can find," I said, anxious to end this conversation and get Demi to my office so I could find out what happened.

"I have the space next to the coffee shop that's empty. There's paper over the front window because it's vacant until I can figure out what to do with it. It's not fancy, and it's pretty bare-bones, but it could work if you want privacy."

"Like I said… I like this girl. We'll take it, Beans." Joey laughed and clapped her on the shoulder. "You just might be the Golden Boy's lucky charm."

I rolled my eyes, even though I thought he was right. "I'll see you tomorrow morning, all right? I'm going to go eat some protein."

"Sure, you are," Butch said with a chuckle. "Good job

today. You're on track, and we'll just keep pushing until the fight."

I nodded, did that half-bro hug, handshake thing, and then led Demi to my office. She wasn't working out with Pinky tonight, and we'd planned for her to meet me here after work. I shut the door, set the bag on the table, and dropped to sit on the couch, pulling her onto my lap.

"Sorry, I'm all sweaty," I said as I wrapped my arms around her. "Tell me what happened."

She took a minute as she ran her fingers along the palm of my hand. "He admitted it. All of it."

I just held her there, knowing that it had to hurt like hell to learn that someone you loved wasn't who you thought they were. "I'm sorry."

"Don't be." She turned on my lap so she was facing me. "The other kid that was with Slade that day was Ronny Waterstone."

"The same guy who attacked you? Looks like he's always been a piece of shit."

She nodded. "I guess I shouldn't be surprised. Obviously, a leopard doesn't change its spots. My father said that he originally thought you and River were involved, and he was just doing his part to keep Slade and Ronny out of it. Apparently, Slade was riddled with guilt and went to my dad and told him that you weren't involved. My dad said he hired an attorney to get you and River out of there sooner. As if that makes everything better."

I nodded. "That could be true. My mom was trying also, but your dad would have had a lot more pull than she did. Listen, Demi, I don't want to come between you and your family. I didn't tell you about this because I wanted you to fix it. I told you because I'm crazy about you, and I needed you to know why I had an issue with your brother and your father. But we can't turn back the clock. It is what it is. It happened. It sucked. But we survived, and we're stronger for it. And you're sitting on my lap now, making sure I eat right, so, at the end of the day, I won." I smirked, and she smiled a real smile for the first time since she'd gotten here.

"I think we both won," she said. "And my mom and grandfather were really upset. They didn't know anything about it. My father packed his bags and left for the city to give my mom some time to process. I've never seen her so angry."

Shit. I hadn't expected that. I figured they were either all involved, or they'd all supported him for doing what he could to protect his own kid.

"I'm sorry about that. I'm sure this has to be upsetting for you."

She shook her head. "What's upsetting for me is what he did to you. I won't speak to him until he apologizes to you and River."

"I don't need an apology from him, and neither does River." The man didn't have any place in my world now, aside from the fact that I was pretty certain I was falling in love with his daughter. "Did you ask him about the restraining order? Because I had River run Ronny's name in the system with a police buddy of ours. There is nothing pulling up for a restraining order."

She nodded, and her eyes welled with emotion. "Yeah. He admitted he lied about that, too. Apparently, I don't really know my father at all. He just called Ronny and threatened him directly."

I wrapped my arms tighter around her and tucked her head beneath my chin. I hated the guy, but I knew that she loved him, and for that reason, I tried to say something to soothe her. "Listen, my dad fucked up a lot when I was young, but he turned things around later in life. He owned it, and he did better those last few years of his life. Don't try to predict the future. Just take it one day at a time."

"You should be bashing him after what he did. Why are you being so nice?"

"I'm not that nice, Demi. I don't care for him, but I care for you. And I know you love him, even if you're angry at him right now."

"Wow, that was very romantic, Romeo Knight. You're full of surprises." She pushed back and rested her forehead against mine.

"You're full of surprises, too," I said.

"How so?"

"You're just—" I took her face in my hands and looked into those gorgeous green eyes. "You're kind, and you're beautiful, and you're strong all at the same time. I'm not used to that."

"Not used to what?" She raised a brow, eyes searching mine.

"Feeling this way," I admitted.

"Me either." She leaned down and kissed me. And then she pulled back. "Can we stop by and see River before we call it a day? I'd like to speak to him."

"You don't need to do that. You don't owe anyone anything. He doesn't blame you either. We were wrong to hold it against your whole family when you had nothing to do with it."

"I get it. But he's your best friend. Can you just take me there so I can say my piece?"

"Sure. Let me eat a few bites of this because my stomach is rumbling. And then I'll take you over there. You want to ride on the back of my bike? You've never been on it before."

"Very sexy. A boxer with a motorcycle. Let's do it."

I devoured two pieces of chicken and some salmon, and we made our way out to the alley. I grabbed the helmet that I kept for my sister at the house and pulled it over Demi's head, and she slid onto the back of my bike.

We drove the few blocks to River's place near the water, and I loved feeling her body pressed against mine. The way her arms came around my waist and her hands fisted in my hoodie. We pulled up in front of River's place, and I helped her off the bike before leading her to the door. River could be an intimidating guy. A loose cannon at times.

But he knew how I felt about her, and he'd hear her out.

"Don't be nervous. He looks more intimidating than he is."

We approached the front porch.

"I'm not nervous," she said confidently as I rang the bell.

He pulled open the door. His shirt was off, his arm covered in tattoos, and he raised a brow. He was an enigma. A brilliant lawyer who'd buried himself in the books to get through law school. Yet he was a total wild card outside of his profession and always had been. He never liked being put into a box.

"If it isn't the Golden Boy and his little lady." He smirked. "This is a pleasant surprise."

There was music playing in the background, and a woman's voice called out to him. "Is that dinner, handsome?"

I laughed. My best friend was a player, just like his little brother. Neither of them had ever had a serious relationship in all the time I'd known them. I had a feeling it had to do with their upbringing, but it worked for them, so I wouldn't judge. "We won't keep you. Demi just asked if I'd bring her over here to talk to you real quick."

"What's up, Crawford?" He leaned against the door frame, and she smiled.

"I wanted to apologize for what my brother and my father did to you and Romeo. I confronted him today, and he didn't deny it. I want you to know that I'm sorry, and I think it's horrible and disgusting, as did my mother and my grandfather when they found out. If I could turn back time, I would. But I hope you won't hold my father's actions against me because this one is pretty important to me, and I know he's important to you." She flicked her thumb at me, and I wrapped my arms around her, rubbing my scruff against her neck.

"This one has a name," I said, and she broke out into a fit of laughter.

River looked between us and then set his eyes on Demi. "Listen, if I held the actions of parents against their kids, I'd have to disown my best friends."

I shot him the bird, and a wide grin spread across his face. "I misjudged you, and that's on me. I'm glad you two figured your shit out. It's nice to see my boy happy. You and I have no beef, Demi."

"Thank you. That means a lot to me. And you can call me Beans now." She smirked.

"River, are you coming?" a woman called out from somewhere in the house.

"That's what she said!" he shouted back. "Now, take him home and make him shower. You stink, Golden Boy."

He held his fist up for me to pound it, and he did the same thing to Demi. But she surprised us both when she lunged at him, wrapping her arms around him. She sniffed a few times, and he looked at me with wide eyes. River wasn't used to dealing with emotions, so this was foreign.

But more surprising than her hugging him was what he did next.

He wrapped his arms around her and looked up at me. "I think she's a keeper."

I barked out a laugh. "Yeah, you and everyone else."

She pulled back and swiped at her tears. "Thanks for hearing me out."

I took her hand in mine and led her toward my bike parked in the driveway.

"Hey, Beans," he called out, and we both turned around.
"Yeah?"

"I assume I get a discount on the fancy drinks now that you're one of us."

"Finally. Someone who doesn't have a chip on their shoulder about a discount. You can count on it."

"You're a goddamn lawyer. Pay the girl for her coffee, asshole."

"See you tomorrow," River said with a laugh before shutting the door.

"Feel better?" I asked her as I pulled the helmet over her head.

"Yeah. Now, let's get you home and get you showered so you can have your way with me."

I gripped her by the hips as she squealed, and I set her on the back of my bike, then burned out of the driveway because I couldn't get her home fast enough.

And the sound of her laughter filled the air around me.

eighteen

· · ·

Demi

WE'D STOPPED by Romeo's place to grab some clothes, and he agreed to sleep at my house tonight. I had a bathtub, and I'd convinced him that it would help his sore muscles.

He informed me that he hadn't taken a bath since he was three years old.

"How is that possible?" I asked, filling the clawfoot tub and setting out two towels for us.

"I'm a boxer. And a dude. I'm not into bubble baths." He tugged his hoodie over his head.

"Just wait. You're going to be all about the bathtub after this."

"You want to bet on that? I don't see it happening. And I'm not getting in there unless you get in with me. But I'm not sure how two people can fit in that thing."

"Wow. A shower and a bath all on the same day. Look at you, knocking things off my bucket list."

"Well, it'll be a first for me, too. I've never bathed with a woman."

He reached for my sweater and pulled it over my head, and we both got undressed. "I like being your first something, too," I admitted, as I turned off the water. "You get in first, and I'll just squeeze in there with you."

He howled when he put his toe in the water. This big, tough guy, who fought for a living, was whining about a little hot water. My head fell back in laughter when he winced as he adjusted to the temperature and settled into the tub. He leaned back, and his wide shoulders flexed as he draped his arms over the side of the tub.

"Get in here with me," he said, and I climbed in and settled between his legs.

"Ohhhh. I didn't realize you could get turned on in hot water." I chuckled as his erection pressed against my lower back.

"If you're naked, it doesn't matter where I am; my dick responds to you."

I rolled over onto my stomach so I could face him. "Is it weird that we've showered and bathed together, and we've never had sex?"

"Nothing about this is normal for me. I'm usually the guy who leads with sex. But I like that we've taken our time. I told you that this feels different to me, and it's the truth."

"It's been a wild ride already, hasn't it?"

"We made it over the hurdle of our past, and we're still standing. So that says a lot."

"What about all the boxing groupies that are hanging out at the gym? You sure you want to be tied down when you're practically famous now?" I teased. I knew Romeo was a straight shooter. He wouldn't have let things go this far or told me about my family if he wasn't all in.

"Boxing groupies..." He smirked, and he was so sexy I rocked against him before I could stop myself. His erection swelled against my lower belly, and I slid forward, settling him between my thighs as he groaned. "The only boxing groupie I'm interested in is you."

"Good. Because I'm all in." I rubbed my nose against his. "I don't want to wait anymore. I want you. All of you."

He moved so fast I couldn't even process what was happening. Water sloshed over the side of the tub as he pushed to his feet and managed to take me with him. Laughter filled the space around us, and he had us both out of the tub within seconds. He wrapped me in a towel, tied one around his waist, and scooped me up.

"I want all of you, too." He tossed me onto my bed, and I gasped.

"Then what are you waiting for?"

"There's no going back once we cross this line." His voice was all tease. "And I have an insatiable appetite when it comes to you."

"The feeling's mutual." My breaths were coming hard and fast now, as he hovered above me.

"I…" His hand moved to the side of my face, and he looked more serious than I'd ever seen him look before. "I love you, Demi."

My heart raced so fast at his words, and I felt so much for this man that it almost overwhelmed me at times. "I love you, too. I have for a while."

"Yeah?"

"Yeah."

"I've never told a woman that I loved them outside of my family. Maybe that's why all my past relationships were so bad." He chuckled.

"Yeah. Fighting and love don't always go together, although we started off pretty rocky, didn't we?"

"That was just me being an asshole. But how about I make that up to you right now?"

"You already have, but I'm ready for more. For everything."

"Me, too, baby." He leaned down and kissed me as my hands trailed up his back. My body was already tingling with

Laura Pavlov

anticipation, and he'd barely touched me. He pulled back and gently opened the towel. His heated gaze scanned down my body slowly.

His lips found mine again, and he kissed me, gently this time. He kissed my cheeks and my forehead and the tip of my nose before his tongue traced along the line of my jaw and down my neck.

It was difficult to breathe. He took his time on my breasts, devouring them with his mouth and his tongue. I nearly arched off the bed, and he chuckled against my skin as he kissed his way down my abdomen and my thighs. My entire body trembled with desire.

"Romeo, please," I whispered. I couldn't take much more.

He pulled me down to the edge of the bed and pushed to his feet, dropping his towel and stroking himself a few times. "Do I affect you the way you affect me?"

"Holy shit," I groaned, just as he pushed my legs apart and dipped his fingers down my slit.

"Yes. So fucking wet. I need to taste you first."

Oral sex had never been my thing, but I nodded because I had a hunch that anything with this man was going to be my thing.

"Are you as sweet as I think you are?" He dropped to his knees, hiked my legs over his shoulders, and looked up at me.

My heart was beating loudly in my ears, and my fingers tangled in his hair. He leaned forward, and his tongue took the place of where his fingers had just been, as he licked across my most sensitive area.

I nearly came off the bed in a jolt. But Romeo was just getting started. His hands gripped my hips, and he teased me with his tongue before dipping a finger inside and slowly bringing it out as his lips sealed over my clit. He brought me to the edge before pulling back.

Again and again.

Over and over.

I was covered in a layer of sweat and was so turned on that I couldn't see straight.

I tugged at his hair, begging him for more.

And that was when he slipped his tongue inside me, his thumb circling my clit. The sensation was too much.

I bucked against him as the brightest lights exploded behind my eyes and a cry escaped my lips. I rocked against him as I rode out every last bit of pleasure.

And he stayed right there.

My arms were tingling.

My legs were tingling.

My head was spinning.

And I'd never felt a sensation like this.

Nothing even close.

When my breathing calmed, he lifted his head, his mouth glossy with my desire. His lips turned up the tiniest bit, and he just watched me as if I were the only woman to ever exist.

"If nothing good ever happens to me again, I'd still be the luckiest guy in the fucking world." He crawled up beside me and pulled me into his arms.

His erection was pressing against my lower belly, and my hand slipped between us to stroke him.

"That was amazing," I said, my head tipped back to look at him.

His eyes were half-mast as my hand moved up and down his shaft.

"I need to be inside you right now." His hand gripped my chin, and he claimed my mouth. His tongue slid in and out, matching the rhythm of my hand.

He pulled back, and I released my grip on him as he moved to his feet. He reached for his wallet in his sweatpants and pulled out a condom, tearing the edge with his teeth. I sat forward, watching as he slid the latex down his long, thick length. His eyes never left mine.

"Tell me how you like it," he asked, as he climbed over

me. "I want it to feel as good for you as it's going to feel for me."

"How do you know it's going to feel good for you?" My voice was huskier than usual.

"Because I could come from just watching you fall apart. Your fucking body turns me on so much it won't matter what you do. Tell me what you like."

"You. That's what I like. As long as I'm with you, that's all I need. All I want." My teeth sank into my bottom lip, and my hand rested on his cheek.

This sexy grin spread across his face. "I'm going to make you feel so fucking good."

"Counting on it."

He chuckled as he settled between my thighs, teasing my entrance with the tip of his dick. "But you need to tell me if it hurts or if I need to stop."

He was large, and I knew he was worried that he'd hurt me, but I wasn't worried. I trusted him.

And I wanted him so badly I could taste it.

He moved forward, the veins on his neck pulsing. He was clearly using every ounce of restraint to go slowly.

His eyes were on me. They were so dark they almost looked black as he pressed inside me.

Inch by glorious inch.

"Breathe, baby," he whispered, waiting for me to do what he said. "You can take it."

I let out a breath and reached around to his ass to urge him on. "Do not stop."

It came out as more of a command than a request, and his lips twitched.

One final thrust and he was all the way in. He didn't move at all, allowing my body to adjust to his size. A layer of sweat covered my forehead.

It was both pleasure and pain.

And I only wanted more.

I arched into him before tugging his mouth down to mine. His tongue slipped inside my mouth, tangling with mine, as he pulled out of me and then slowly pushed back in.

Over and over.

Until we found our rhythm.

And I met him thrust for thrust.

That was when he startled me with one quick movement. He flipped me over on top of him as he shifted to lie on his back. I sat above him, one leg on each side, as I straddled him.

"I want you to ride me. Set the pace. Show me what you like." His large hands covered my breasts, and he tweaked my nipples with the tips of his fingers. My head fell back as I arched into his touch. I slid up slowly and then back down, rocking my hips back and forth in the process. My hands braced the tops of his thighs as I arched further back, getting lost in the moment.

Faster.

Harder.

More.

His hands moved to my hips as he guided me up and down his dick. His thumb moved to my clit, knowing exactly what I needed.

My legs started to shake, and our breaths were the only audible sound in the room.

Panting and groaning, we moved together as one.

"You were fucking made for me," he said, as he sat forward, and his mouth sealed over my breast.

I completely lost control.

My body shook as the most incredible orgasm coursed through every inch of me.

Romeo thrust once more before a guttural sound left his mouth, and he grunted my name as he followed me right over the edge.

And nothing had ever felt better as we continued to rock into one another.

I somehow knew in that moment that nothing would ever be the same.

I loved him in a way I never knew was possible.

He thought I was made for him, but he was made for me.

Because we fit in a way I never had with anyone else.

In a way that made me feel complete.

And loved.

And wanted.

I hoped we could stay right here forever.

nineteen

. . .

Romeo

HOLY.

Shit.

I'd had some good sex in my life. Fantastic sex, even.

But this. This was next level. This connection.

This girl.

Her body. Her mouth. Her eyes. Her pussy. Her laugh. Her voice.

I loved it all.

I'd always assumed I wasn't meant to love anyone outside of my family and my friends. I'd kept my circle small intentionally.

I didn't trust easily.

I just didn't know that I was capable of feeling this way about another person.

The women I'd dated in the past had said I was cold and closed off—and they'd been right.

Because I hadn't been with the right fucking woman.

Until now.

I held her against my chest until our breathing slowed.

"Is it bad for you to have a lot of sex when you're training so hard?"

I chuckled and kissed the top of her head before sliding out of her and moving to my feet to dispose of the condom in the bathroom.

"I probably shouldn't have sex the night before the fight, but it's not an issue doing it every day until then." I stopped to stand in front of her, and my eyes raked over her gorgeous body. I wanted to memorize every lean muscle and curve.

She patted her bed for me to lie beside her, and she settled her head on my chest. "Good to know. I think we need to do that as often as possible. Like, I could make that my full-time job." I could hear the humor in her voice, and I tipped her chin up to kiss her.

"I wouldn't argue with that. Sell the coffeehouse and just stay naked in bed, waiting for me to ravish you every day? Sign me up."

My fingers ran down her arm. Her skin was so soft, her body so feminine. I'd never laid eyes on anyone more beautiful.

And completely unassuming, which made her even more attractive.

If that were even possible.

"I want to go to your fight," she said, completely out of nowhere.

I traced along her dainty fingers before wrapping her up a little tighter in my arms. "Where'd that come from?"

"I think about it, you know? About seeing you out there. I'm nervous to see you get hit because I'll want to dive into the ring and help you. And kick his ass if he lays a hand on you. Which, obviously, it's a fight, so that's inevitable. You'll have to take some punches, and that worries me. But I want to be there for you."

"Wow, you really have been thinking about this." I chuckled. "I'll be honest with you because I want you to know what it's like. He's a badass fighter, Demi. And I'm going to put up the best fight I can, but I'm not favored in any of the odds to win this fight. They want someone who can go a few rounds with him and put on a good show. And if seeing me get hit a shit ton of times is going to upset you, I think you should stay home. Or you can wait at the hotel for me, too."

"I don't want you to get hit," she said, pressing her elbows to my chest so she could look at me.

"It's a fight. Escaping without a hit is not an option. I'm just hoping I put up a good fight and hurt him a little, too."

"I know you said people have been distracting you on your runs, and it can get frustrating."

"Yeah, I think everyone is just reacting to all the hype from Leo, you know?"

"I know I mentioned it before, but my family has a lot of land, and it's right on the lake. There are trails, and it's really peaceful." She held her finger to my lips when I started to interrupt because I was not going to be running on her father's property. The asshole would probably shoot me for trespassing. "My dad isn't even staying at home right now. My mom feels horrible about what happened, and so does Gramps. My grandparents' home backs up to my parents' property line, so there is a lot of open space. You are welcome there, Romeo. And I want them to know you because they're going to love you just like I do."

"If your father doesn't accidentally shoot me for corrupting his daughter and outing his dark secrets."

"Well, he'd have to get past me. You wouldn't be alone," she said with a laugh. "I'd be riding Teacup. She's an older Arabian horse, so she's not as fast as she used to be, but she can definitely outrun you."

I chuckled. "I'll think about it."

"Okay. Let's get some sleep for now. You've got an early workout, and I've got to get to work early tomorrow because I missed a few hours today."

"How are you feeling about everything? You haven't said much. It can't be easy hearing your dad admit to everything."

"I don't know how I feel. Sad about what he did. Relieved that he owned it. Hopeful that maybe we can all move forward now that it's out there. He can't take back what he did, but he can try to do better moving forward."

She was so honest and positive and full of hope.

I doubted her dad would be anxious to make amends. He wasn't mad at himself for what he did; he was mad that he'd been caught.

But Demi didn't see the world as the jaded place that I did.

And I wouldn't tarnish it for her.

I wouldn't try to change one hair on her gorgeous head.

"One day at a time, all right?"

I worried about the fact that some fucker who'd attacked her was still out there. There was no restraining order and nothing keeping him from coming around.

And then we had her brother, who was an addict and had already broken into her shop once before, and that dude was dangerous in his own right.

Her father had admitted what he did, but who the hell knew what he was going to do in response or if he'd choose to retaliate or come after me for telling her what he'd done. I didn't have one doubt in my mind that he wouldn't want me with his daughter.

But I wasn't going anywhere.

I'd just have to prepare to battle a lot more people than I'd planned on.

I was training hard for my fight with Leo, but I had a feeling he wouldn't be the worst coming my way.

————

Leo was at it again. He'd been interviewed on a national sports station, and he'd basically guaranteed that he'd knock me out in round one. He'd offered me an additional million dollars if I could go three rounds, and he'd offered up his entire purse if I could go the entire twelve rounds with him.

I didn't know how much money Leo had, but throwing around millions of dollars when you didn't have to was stupid where I came from.

The guys were all here, eating pizza and salad. My body ached from my run this morning and the beating I'd taken last night, sparring with four different guys with one arm tied behind my back to make it more challenging. I'd taken more body shots than anyone should take in one sitting.

But it was all for the greater good.

Joey had decided I needed an afternoon off after getting worked over last night and then running hard this morning.

"Let him run his mouth. It works in your favor. He's such a cocky piece of shit," River said, reaching for another slice of pepperoni.

"Agreed. Why in the fuck would you offer someone millions of dollars when you don't have to? You already agreed to fight the dude. Just show up and fight, asshole," Hayes hissed.

"Listen, I think it's great. The entire town is wearing Golden Boy gear, and there's a goddamn mural of you painted on the side of The Golden Goose. His bullying ass is fueling everyone in Magnolia Falls to rally behind you," Kingston said over a mouthful of food.

"I saw a bunch of people interviewed on some morning show, and they were all rooting for you to kick his ass. I think you've got more than this town supporting you. Hell, the whole country is talking about this fight," Nash said. "And for the record, Cutler made me buy seven fucking T-shirts with your name on them so he could wear one every day of the week."

"That's Beefcake to you," I said over my laughter. "Listen, the guy can fight. And I don't even know what to expect when I get in that ring. I mean, I hope like hell I can last more than one round. But I've never fought anyone like Leo before, so I don't have a fucking clue. All I can do is work hard and leave it all out there."

"Don't sell yourself short. You were the kid in the back alley who fought off three dudes way bigger than you when you were young. He can talk all he wants, but you're going to put up a damn good fight, Romeo. I don't have one doubt about that." Kingston reached for his drink.

"Well, good, because I think I've got enough doubts running through my mind for all of us." I leaned back against the couch. All this talk and coverage on the news was getting to me. I'd only done one interview with Brinkley, and Joey had convinced me to do an interview next week with a national news channel that would be traveling to Magnolia Falls to meet me. I wasn't looking forward to it.

"You going to let Beans go to the fight? I saw the way she looked last night when you were in the ring with those guys." River leaned forward, arms resting on his knees. I loved that they all called her by her nickname now. They'd welcomed her into the fold like she'd always been one of us.

"You mean when Joey let them beat the shit out of him? I don't get that. You had your goddamn arm tied behind your back," Kingston said. "I noticed Demi's eyes were welling up with tears; that's why I got her out of there. But if I'm being honest, I felt like I was going to lose it, too."

Everyone chuckled at that. Kingston was a teddy bear beneath his gruff exterior.

"Yeah, Nash had to stop me because I was about ready to climb in there and start throwing some punches. It's instinct, I guess." River shrugged. "But we've all seen you fight before. She hasn't. You think she's up for it, dude?"

I ran a hand through my hair. "I don't think she should go, but she's stubborn as shit. I told her not to come last night, and she came right through the back door anyway."

"Is she still not talking to her father?" Nash asked.

"Nope. He's staying in the city, and she hasn't spoken to him. Her mother isn't speaking to him either. Our little secret has fucked up her entire family."

"No fucking way I'm buying that shit. What they did to you and River—this is just karma biting him in the ass. His daughter falls in fucking love with the kid he put into a shitty prison for teens for a crime his own son committed. That shit is real, and he needs to feel it. I hope it haunts his goddamn dreams for years." Hayes leaned back against the couch and crossed one leg over the other as if what he'd just said was no big deal.

"Her brother wants her to come to some family therapy session at his rehab out in Boston. And that's the thing with Demi; she's pissed at him for everything that's happened, but she doesn't give up on people. She wants to go, but I don't want her to go alone. What if he's not even in rehab? What if that other fucker shows up to mess with her?" I said, because we were all aware that Ronny was still a loose end that hadn't been dealt with. From my experience, loose ends didn't just go away.

"You want one of us to go so you can train, and we can keep an eye on her?" River asked.

Like I said, these guys always had my back. And I'd always have theirs.

And now they had Demi's back, and I fucking loved it.

"Let me think about it. I'm leaning toward going with her. We can be back in a day, and at least I'll be waiting outside if she needs me."

"Never thought I'd see the day our Golden Boy would fall hard, and for a nice girl, too." Kingston whistled over his laughter.

"Yeah, we were used to you dating crazy women who might burn your house down if you didn't return their call quickly enough." River barked out a laugh.

We were all giving one another a hard time about our dating track records when Pinky knocked on the door.

"What's up?" I asked.

"Uhhh…" He glanced around. "Governor Miller is here, and he asked if he could speak to you."

Demi's grandfather.

He wasn't the governor anymore, but apparently, that title stays with you. I pushed to my feet, and so did the guys.

They clapped me on the shoulder, grabbed their plates, and dropped them into the trash while Pinky went to get Demi's grandfather and bring him back to my office.

I wasn't sure what this was about. Maybe he was going to ask me to keep my story to myself. I didn't have any plans to share it with anyone else.

"Take no shit," River whisper-hissed in my ear before leading the guys out.

Governor Miller stepped into my office. Pinky's eyes were wide as he stood behind him, and I motioned for him to close the door.

"Thanks for seeing me, Romeo." He extended a hand.

"Nice to meet you, Governor."

"Please, call me Carson," he said, and I motioned for him to sit down. He took the chair as I moved across from him to sit on the couch.

"Okay, what can I do for you, Carson?" I cleared my throat, preparing for the threat or the bomb that he would drop.

"You can't do anything for me, son. I'm here to see what I can do for you." He was in his late seventies, and he had the same green eyes as Demi's.

"I don't need anything."

"Well, I'm going to start with an apology first. I need you to know that I do not support what my son-in-law did to you and your friend, River. I plan to go and apologize to him in person, as well. I never cared for Jack when he started dating my daughter in high school. But she was smitten; you know how teenage girls can be."

"I have a younger sister, so I know all too well."

"But they've been together for a long time, and he gave me two of my greatest gifts. Demi and Slade." He held his hand up, even though I made no attempt to interrupt. "Slade is a lost soul, but I don't use love as a weapon. He's my grandson, and I'll always do what I can to help him. But I do not condone what either one of them did. At least Slade has the excuse of being young and an addict, but his father made a very poor decision, and it's one that he has to live with now."

I nodded. "I don't expect anything from all of this. I had to tell Demi the truth if we were going to be together. And trust me, I tried like hell not to go there."

He chuckled. "That girl is all sunshine and goodness, isn't she? Always has been. Sees the good in everyone. Loves hard and works hard. And she's always known right from wrong. She's always known who she is."

"Agreed. I don't know what the hell she's doing with me, but I'm not arguing."

"She's a good judge of character. She's been blindsided by her father, and frankly, so have I. I wouldn't have guessed he'd do what he did. And being a politician, that doesn't happen often. So, I'm here on behalf of my family to tell you that I'm sorry for what happened. It's unacceptable. Demi told me that she'd like you to come out to the house and you don't feel comfortable, and I understand why you wouldn't, but I came here to tell you that we would welcome you coming to our home. My wife is devastated by this latest news, and we'd like to try to make it right. You're important to Demi, which means you're important to us."

This was probably the last thing on the planet I would have expected.

"Thank you. I appreciate that. She wants me to come out and run with her while she's riding horseback." I chuckled.

"Let me just say this: You're much more welcome than her father is at the moment. He's a smart man; he'll stay away for a while. He's ashamed of his actions, whether it be because of what he did or the fact that he got caught—I don't know for certain which it is. But he knows he messed up. That's why he's hiding away."

I wasn't sure if that was true, but Carson Miller seemed like a straight shooter.

"I'll definitely come by with Demi soon." I cleared my throat. "But I do have another concern."

"Let's hear it."

"Ronny Waterstone. I know Demi shared what happened, and I don't like that he's just out there walking around."

"We're on the same page, then. His grandfather and his father have received a call from me. There will be no further business interactions on my end, and I reached out to a police officer friend to see if we can do anything about a restraining order, but we're going to need Demi to get this documented if we want to do that. He's a piece-of-shit kid. I don't think he'd be brave enough to come near her now that he knows we're all aware of what happened, but I wouldn't have thought he'd do what he's done, so I can't say for certain. I will crush that little pissant if he comes near her, though. But I have a hunch he'd have to survive you first."

I nodded and felt my lips turn up in the corners. "You'd be correct. What about Demi's father's business ventures with Ronny's father?"

"I have not spoken to Jack since everything came to light. I'm too angry at the moment. But after my conversation with Ronny's father and grandfather, I don't believe they're going to be doing anything because they were very disturbed by the information."

"All right. That's good to know."

"So, you've got this fight coming up, and my grand-daughter tells me you're training hard. How about you come and have a big T-bone steak with us this weekend?"

I thought about it. "Okay. I'd like that."

"Sounds good. I'll be heading over to River's law office to see if I can get him to come out to the ranch, as well, and maybe he'll even join us for steaks."

River wouldn't normally be into that, but he had a soft spot for Demi, so I figured he'd probably agree, seeing as this was her grandfather.

I offered him my hand, but he pulled me in for a hug, which shocked the shit out of me.

In a way, it felt like that bad chapter in our lives was finally being put to rest.

twenty

. . .

Demi

"THIS MIGHT BE the oddest group, going to the grandparents' for a Sunday barbecue, huh?" River teased from the driver's seat as he pulled into my grandparents' long, circular driveway.

Romeo sat up front, and I was sitting in the back with Cutler, who only responded to Beefcake, so I was going with it.

"I think it's a perfect group." My grandfather had personally gone over to apologize to both Romeo and River and invited them over for lunch. He'd extended the invite to all the guys, but Nash and Kingston were working on a big custom renovation, and Hayes was on duty at the firehouse today. So, we'd brought Cutler with us, and he was thrilled about it.

"I think it's perfect, too, Demi. And you said they have horses? I've only been on the back of Uncle Ro's bike, and he wouldn't let us go anywhere because it's not safe for kids. I've never been on a horse," the little guy said. He was so cute it was impossible not to smile around him. He was sporting one of the many T-shirts being sold in town to support Romeo, and this one read:

Magnolia Falls' Golden Boy… He's a real knockout.

Cutler had the shirt tucked into his dark jeans, a black leather coat, and some black Dr. Martens. I mean, this kid was as cool as you get. His hair was slicked back with a ton of gel, and his little cherub cheeks were tinted pink. He looked like a mini version of all five of these guys melded together.

"Yes. I can take you out for a ride if you want. And my grandparents are going to love you."

"What's not to love about Beefcake?" he said with a wink. I mean, the swagger on this kid was unbelievable.

Everyone laughed, and we got out of the car. River and Romeo seemed far more tense than Cutler, who took my hand and waggled his brows at Romeo, who reached for my other hand.

"Listen, I'm doing the whole lunch at the mansion thing for you, Beans. But don't make me suffer through a pissing match with you two." River smirked at Romeo and Cutler.

"I know she's Uncle Ro's girl, but he said she could be my girl, too." Cutler came to a stop and gaped up at the large house in front of him. "My dad told me to use my manners, and now I know why. This is a giant house."

"You use your manners no matter the size of the house. You know that," Romeo said, raising a brow.

"Yep. That's right. But big houses need big manners."

I shook my head and laughed as we walked up the steps, and I pushed the door open. "Hey, Gramps and Grammie! We're here."

Sheila came to the door. She'd worked for my grandparents since I was a little girl, and she took Cutler's coat, as the rest of us were not wearing one. The weather was starting to get nicer now, and the sun was shining today.

"I like your shirt," Sheila said to Cutler.

"It's for my Uncle Ro. He's got a big fight coming up." He flicked his thumb at Romeo and beamed up at him with so much pride.

"Oh, I know. It's all anyone in town is talking about," she said, and I introduced everyone to her.

Romeo tried to act like all the attention wasn't getting to him, but I knew differently. Leo had pulled some cheap shots this week. He'd somehow found Keith Knight's mug shot from when he'd been arrested for his third DUI and was later sent to prison. He'd blasted it on every social media platform and said the only way Romeo would make it one round of this fight was if he did something shady, which he'd said ran in the family. The caption read: *The small-town golden boy will be praying for jail time when I put his ass in the hospital.*

I hated this guy with a passion. I'd never felt this kind of disdain. It made no sense to me that he'd all but bullied him into agreeing to fight him, only to taunt him every single day since.

River had calmed me down when Romeo had gone for a run this morning and told me it was all for show and not to worry. I'd grown close to Romeo's friends, and they felt more like family now. We met almost every day after work to watch Romeo's second practice and cheer him on when we could.

Sheila led us out to the backyard, where my grandparents and my mom were sitting, drinking sun tea and chatting with Valentina and Mimi who'd obviously beat us here. They all seemed to be getting on just fine without us.

Everyone pushed to their feet, and we made introductions all around. My grandmother and my mom gave Romeo and River extra-long hugs, and I didn't miss the emotion in their welled-up eyes when they pulled away. My mom bent down and greeted Cutler.

"And who is this handsome young man?"

"You can call me Beefcake, ma'am," he said, a wide grin on his face.

"Beefcake, huh? What's your last name?" my grandfather asked with a chuckle.

"Heart. Beefcake Heart. And I'm all heart, sir. You can

even ask my uncles and my girl, Demi. They'll tell you the truth."

Valentina hugged me and scooped up Cutler to give him a hug, as well. They were clearly close because he called her Titi, and then he kissed Romeo's grandmother on the cheek and called her Gigi.

Ben was barbecuing steaks, like he did every Sunday afternoon. He was Sheila's husband, and they lived in the guesthouse on the property. The table was set beautifully, as always. My grandmother loved to entertain, and she and my mom were telling everyone about their plans for the white party this year.

"I've always wanted to come, but I usually have to work or something comes up," Valentina said.

"This year, you'll have to come. It's a fun celebration for everyone in town," Grammie said proudly, and her eyes landed on Romeo. "And I'm hoping you and your friends will attend this year."

River barked out a laugh. "Yeah, white parties aren't normally our thing. Not that we ever felt like coming here was a good idea."

He never stood on ceremony. He may as well have just said that they didn't come because our family had framed him and Romeo for a crime they didn't commit, and there was no love there.

At least until now.

Romeo's hand found mine as it rested between us on the outdoor couches, and he intertwined our fingers. Almost like he knew the conversation was difficult for me to hear.

But it was him I was worried about.

"Well, now that we all know what happened, we can move forward. We would really like you all to be here, and if you don't want to wear white, we'll be fine with that, too," Gramps said.

My grandmother huffed. "Just a white shirt, you know, to

stay on theme."

Everyone laughed some more.

"So, let's talk about the other elephant in the room. That guy you're fighting is a real piece of work, Romeo. I don't understand all that social media baloney, but pulling out a deceased man's mug shot is not okay." Gramps had no filter and was going to go right at it.

"Leo's trying to get under his skin. He's been doing it all along, which makes me wonder if there's a reason," River said as he sipped his tea.

"It's pretty disgusting. Tia called this morning and was really upset about it. Why do you think he's going to such lengths to hurt us?" Valentina asked.

River's gaze softened as he looked at Romeo's mother. It was obvious they were all close. "It's all about messing with Romeo. Making this a big show so it draws a lot of attention, which equals a lot of money. But the way he's doing it"—he looked out at the miles-long green pasture that led down to the water—"makes me wonder if he's as tough as he pretends to be. And maybe half of his strategy is just to get into some-one's head."

"I agree with that." Gramps nodded and looked over at Romeo. "A man who was putting in the work would stay focused, like you're doing with your training. Less talk and more work."

"Listen, I haven't fought in a while. All I can do is prepare the best I can, show up, and hope I can go the distance. I'm not under the delusion that I'm the more skilled fighter. He's got experience on his side. He's been a professional fighter for many years, and he wants to go for the belt. I want to leave in one piece and not embarrass myself. We have different goals."

My heart squeezed at his words. I knew this had to be terrifying, hearing some asshole talk about how badly he planned to hurt you every day. But Romeo took it all in stride.

"You could never embarrass yourself," I said. "You've

stepped up, and you're working unbelievably hard. It's so impressive. And you don't engage with his nonsense, which says a lot about you."

"Trust me. I engage in my head," he said, as he sipped his tea, and he suddenly looked like he was a million miles away.

"My daddy's not letting me go to the fight. I'm staying home with Titi and Gigi because they don't want to see Uncle Ro fight, but I do. And we're watching on TV."

Romeo's mom looked away, and I knew she was just as nervous as I was. But I was going to that fight come hell or high water. I'd be there every step of the way, cheering him on.

"That's right. We'll be watching from home," Valentina said, her voice cracking a bit on her words.

Thankfully, Ben and Sheila chose that time to call everyone to the table. We spent the next hour eating and talking and laughing. The conversation had lightened.

"I don't know why I have to be eighteen years old to get the *Ride or Die* tattoo like my uncles. Do you think that's fair, Demi?"

"Look at you going to the softie in the group to try to get your way, Beefcake," River said as he dropped his corn on the cob onto his plate.

"Hey. I'm not a softie."

Romeo glanced over at me and smiled, and my stomach flipped, per usual. There was something about the way that he looked at me. Like I was the only girl in the whole world. Like he'd move heaven and earth for me if I asked him to.

"You're a softie for Beefcake, baby." He smirked.

"Well, you know I like to take your side," I said to Cutler, who was sitting between my mom and my grandmother, who were both enamored with him. "But I agree with your daddy. I do think you should be an adult before you do anything permanent to your body."

"Demi, you're my girl. You aren't on my side?" His little

brows pinched together, and everyone was laughing at the devastated look he was flashing me. "I want to have it before Uncle Ro's fight."

"I didn't say that. I think we could do something *not permanent* if your daddy was okay with it. I'll text him and see what I can work out for you."

Cutler fist-pumped the sky, and my grandfather shook his head. "This kid is going to be running the world someday. You just flipped her without even trying. And my granddaughter doesn't sway all that easily."

More laughter.

I pulled out my phone and sent a text to Nash.

> Hey. Beefcake is devastated about waiting a lifetime for his RoD tattoo. What if we use a Sharpie and make the little guy's dreams come true for the fight? He can watch from home and sport a fake tattoo.

NASH

> Damn. This kid doesn't stop. I mean, I'm allowing him to go by the name Beefcake, so a Sharpie tattoo is the least of my worries. Just make sure it's hidden so I don't get shit from his teacher.

> You're such a softie.

NASH

> Takes one to know one. How's Romeo doing with the shit that broke this morning?

> Acting like he isn't bothered, but he's bothered.

NASH

> Yeah. That's what I figured. We're all worried about him bottling this shit up.

> I'll get him to talk about it. I just need some time.

NASH

Glad he's got you by his side.

> Glad he's got you guys by his side, too.

He liked the text, and I dropped my phone back down on the table.

"It's a go, Beefcake. I'll draw the tattoo on your arm with a Sharpie the week of the fight. You'll be supporting Uncle Ro from Magnolia Falls," I said.

Romeo glanced over at me, his tongue sliding along his bottom lip, and I squeezed my thighs together in response.

The way this man made me feel was unexplainable.

Every damn day, too.

We couldn't get enough of one another.

"You really are my girl, Demi." Cutler moved to his feet and looked around the table. "May I be excused? I want my girl to show me how to ride a horse so I can propose to her someday on horseback."

Romeo's head fell back in laughter, and it was the first real laugh I'd heard from him today. "How can I compete with this?"

"You've already won. I'm all yours," I whispered into his ear.

I took Cutler's hand in mine and led him toward the barn. Everything felt lighter today than I'd expected with Romeo and River and my family.

They'd all made peace, and there were no issues.

And it felt like we were finally putting all the darkness behind us.

twenty-one

. . .

Romeo

> Demi and I took Cutler to Demi's grandparents' house, and the kid rode a horse on his own like he was a fucking jockey.

RIVER

You mean Beefcake?

> My bad.

NASH

Thanks for doing that. He loves those fucking horses now. Are you still running out there?

> Yeah. Demi has me racing her while she's on a goddamn horse and taunts me when she stays just a few feet ahead of me.

KINGSTON

Love that girl. She knows how to push you. Should we have her get the RoD tattoo?

HAYES

I don't see Beans rocking a RoD tattoo. Not
her style. But I think it's tattooed on her soul,
if I'm being honest.

KINGSTON

Damn. Hayes just went deep again.

I'D BE LYING if I didn't admit that it meant something to
me that they loved my girl so fiercely. I'd never dated anyone
they even remotely liked. Demi had become one of us.

HAYES

What can I say? I can go deep when
necessary. What happened with Lionel at
the bar?

RIVER

Fucking Lionel. Jenna Tate is suing him
because she slipped on some sort of slime or
slush or some shit behind the bar. All he had
to do was pay her medical bill. It was a work
accident. But his stubborn ass let this turn
into a shit show.

> That sounds about right. Lionel likes to see
> how far he can push things. Is he going to
> have to pay a lot?

RIVER

He'll probably end up paying twice as much
as it would have cost him if he'd just taken
care of shit when it happened. If she wants
to push things, she could probably own the
damn place at the end of the day. But he's
still complaining about the whole thing and
continues to try to fight it.

We'd been friends with the Whiskey Falls bar owner for a

long time, and he'd gone to River to represent him in the ridiculous lawsuit that should never have gone this far.

KINGSTON

Jenna Tate is hot.

RIVER

Where the fuck did that come from? We're talking about the lawsuit, not how hot she is, dicknut.

KINGSTON

Hey, I call it as I see it.

HAYES

Jenna Tate has got to be in her mid-forties. What the fuck is wrong with you?

KINGSTON

Hey, I love me a hot cougar! I do not discriminate. Age is just a number.

NASH

Get your ass back to work, you fucking horndog.

KINGSTON

Ball breaker. <middle finger emoji>

RIVER

Are we meeting at Whiskey Falls tonight?

I'll meet you there after my workout.

They all replied with a thumbs-up emoji, and I got back to work. I was drowning in paperwork, as the long workouts were taking a toll, and I was exhausted. I was thankful that Pinky had stepped up at the gym, and we'd brought on Dallas

Johnson to help with training some of the fighters. I wasn't training anyone now, as the countdown was on. I had less than four weeks until the fight, and I still had a lot of work to do.

I spent the next two hours paying bills and ordering some new equipment for the gym. We'd grown in size a lot since I'd started training for the fight; everyone wanted to work out at Knockout now.

I grabbed my bag and headed across the alley to meet Joey. I glanced at my phone, realizing I hadn't heard from Demi in a little bit, which wasn't the norm, but it probably meant that she'd been slammed this afternoon. Using the empty space next to her coffee shop for my second workout had been really helpful. There were no distractions there. And Joey and Butch could focus on kicking my ass with no audience, aside from my girlfriend and the guys when they came by to cheer me on.

There was a car that I didn't recognize parked out front, and for whatever reason, alarm bells were going off. You didn't see a lot of Bentleys in Magnolia Falls because the people here weren't pretentious pricks.

I glanced inside and saw Oscar Daily standing near the counter, studying a man who had his back to me. Peyton was standing beside Demi, her shoulders stiff, and when I took in the expression on Demi's face, I fucking knew.

I didn't know how, but that was all it took.

I pulled the door open and dropped my bag and charged the asshole.

"Is this the fucking guy?" I shouted. Demi's eyes were wide, but she gave me the slightest nod.

"Who the fuck are you?" the prick asked, but I was already on him. I wrapped my arm around his throat and pulled tight against his windpipe.

"I'm your worst fucking nightmare!" I shouted as I dragged him backward toward the entrance.

I shoved him out the front door as he screamed like a little bitch. "Do you have any fucking clue who I am?"

The balls on this asshole.

And as I took him in, I had a flashback of all those years ago in The Daily Market when he and Slade vandalized the store.

"That's the reason you're out here, dickhead. I know exactly who the fuck you are. And you were warned to stay away from her. And you should be warned to stay the fuck away from me."

People were gathering around now, as the commotion had obviously drawn attention. Demi, Peyton, and Oscar were standing beside me.

"The fuck, D? This is your boyfriend? This fucking little pansy-ass fighter?" He pushed to his feet and brushed off his navy suit.

"Fuck you, Ronny," Demi spewed. It was hot as hell seeing her stand up to the asshole. "He's also the guy you let take the fall for what you did all those years ago. Your secrets are catching up with you."

"I don't have a clue what the fuck you're talking about. I came here to talk some sense into you. You made something big out of something little. It was no big deal. And now you've caused a lot of problems for both of our families. Are you happy about this? Our grandfathers have been friends for fifty-some years, and now they aren't speaking." He pulled his keys out of his pocket as he waited for her to respond.

"Yeah, I'd say I'm the happiest I've ever been." She pushed her shoulders back and glared at him. "And I didn't make something big out of what happened. I should have reported you and gone public when it happened months ago."

"Fuck you, D!" he shouted, and I noticed that people had their phones out now and appeared to be filming the altercation. But I sure as shit wasn't going to let him talk to her that way. I wanted to put his face through the front window, but I knew guys like this. He'd end up the victim in the situation. His money and his family's power had already cost me in the past.

I moved closer, standing several inches taller than him. "No one cares who your daddy is here, Ronny. You were an asshole years ago, and you're an asshole today. You like to take advantage of women, don't you, you piece of shit? You were warned not to come near her."

"I will fucking destroy you," he hissed. "You have no idea who you're messing with."

"You don't fucking step one foot in her shop, do you hear me? Not one foot, you sick fuck."

Sirens sounded in the distance as they closed in.

"I called the police," Peyton said.

Oscar looked rattled, and Demi looked—angry.

The police car rolled up, and every once in a while, a blind squirrel finds a nut because Brett Rogers stepped out of his police car and moved to stand between me and Ronny the douchebag.

"What's going on, Romeo?"

"This guy isn't allowed to be here. He's been warned."

"You not supposed to be here?" Brett asked, just as River came jogging over from across the street. He must have heard something. He was that guy.

He always just showed up when you needed him.

"She doesn't have a fucking thing on me. Do you know who Senator Waterstone is, Officer Dipshit?" Ronny spewed. "That would be my grandfather, and you're going to be in some deep shit if you don't arrest this son of a bitch for putting his hands on me."

"We may not have paperwork filed, but Ronny knows he isn't supposed to come near me." Demi tipped her chin up. "He knows what he did. That's why he's here. He wants me to lie for him. It's what everyone does for him."

"Call her father. He's with my father now, and they're trying to figure this shit out. Do you really think her father would be having dinner with mine if he thought I was a risk to his daughter?" He smirked.

"You piece of shit," I hissed.

"I want this man arrested. He assaulted me," Ronny said. "And didn't your father spend time behind bars? That's right, you did, too, back in the day. I guess it runs in the family."

Brett glanced around at the locals, who were watching this all go down. "Well, did anyone here see Romeo assault the senator's charming grandson?"

Oscar spoke first. "I've been here the whole time, and Romeo has been nothing but friendly since he came in to get his coffee. This senator's grandson started the argument."

River barked out a laugh and nodded.

"Yes. That's exactly what happened," Janelle said. She owned the flower shop, Sweet Magnolia, and I did a double-take of the hat she was wearing that read:

I'm just here for the Magnolia Falls Golden Boy.

"I'm the one who called the police, and I called before Romeo even showed up. Demi was scared of this guy the minute he walked through the door." Peyton crossed her arms over her chest.

"This is bullshit. A bunch of small-town hicks defending their white-trash fighter. Are you kidding me right now, D? Are you seriously with this guy?"

"Like I told you the night you tried to attack me," she said, stepping forward and looking him directly in the eyes. "Stay the fuck away from me, Ronny. You just made this whole thing public, so you only have yourself to blame."

"I wonder what your father will think of you involving your fucking garbage boyfriend in family business?"

The way that he was looking at her, the evil I saw in his eyes—I couldn't stand here and not do something for one minute longer. He wasn't scared enough.

My job wasn't done.

"Hey, Brett, I think everything is fine here. But Janelle seems shaken up. Maybe you could walk her back to the shop?"

Ronny's eyes gaped between me and Brett.

"Yeah. It's my duty as Officer Dipshit to make sure the locals feel safe." He held his arm up, and Janelle chuckled and wrapped her hand around his elbow, and they walked away. "Come on, everyone. Show's over."

The few locals who'd been standing there turned and walked away, and Oscar looked over at me and nodded before leaving with the group.

Understanding reached Ronny's gaze, and he made a run for it, but I was faster. I grabbed him, pulling him around to the alley and shoving him hard into the brick wall. He cried out, but he didn't fight back, just as I'd figured he'd do.

He liked to beat up on people smaller than him.

Women in particular.

River was right there beside me. Like he always was.

"River, do you recognize this prick?" I held my forearm against his throat.

"This is the prick who framed us all those years ago," he said, leaning close to his face and looking him in the eyes. "But we survived that shit. But now, you've messed with Romeo's girl. She's one of us, and we just won't allow that, will we, brother?"

"We will not. You think you can take advantage of women? You think anyone gives a shit about who your grandfather is here?" I leaned close to his ear.

Now it was River's turn. "You need to understand something. We don't give a shit about prison, nor are we afraid of a good fight, so I'd suggest you get your fucking ass out of this town and stay the fuck away from Demi Crawford, or we will haunt your fucking nightmares. I will spend my days making your life a living hell. Do you hear me?"

River was an intimidating dude. His arms were covered in tats, his eyes were hard, and he never backed down.

I felt the same rage as he did. I wanted to beat the shit out of Ronny, but I heard Demi's voice call out behind me, and she was begging me to let him leave.

River's hand squeezed my shoulder.

"He gets the message. Don't give him anything to come back on you. We know where to find him, don't we? And after that little scene you just caused goes public, women all over will find out exactly who you are." River smirked.

I took a step back and shoved him toward the sidewalk, and the little fucker ran to his car. He glanced over at Demi but didn't say a word. I waited until he drove off.

"You all right?" I asked her, as she stepped into my arms.

"Yeah. I'm fine. I can't believe my dad is with his father right now. I thought he was trying to fix our family." She sniffed.

"You can't trust that dude, Beans. He could be making that shit up," River said, shocking the shit out of me as he tried to make her feel better about her father.

"He's right," I said after we stepped inside. "Don't base your feelings for your father off that guy. I wouldn't trust a word he says."

"Well, a lot of people just witnessed that argument, so Ronny just made all this public by showing up here. And that's not going to sit well with him or his family."

"Not our problem," I said.

I stayed with her until she locked up, and we made our way over to meet Joey for practice.

And in the hours I was working out, a shitstorm had started.

The viral video was now national news.

And between Leo and Ronny, I was all everyone was talking about.

twenty-two

. . .

Demi

THIS LAST WEEK had been absolute madness, and Romeo was definitely feeling the pressure. The entire town was promoting the fight now. If you wore one of the Golden Boy shirts, you would receive ten percent off at Whiskey Falls bar and The Golden Goose.

Someone had posted a video of Ronny and Romeo arguing on social media, and it had taken on a life of its own. Leo had jumped on the bandwagon and had been thrilled to point out that he knew Romeo's weakness now.

Me.

He posted photos of the altercation where Romeo kept me tucked right behind him. He made a video playing the clip over and over of Romeo telling Ronny to stay the fuck away from me. And people ate it up. It had gathered millions of views, and local news channels were asking to come and interview Romeo daily.

It was a lot.

But my boyfriend had kept his head down and tried to ignore all the noise and focus on his training. Joey had stepped things up, as these final weeks of practice were grueling. Romeo was training harder than ever, and yesterday,

Teacup and I had barely been able to stay ahead of him on his seven-mile run. The weather was warming up, and I loved being able to help with this part of his training. When he ran through town, everyone was out there, cheering and honking their horns, but out at my grandparents' house, it was peaceful and quiet. He could clear his head and focus on his run.

And I got to enjoy the view.

He was chiseled perfection.

I watched him sleep as he rolled toward me, his eyes blinking open as his hand found my hip and he pulled me closer. It was the first day in weeks that we'd been able to sleep in, which wasn't even really sleeping in, because the sun hadn't come up yet. But normally, he was up at 4:00 a.m. to get his run in early. Joey thought he needed the rest this morning and wanted him to take a day off from running, but he'd be in the gym later today.

"Hey, baby. Are you watching me sleep?"

I snuggled up against him. Cedar and sage were now my kryptonite. My fingers roamed his chest, and he groaned.

"Yes. You rarely sleep, so I was enjoying the view. Are you sore?"

"I think I'm in a constant state of discomfort, if I'm being honest." He chuckled. "I'm always a little sore."

"Well, those guys really pushed you hard last night, and you ran hard in the morning, too. Can you take a day off from work today?"

"Nope. I need to catch up on payroll and the books and get the schedule going for next week. We just keep growing, so I need to hire another trainer."

My fingers were trailing along his shoulder and down his arm, and I pushed to sit up. "How about I give you a massage before we both have to get up?"

"How about I bury my face between your thighs and start my day with you on my lips?"

"Massage first. Pleasure second," I teased, as my teeth sank into my bottom lip at the thought of it.

Romeo always knew how to please me. Even when he was exhausted. Even when I knew he should just get some sleep. He said that he slept best after hearing me cry out his name.

How could I argue with that?

I urged him to roll onto his stomach, and I moved to the bathroom to grab some lotion and then climbed on top of him, straddling his waist. I squeezed the lotion into my palm and rubbed my hands together before pressing down on his shoulders, causing him to groan.

I worked his muscles slowly before moving down his back.

"That feels so fucking good," he said.

"It will help loosen you up, too." I pulled his briefs down, and my fingers dug into his firm butt.

"Wow. You're really going there, aren't you?" He chuckled as I moved down his thighs, adding more lotion to my hands.

"I want to make you feel better. I know how exhausted you are."

"The best I feel every single day is when I'm with you. When I tune out all the noise. When I'm sitting on the couch, watching a movie with you. When I'm watching you eat or laugh. And, of course, my all-time favorite time of day is watching you fall apart when I'm buried deep inside you," he said, his voice deep and gruff.

"I feel best when I'm with you, too," I whispered. My feelings were so deep for this man that I found it over-whelming at times. "Are you going to miss me when I'm gone?"

I was going to meet Slade for his family counseling session. He'd asked me to come, and he was there, doing his part, so I'd agreed. I had a lot to say to him and a lot of anger over what I'd learned since he'd been gone, but it didn't mean that I didn't love him.

"I wanted to talk to you about that," he said, rolling onto his back, and I squeezed some more lotion into my hands.

"Okay." I settled on top of him again, one leg on each side of his waist before leaning down and pressing my palms into the tops of his shoulders.

"I talked to Lincoln, and he and Brinkley happen to be going to New York at the same time. They said they could pick us up, and we could fly with them on their plane, and they'd take us to Boston. And then they'd fly us back on our own because they're staying for a few days since my brother has meetings there and Brinkley's got work."

His brother was a famous NFL player, but I hadn't met him yet. Romeo talked about him and Brinkley often.

"Really? That's so nice. You really want to come with me?" I asked, pausing as I worked my fingers over his chest. I hadn't asked him to do that. He had issues with my brother that were fair, and I didn't expect him to want to support Slade in any way. Not to mention his training was a full-time job, on top of running the gym.

"I love you, and you've supported me through all this shit with the fight. Now you've been dragged into the middle of Leo's madness, and he's talking about you every fucking day. You're out on Teacup, early in the mornings, racing my ass before work. I want to support you, too, baby. This works both ways." His tongue swiped out to wet his bottom lip, and his hooded gaze had me squirming as I rocked against him, finding him hard as a rock beneath me.

Everywhere.

"This is a little different. I'm going to visit a man who made your life a living hell all those years ago."

"He's your brother, and I know that you love him. And I love every part of you, Demi Crawford. Even the part that forgives people who don't always deserve it." His gaze softened. "You're meeting with your dad after work today, right?"

"Yes. He says he has a lot to say to me, and I want to hear him out. I know he and my mom have started marriage counseling. It's all just… messy, you know?" I sighed. "And I love you, too. All of you. Even the part of you that doesn't want to tell me how much pressure you feel. How exhausted you are. How frustrated you are by Leo's taunting. And now you've got Ronny freaking Waterstone posting about us, too. It's a lot."

"It'll all settle down after the fight is over. Ronny's trying to save face because now the whole world knows he's a fucking creep. He can blame us for this coming out all he wants, but if he'd stayed the fuck away from you, none of this would have happened."

"I could not agree more. He brought it on himself." I slid down his body and worked his abdomen, one muscle at a time. Now, I was trailing my lips behind my fingers, and Romeo sucked in a breath. I moved down his thighs, taking my time on each leg.

I crawled between his legs and pulled the front of his briefs down, and his dick jolted in response, standing straight up.

I wrapped my fingers around his thick length and stroked him up and down as my gaze locked with his.

"Fuck, baby," he whisper-hissed. "Why does everything you do feel so fucking good?"

I loved that I affected him the way that he affected me.

It made me feel sexy and powerful.

This man was everything I wanted.

Everything I needed.

I pumped him faster, and he reached for me. "I need to be inside you. Right. Fucking. Now."

I reached into my nightstand drawer and pulled out a condom before tearing the top off with my teeth. I rolled it down his throbbing erection, and his eyes never left mine.

Then his hands found each side of my hips and lifted me effortlessly, lining me up right above him.

He slid me down slowly, filling me completely. My head fell back, and I rocked up and down as we found our rhythm.

He sat forward and wrapped his lips around one hard peak, teasing and licking, before moving to the other side.

I was so turned on I could barely see straight.

His hand moved between us, knowing exactly what I needed, just like he always did. He pressed his fingers against my clit, and I gasped. I was already so close.

He leaned back to look at me. "Come all over my cock, baby. I want to feel you."

That was all it took.

His hands. His fingers. His mouth.

Romeo.

It was too much.

I dug my nails into his shoulders, and his name left my lips on a cry as my entire body went over the edge.

My vision blurred.

I continued to move as he gripped my hips and thrust into me.

One.

Two.

Three.

It was my name on his lips when he followed me over the edge.

He rocked me against him over and over, riding out every last bit of pleasure.

And I was completely lost in this man.

———

I found my father in his study, and I walked in as he moved to his feet. I held up my hand to stop him. We needed to talk, not hug. I had a lot of questions, and I wanted to keep my head clear for this conversation.

"Let's talk first," I said, sitting in the chair across from him.

My mom had said he'd meet me here after their session, as they were still going through a lot, and it would take some time. She was over at my grandparents' house, working on the white party with Grammie and the decorating committee.

"Thanks for coming over to see me." He sat down, and his eyes looked sad. Tired. I pushed away the urge to tell him that everything would be okay. That I could forgive him.

Because we had a long way to go.

"Of course. But let's start with Ronny. He'd made it sound like you two were good, and he was heading over to meet you the day he came to the coffee shop."

"Demi." He cleared his throat. "I've made a lot of mistakes, and not doing more about what you'd shared with me regarding what had happened with Ronny is my biggest regret."

"Not sending two innocent teenagers away from their families for months? It's the Ronny incident that you're most upset about?" I folded my arms over my chest and raised a brow.

Yeah. Things are about to get real. I'm not holding back.

"One thing at a time, sweetheart. I said I've made many mistakes. But I should have reported Ronny. I did call him immediately after I spoke to you that night, but he didn't respond until the following morning. He told me he'd blacked out and had forgotten where he'd been the night before. He agreed to see a therapist and genuinely seemed to feel terrible about what had happened. I didn't want a police report to be filed because I knew it would humiliate him and his family. But I was wrong. I put your safety on the line. I never thought he'd show up here."

"Well, he came to meet you recently, right, Dad?"

He nodded the slightest bit. "Patrick came into town and

asked Ronny to be there, too. He wanted his son to apologize to both of us. I told him that you weren't currently speaking to me, so I guess he took it upon himself to go to the coffee shop and address the issues himself."

"That's not what he did. He came in angry and told me that I'd messed everything up for both of our families. That there was a lot of money on the line, and I'd caused all these issues over nothing. He still thinks he did nothing wrong. You get that, don't you? Have you seen the things he's posting on social media now? About me? *Your daughter.* That I was a tease and that I've twisted the whole thing. The stuff he's saying about Romeo being the son of a jailbird. That he's trash and so am I." A tear ran down my cheek. I'd tried to put on a brave face, but it was all taking a toll. I was tired of all of it.

"I'm very aware. I have Sam reaching out to him today." Sam Simmons was my father's attorney at the investment company that he ran. "He is going to take those posts down, or he is going to get slammed with a defamation of character lawsuit. I have ended all business ventures with Patrick and their family moving forward. I should have done that sooner, but I'm trying my best to repair our family, Demi."

I nodded. It was a start.

"Okay. And how exactly are you planning to repair things with Romeo and River?"

"Your mother tells me you're dating him and that it's gotten serious." He cleared his throat. "You do know that his father served time, and he and River were not innocent kids back then. They'd ditched school and had reputations for getting into fights."

"Well, your son and Ronny ditched school that day, as well, didn't they? And Romeo was going through a hard time. His father had just gone to prison, Dad. His family was falling apart, and you made everything worse. Who cares if a teenager ditched school all those years ago?"

"His father had three DUIs and could have killed someone."

"And my father is a liar who sent two teenagers to a hell-hole to save his son and his pathetic friend."

His brows narrowed as he studied me. Anger flashed across his gaze, but he quickly fixed his features. "I am truly sorry for what I did. I did not want your mother to suffer because Slade made a stupid mistake. I was trying to protect my son. My wife. My family."

"At the expense of someone else's." I shrugged. There were no tears left to cry for my father in this moment. "Dad, that is *not* okay." There was a disconnect here, and he wasn't understanding the magnitude of his actions. "He's such a good man, Dad. And you owe him an apology—you owe *both* of them an apology."

He looked away, staring out the window at the water in the distance. "So, this really is serious between you two, then? You're in love with a boxer. One who has no college degree or plans for the future outside of getting into a ring and getting punched in the head. Are you doing this just to prove a point to me?"

A maniacal laugh left my lips, one I didn't know I was even capable of. "You're serious? You think I'm in love with Romeo because I want to teach you a lesson?"

I pushed to my feet. I didn't know that I could leave this house more disgusted than I'd been when I'd arrived.

"Demi. Stop. That's not what I meant."

I whipped around. "You don't even know him. You judged him back then, and you're judging him now. Judging me!" I was pissed. "So what if he doesn't have a college degree? Ronny has one. Slade has one. And look at their goddamn lives. Romeo is a professional boxer. He runs the gym his father started so that he can help take care of his family. He's honest and hardworking and strong. And I love everything about him. Shame on you for thinking that money and power make someone a man. I don't know that Mom is looking at you the way that I look at Romeo lately," I spewed. "Let's face it, Dad. You were going to let Ronny get away with what he did to me because it was going to cost you money. If I hadn't fought him off, and Liz hadn't been home and walked in, he most likely would have forced himself on me, Dad. But at least he has a college education, right?"

I stormed out of his office and found my mother standing in the entryway.

"Demi Crawford, you get back in here right now. This conversation is not over!" he shouted as he followed me into the foyer.

My mom looked between us, exhaustion written on her features.

"It's time for you to go," she said to my father as she glanced at the front door.

"Agreed," he said as he looked at me. "You come back when you can show me some goddamn respect."

My mother chuckled. "I was talking to you, Jack. And from now on, I'll meet you at our therapy appointments. You are not welcome here."

He sighed and shook his head. And then he marched out of the office, grabbed his keys, and stormed out the front door.

"I've made a mess of our family, haven't I?" I whispered.

"Nope. You've done nothing wrong. Your father has made a mess of our family all on his own."

She wrapped her arms around me, and I wondered if our family would ever recover.

twenty-three

· · ·

Romeo

"THIS IS SO NICE OF YOU," Demi said, as we munched on breakfast on the plane with Lincoln and Brinkley.

"I've been looking forward to meeting you, and this will give us a few hours together," Brinkley said. My sister-in-law was an amazing woman. She'd played a huge role in Lincoln and me building the strong relationship that we had now. If it had been up to the two of us, we'd probably have been too stubborn to give it a chance.

"Yeah, me, too. Romeo talks about you guys all the time," my girlfriend said as she smiled up at both of them.

"Easy now. I don't talk about them all the time." I rolled my eyes, and everyone chuckled.

We spent the next few hours talking about the fight and all the shit that had been going down.

"Man, I've got to give it to you, Romeo. You've sure managed to piss off some powerful people." Lincoln shook his head as he sipped his mimosa because he was a bougie fucker who happened to be in the off-season at the moment.

Demi pulled out a protein shake from her little carry-on cooler and handed it to me, which earned her even more laughs. "Drink up, Champ. You had a hard run this morning."

"Yeah, you keep laughing, brother, while you drink your bubbly and enjoy the moment."

"I plan on it. So, how is he handling the pressure? I know the training is going well. But the bullshit with the senator's grandson and now Leo taunting both of you. It's a bit relentless, yeah?"

"Hey, why are you acting like I'm not sitting right next to her?"

"Because I want to hear it from her. You keep telling me you're fine, and I need to know if it's true. You spend all your free time with Demi, so I think she would know."

I shook my head and drank my shake and huffed beside her. Everyone was so fucking worried about how I was handling the heckling. I grew up with a father who was an addict and went to prison. I had thick skin. I'd spent months in a juvenile detention center, surviving things most kids couldn't begin to fathom.

My concern was my girl.

Her getting overwhelmed by it.

I could handle anything. But I hated that I'd dragged her into my shit.

Her hand found mine, and she intertwined our fingers. "He's handling it all really well. I don't think it's pleasant by any stretch of the word, but he shakes it off. He's been working incredibly hard, and it's inspiring to see someone push themselves, day in and day out, to the brink."

"It must run in the family," Lincoln said as he waggled his brows at me, and I flashed him the bird.

"I'm impressed, Romeo. You've stepped up to the challenge. And what Leo is doing says a lot more about him than it does about you. You're training while he's doing a lot of talking."

"I don't think Leo is too worried about this fight. The truth is, the dude is a badass, and he knows it. So, he spends a lot of time getting into his opponent's head. It's a strategy. One that probably works often."

"Is it working this time?" Lincoln asked.

"I don't like him talking about Demi," I said. That was really all there was to say. The other shit was just water under the bridge. He wasn't saying anything I hadn't heard before.

My girlfriend turned to look at me, her gaze wet with emotion. "Well, I don't like him talking about you, so we're even."

"Damn. You two are so freaking cute. I can barely stand it," Brinkley said, fanning her face. "So, Romeo told us a little bit about the stuff that happened with your father, and I'm sorry that you're going through that. And obviously, all that happened with Ronny Waterstone sounds like it was pretty scary, as well. Trust me when I tell you, I can spot a slimeball a mile away. And that guy is a slimeball."

"She's not kidding. She's got a gift for reading people."

"That's right, Captain. I read you like a freaking book, didn't I?" Her voice was all tease as she leaned against my brother, who wrapped an arm around her.

Demi watched them with a wide grin on her face. "You guys are pretty freaking cute yourselves. And the stuff that happened with my family was hard on Romeo and River. No one else. It's probably hard to fathom right now, but my father is not all bad. There's a decent man beneath all of this, so I think that's what hurts the most. There is goodness there, but it's clouded over right now by these awful things that he's done. And his lack of remorse is what gets me most."

My chest squeezed at her words. She hadn't told me much about her meeting with her father, just that it hadn't gone well. I assumed that meant he had a problem with me, and she wasn't going to be okay with that.

That didn't sit well with me. I loved Demi, and I knew her family meant a lot to her. I worried this would be something that would eventually come between us at some point, but I was trying to keep my mouth shut. The truth had come out, and she had to process it and move forward however she wanted to. I didn't need to make amends with her father or her brother, but I didn't know if *she* would need that from me when push came to shove.

If all of us being one big, happy family was the end goal for her, I didn't want to be the one to break it to her that it wouldn't be happening.

At least, I didn't see a way that we would ever get there.

I cleared my throat. "Our father, the man Lincoln never knew, made a lot of mistakes. I've shared that with all of you. But there was a good man beneath all of that. He had a big heart. He loved his family. He just didn't always feel worthy of love, so he punished himself over and over. Numbed himself and then struggled to escape that." I glanced out the window; white clouds swirling in blue skies surrounded us. "But I understand what you're saying. Our last few years together were good. He supported my boxing career, and he adored Tia. He deeply regretted what he did to Linc. So… just try to remember the good things your dad has done, you know? It helps when you allow yourself to remember that there is good with the bad."

Brinkley tilted her head to the side and smiled at me. Lincoln had been staring out the window and looked over at me and nodded. And Demi, she thought it over, and then her lips turned up in the corners.

"He did have his attorney threaten to sue Ronny, so let's focus on that."

My brother and Brinkley both laughed, but I didn't. A lot of the shit happening to Demi right now was because of me. Ronny's story wouldn't be getting all this attention if Leo hadn't jumped on board. Hell, I was the reason everything with Ronny had even gone public.

I'd pulled this girl into all my shit, and it was a heavy weight to bear.

"I hope he serves him up a big plate of shut the fuck up." Brinkley clinked her glass with Lincoln's, and that had all of us laughing now.

"Me, too. And thanks for getting us there to see my brother so quickly."

"Not a problem at all. The plane will be at the hangar not too far from your hotel tomorrow morning. I know you both have to get back for work and his training," Lincoln said, his gaze landing on me. "You're going to work out at the hotel while she's with her brother at the rehab?"

"No. I'm going to sit outside of that place until she comes out and I know she's okay. And then we'll go to the hotel, and I'll do my afternoon workout because Joey is pissed that I'm not going to be there for one goddamn afternoon. He sent me the workout from hell to make up for it. It'll take me a few hours, but I'll get it done."

"You don't have to wait there for me," Demi said, her brows pinched together. "I can meet you back at the hotel."

"Not happening. Not with Leo talking about you to everyone who will listen, and Ronny out there wanting revenge on both of us. For all we know, he talks to Slade and knows you're coming. It's not a chance I'm willing to take."

"Is that why you came with me? You were worried?"

"It's not the only reason, but it is one of the reasons." I leaned over and kissed the top of her head. "But the main reason is that I love you, and I want to keep you close."

"I wouldn't have guessed you for a clingy little fucker," Lincoln said as he barked out a laugh.

"Whatever. The apple doesn't fall far from the tree, from what I can see." I raised a brow at his sappy ass.

We spent the rest of the flight talking and laughing, and I could tell that they adored Demi, which I knew they would.

She'd be meeting Tia this weekend, and my little sister couldn't wait to come home and hang out with my girlfriend.

When we arrived in Boston, we said our goodbyes. Demi and Brinkley had exchanged numbers and were fast friends.

"I'll see you next week," Lincoln said, leaning close so only I could hear him. "Proud of you, brother. Just keep doing what you're doing, and you're going to be just fine."

I hoped like hell that he was right. My goal was to leave Vegas in one piece, still breathing. I knew I could take a beating; I'd proven it over the last few months. But I'd never been in a ring with someone like Leo Burns. So, I would just keep pushing harder. Every last bit of work I could squeeze in, I would do.

When we arrived at the rehab center, I kissed Demi hard and told her I'd be waiting for her outside. I spent the next hour and a half doing wind sprints out in the grass, push-ups, sit-ups, anything I could squeeze in.

I glanced at my phone when it vibrated, expecting it to be Demi telling me how it was going, but it was the RoD group chat.

NASH

Cutler's teacher called me in to tell me that he got into a fight at school. He's not even six fucking years old. And twenty bucks to whoever guesses what the fight was about.

KINGSTON

Someone called him Cutler instead of Beefcake?

RIVER

Did someone touch his gelled hair? You know he's funny about anyone messing with his hair.

> Someone took his leather coat? He's
> protective over that jacket, man.

HAYES

They talked shit about one of us. Because
Little Dude does not tolerate that.

NASH

A little fucker in his class said that his daddy
told him that Leo was going to knock Romeo
out. These kids are in kindergarten, for fuck's
sake.

My chest squeezed. I loved that fucking kid so much.

> What happened?

NASH

He punched the kid in the stomach and then
told him to watch his mouth when speaking
about his Uncle Ro. He lost Fun Friday for
two weeks.

> Well, he'll be getting Fun Saturday with Uncle
> Ro for the rest of his life. The kid's got some
> balls.

KINGSTON

He's so fucking loyal. I'll take on Fun
Sundays, moving forward. How dare they
take Fridays away from him!

RIVER

I want the name of the kid he punched so I
can figure out who his fucking father is.

HAYES

Agreed. That's the dude who should be
missing Fun Friday. The dumb fuck doesn't
have a clue what he's talking about.

I mean, in his defense, you've got Leo hyping people up. He's very confident about the outcome of this fight.

KINGSTON

Don't go there, brother. First goal: Go the distance. Just hold your own and take it one round at a time.

HAYES

You drunk, King?

NASH

He's sitting here in the office with me, and he looks a little constipated and weird.

KINGSTON

I get emotional thinking about our boy in the ring. Because you've worked so hard, and we're all fucking proud of you. Call me constipated again, and I will take a shit in your car, Nash.

RIVER

Is Beans meeting with her demon brother now?

KINGSTON

Damn it. I get emotional about our girl, too. She's a good one, Romeo. I say we keep her forever.

NASH

She's not a dog, dipshit. But our boy did survive some really crazy shit in the past with the women he dated before now.

HAYES

At least one of us found a girl that we all like.

> Yeah, I'm here. She's inside now. I'm just
> doing some drills outside while I wait for her.

RIVER

> Stay focused, brother. You've got this. Text
> when you get home tomorrow. I'll stop by
> and heckle you for your afternoon workout.

> Counting on it.

My notifications started blowing up when I ended the call, and I clicked on it to see Leo running his mouth once again. My messages were flooded with people telling me they were rooting for me and that they hoped I'd shut his ass up.

A news notification landed at the top of my screen, and I tapped on it.

My mouth fell open as I read the words in front of me.

Six women had come forward to file complaints about Ronny Waterstone. I wasn't surprised that there were more women who'd experienced what he'd done to Demi, but I was surprised that they were coming forward against him because of who his family was. Hell, Demi's father didn't want to speak out against them. But apparently, realizing that they weren't alone and that he'd been called out for what he did to Demi, they'd found the confidence to speak up, as well.

It made me fucking proud of her.

His family hadn't commented yet, but I hoped his world would come crashing down very soon.

I looked up to see the door swing open, and I tucked my phone into my back pocket. Demi's eyes were puffy, but she was smiling, and everything in me settled. All the bullshit surrounding the fight. My anger toward Ronny. It all dissipated when her eyes locked with mine.

"Hey, you doing okay?" I asked as I moved toward her.

"Yeah. Can I ask you for a huge favor?"

"Name it," I said.

"Come inside with me. Slade wants to speak to you."

There wasn't anything I wouldn't do for this girl. But this was not something I was looking forward to.

I nodded and took her hand.

Because if she needed me, I'd always say yes.

twenty-four

. . .

Demi

MY HAND WAS WRAPPED in Romeo's, and I could feel the tension radiating from his shoulders. But he'd agreed to come inside with me.

He could have said no, and I would have respected his wishes.

But he'd said yes.

I wouldn't have asked him to come inside if I thought this would only benefit Slade. He'd lost the right to be my main concern, though I'd still show up for him. But this could potentially be helpful to Romeo, as well.

I didn't explain anything further; I just led him inside to the room where Slade waited with Dr. Schwartz. I'd just spent the last ninety minutes in here talking to my brother. Getting everything off my chest because Dr. Schwartz said that keeping secrets made things worse, and our family had had a whole lot of secrets.

And she'd been right. Because my brother and I had had somewhat of a breakthrough today, as well.

I knocked on the door and led Romeo inside.

Both Slade and his therapist looked surprised that my boyfriend had agreed to join us. I'd told them that I doubted he would be willing to come inside but that I'd ask. I hadn't even had to explain. I'd said I needed a favor, and he'd said yes without hesitation.

I walked over to the couch and motioned for my boyfriend to sit beside me.

"Thank you so much for joining us, Romeo. We wouldn't normally request that someone who barely knows Slade be here, but after all that has been uncovered today, and with you being here for Demi, I think it's appropriate."

"Okay." Romeo cleared his throat. "I'm here because Demi wants me here and for no other reason."

Dr. Schwartz nodded. "That's fair after everything that has been shared today. But regardless of your motivation, I want you to know that it's appreciated."

Slade looked up at me from the chair where he sat across from us before his gaze moved beside me. "I found out today that the truth has come to the surface, and I've got to tell you, it's a fucking relief."

My brother paused to take a sip from his water bottle. He looked good, actually. Sobriety had always looked good on Slade. It just had never lasted long. But maybe today, we'd made some progress.

At least I hoped so.

"I've carried this with me for a long time, Romeo. This horrible thing that I did all those years ago. Fuck," he said, running his hands over his face.

"No holding back," Dr. Schwartz said. "You have him here, and he's willing to listen when he doesn't have to give you the time of day. So, this is your chance to state your piece."

"I was an idiot. Ronny had introduced me to some strong shit back then. It should have been a red flag that he never did a lot of the shit that he was offering me. Or at least he managed it better. But he'd come into town with his dad, who was meeting with my dad, and he'd convinced me to skip school. We'd gotten drunk, and I was high and just a total dumbass—" His words broke on a sob. "I can't believe the shit that I did. I was too fucked-up to know what happened for a while after that. I started numbing myself more and more with each passing day. My dad had said that everything was fine and that he'd taken care of it. But I learned that Patrick and my dad had pinned it on you and River after Ronny told them that two kids ran back inside to help Walt." Slade got up and walked to the desk to reach for some tissue.

He went on to explain what he'd shared with me over the last hour and a half. That when he found out that Romeo and River had been sent to juvenile detention, he went to my dad and lost his shit. He threatened to turn himself in and confess to everything. The guilt was eating him alive. My father had once again said he'd handle it, and he'd hired someone to get them released early. Romeo listened. He didn't show a lot of emotion; he just nodded and let my brother speak.

"Romeo, I fucked up so much. And that was the beginning of a horrible spiral for me. The guilt really did consume my life. I was disgusted with myself, and I think I didn't know how to handle it. So, I grew even more reckless, which led to the boating accident and hurting so many people who didn't deserve it. And then I just needed to be numb. All. The. Time." Slade shocked the hell out of me when he walked toward us, and then he dropped to his knees in front of Romeo and sobbed. "I'm so fucking sorry. I should have come clean. I should never have allowed that to happen. I don't know how to undo all the mistakes I've made. I don't know how to be sober and accept the person that I am. But at least I can finally tell you that I'm sorry."

My brother stayed down on his knees, crying, and Romeo leaned forward and squeezed his shoulder. "Get up, Slade. You don't need to be on your knees for me. Hearing you own it, hearing the hell you've been through, it's a start. But it's what you do now that matters. We can't change the past, but we can control our actions moving forward. You have a family who loves you and a sister who won't give up on you. Put in the work, man. Demi loves you so fucking much. That's why I'm here. And you have a long life ahead of you. There's plenty of time to make things right."

Slade moved to his feet and swiped at his face. "My sister is the best person I know."

"Well, we have something in common, then," Romeo said as he scrubbed a hand behind his neck. "She's worth fighting for, Slade."

He nodded, and I could barely see through all the tears streaming down my face.

My father had known all along that Slade had struggled with this secret. Slade had shared how he'd gone to him numerous times over the years about the guilt that he carried, and my father told him to keep his mouth shut.

But secrets had a way of coming to the surface.

"Thank you for hearing me out. I'm really grateful. I want you to know that I've been following all this stuff with Leo and your fight, and I really hope you kick his ass."

Everyone chuckled, and Romeo glanced over at me, using his thumb to wipe away my tears. "Thanks. The odds are not in my favor, but I'm going to take it one round at a time and hope to leave in one piece."

"I think you might surprise yourself by what Demi tells me about your training. And this Ronny shit… just be aware, he's a devious dude. He's threatened me many times over the years about talking. He has no remorse for anything he does. He's a spoiled, entitled prick who is used to using his family name to get out of the shady shit that he does." He held up his hands. "Trust me. I'm sure people have said the same about me. But I can promise you, I have been haunted by that day for nine years. There has never been one day that I didn't think about it since I realized what had happened."

"Okay. Well, let's see what you do with this now." Romeo raised a brow.

"Fair enough. Thanks for listening." My brother's eyes locked with mine, and I saw a flash of the boy I'd known my whole life. The brother that I'd looked up to and loved. He was still in there.

"Thank you," I said, squeezing Romeo's hand. "We're going to go."

Dr. Schwartz thanked Romeo, as did my brother, and we made our way outside. We didn't say a word as he moved around the rental car and opened the door for me. But I didn't get inside. Instead, I lunged at him, and I wrapped my arms around his neck.

And I completely lost it.

"Thank you for being here. For going in there. For supporting me. No one has ever supported me the way that you have. You just went in there blindly because I asked you to."

He held me there for the longest time before letting go and pulling back to look at me.

"I will always have your back. I love you."

"And I will always have yours. I love you," I said, as I moved into the car and buckled my seat belt as he slid into the driver's side and started the car.

I now understood the tattoo on Romeo's shoulder. The one that all the guys had.

Ride or die.

Because it may not be inked on my arm, but it was etched in my heart.

———

We'd returned home to Magnolia Falls and the whole trip had been a blur as it had been a quick turnaround. I was looking forward to spending some time with Romeo's sister, as she'd come home from school to visit her family.

"Is it hard for you to watch him work this hard?" Tia asked, when we walked next door to the coffee shop. I had a door that connected to the empty space that Romeo was training in now with Joey and Butch.

River and Hayes were there cheering him on, and I could see that Tia was struggling. Romeo worked himself to the bone. He had his arms tied back while he took hits to his body over and over. He did endless drills, including one-handed push-ups with weight on his back and sit-ups where he took hits to the body every time he sat forward. He jumped rope faster than anyone I'd ever seen, and he spent a lot of time on the bag, in the weight room, and sparring. Not to mention starting most days running out at my grandparents' ranch while I sat on Teacup and pushed his pace. The man was a machine. He was training all day now. Even in between workouts, he found a way to lift and to move.

"I'm so proud of him because I've never seen someone work so hard, you know?" I said, as I made us both hot tea and set the cup in front of her. "But yes, there are times that it's difficult to watch."

"They're punching him in the stomach with his hands tied behind his back," Tia said, her eyes welling with emotion.

"Joey is a really great trainer, Tia. And he's preparing Romeo to fight the best way he can. Without the use of both hands, it forces him to move his feet and take the hits that come his way. Joey needs to know he's going to be okay when he gets in that ring. Your brother stepped away from fighting for a long time, and now he's getting into the ring for the first time with a guy who held the belt not that long ago. He has to be prepared, or he will get hurt. I think he knows that."

A pit settled in my stomach just like it always did when I thought about it.

"Does he tell you that he's scared?" she whispered.

"Never. I don't think that's his style. I don't think fear drives him. I think he's realistic. He knows that Leo has a world of experience and is one of the best in the world in their weight class. He's studied Leo's films for weeks. He wants to fight smart. He wants to go the distance. He wants to make himself and everyone he cares about proud. But I don't think he thinks about winning. I think he thinks about being smart and leaving there proud of his performance while also being in one piece."

She nodded. "I hate that he's fighting. But Leo really taunted him, you know? And Romeo is such a proud man. He's always been that way. Even when he went away for those months over that incident." She winced as she looked up at me, and I swallowed hard. I could see the pain in her eyes as she spoke of it. "He was there, telling me and Mom and Mimi not to worry. That he'd be fine. And he had to be terrified, but he never let us see it. He's so damn stoic."

"He's also very smart. He wouldn't be doing this if he didn't think he could handle it. How about we watch it together so we can help each other through it?"

"I don't know if I can be out there, Demi. I might stay back in the locker room. I don't know if I can see him get hit over and over. I've never gone to one of his fights. Are you going to be able to watch?"

I nodded. I understood it. "I think you have to do what you're comfortable with. If he sees that you're upset, that will upset him, as well. I'm planning on being out there. I know it will suck, but I'm going to make myself do it."

She studied me, eyes searching mine. "Wow. You really love him, don't you?"

I chuckled. "How can you tell? Because I'm willing to watch his fight?"

"No. Because I saw you in there a few minutes ago. You put on a brave face, Demi. But your shoulders stiffened every single time they hit him. Your hands were in fists when he was doing those sit-ups and they were smacking him in the stomach. Your lip bled the slightest bit when he was sparring with his hand tied behind his back because you sank your teeth in so hard to keep from reacting. You don't like watching it any more than I do, but you love him so much that you do it. I guess you both have that whole being stoic thing in common."

My chest squeezed at her words. Because she was right. She'd seen right through me.

"We do have more in common than we thought we would."

"I've got to tell you, I've never seen Romeo so happy. And that's saying a lot with all the stress he's been under with the media stuff being impossible to ignore and all this training he's doing. He's crazy about you, and I love it."

"Thank you. I feel the same, and there's been a lot of stress around us since the day we met. But honestly, when I'm with him"—I glanced away as I gathered my thoughts—"I forget about everything else. I just feel content and happy and loved. I know it sounds corny, but it's the truth."

She wrapped an arm around my shoulder. "I'm so happy he stopped being a stubborn ass with you and admitted how he felt. And I'm thrilled that I feel like I might have a new bestie."

"Me, too." I leaned my head against hers just as the door swung open.

"Hey. He's about done. How about we go to Whiskey Falls and grab some appetizers and cocktails for those of us who are old enough?" River smirked before winking at Tia.

"My fake ID is not going to work because Lionel knows I'm not twenty-one."

"Just bring the ID with you and don't drink. I'll take care of Lionel. Your brother is exhausted, and he needs food."

I hopped off my chair and grabbed a protein shake from the refrigerator for Romeo to drink before we left.

River's eyes landed on me when I turned around, and he smiled the slightest bit. He was this badass guy covered in tattoos, but I knew that beneath it all was a big teddy bear.

"Okay, let's go get him some food," Tia said.

We all loved Romeo fiercely. No doubt about it.

twenty-five

. . .

Romeo

I WAS happy to see Tia and Demi getting along so well. My sister had never liked anyone that I'd dated in the past.

But these two seemed to be fast friends.

I was fucking tired from the workout I'd just survived. I'd downed my protein shake and ordered a chicken sandwich, but I was ready to get home and get some sleep.

And then do it all again tomorrow.

Two more weeks of this. My body wouldn't last much longer. I basically trained from morning to night. And Joey was pulling some tricks out of his hat lately that were no fun. Yesterday, he'd had me push a giant tire for miles through town. The man was relentless.

And as exhausted as I felt, I knew without question that I was in the best shape of my life. I was stronger than ever. Benching and lifting weights I'd never thought possible. I was running faster. Boxing harder.

But was it enough?

There was no fucking way to know.

That was what drove me day in and day out. If there was more that I could do, I was going to do it. I was going to leave that ring knowing I'd done everything that I could. The odds weren't looking good for me, and every sports book on the planet had Leo favored by a long shot. But they also didn't know how hard I was training. It didn't mean it would change the outcome, but it meant that I might last longer than people were predicting.

I didn't think one sports commentator had me going longer than three rounds, and most had me being knocked out in round one.

I was going to fight like hell to keep that from happening.

"Well, isn't this an unlikely group of misfits." Lionel tossed some napkins down and looked between us. "You've got one, who isn't old enough to be in a bar, and here she is, sitting with my lawyer, who is a tattooed, shady fucker but happens to be a brilliant legal mind."

Laughter bellowed around the table.

"There are very few bar owners who have a lawyer at their beck and call. If you'd stop getting your ass into trouble, I could just be considered a regular patron." River held up his beer and clinked it with Kingston's.

"Nothing regular about your ass. And Mr. Charming over here…" He flicked his thumb at Kingston. "He started a bar fight three nights ago, and I'm still cleaning up the mess from that shit."

"Hey, hey now." Kingston held up his hands. "That girl was out of control."

Demi's mouth fell open. "The fight was with a woman?"

"Oh, yes. Our precious King is a heartbreaker, and Molly Slickman was not having it. He was talking to Lana Smith and Molly got pissed and tried to hit him with a beer bottle, but he ducked, and it shattered all over the floor. And then Lana decided to defend her man, and a whole goddamn scuffle broke out." Lionel shook his head in disbelief. "I don't get it. You're not that good-looking."

More laughter.

"What can I say? I was just chatting with Lana, and Molly

lost her shit. So needless to say, I went home alone. Violence makes me uncomfortable unless I'm watching Romeo fight." Kingston chuckled before taking a long pull from his glass.

"Please. You were a scrappy motherfucker as a teenager." River rolled his eyes.

"Agreed. You got me into half the fights I was in during high school," I said, tossing a wink to Demi, who was watching with fascination.

"Fine. Enough about me. Anyone else you want to analyze at the table?" Kingston asked as Doreen set our food down.

"Well, these two are an unlikely match, but it seems to be working." Lionel looked between me and Demi and smiled at her. "Don't know how his ugly mug got such a catch, but if I were Romeo, I'd hold on tight."

"Hey, why are you so nice to Beans?" Kingston whined.

"Because she's sweet, and she makes the best coffee."

"Thanks, Lionel. I'll keep the mocha lattes coming," my girlfriend said.

He walked off, and we kept the conversation light.

"You all right, brother?" River asked, turning his attention to me.

"Yeah. I'm just beat. Looking forward to having a beer with you guys in a few weeks."

"Shit. It's probably not supportive of us to drink in front of you," Kingston said, before tipping his head back and chugging his beer. "There. I'm done."

I shook my head and laughed. "Dude. Drink away. It doesn't bother me at all."

"Thank God. After that bar fight story, I could use another one." Kingston held his arm up and ordered another, and River shot him a look.

"So, Demi was telling me about the white party. Is everyone really going for the first time? Because I am all about it. I've tried to get my brother to go with me for years. I'm going to have to find a really cute dress to wear," Tia said, and River, Kingston, and I all groaned at the same time.

"White parties aren't really our thing," I said, glancing over at Demi.

"You're all going. My grandmother is counting on it. Don't even try to worm your way out of it."

"What if my face is all beat up after the fight? You really want me at a fancy party looking like that?"

She finished chewing her food and reached for my hand. "You're always the best-looking guy in the room to me. It doesn't matter what happens in that fight."

"Hey!" Kingston shouted and pointed at himself. "You think him all beat up is better looking than this? Come on now."

"What can I say?" Demi teased. "You're all good-looking, but Romeo just does it for me."

River barked out a laugh. "I'm going to check in with her about this after the fight. But I'm here for a woman who stands by her man."

"They really are too cute for their own good, right?" Tia said, as she beamed at me and Demi, and I tossed my napkin onto the table.

I was struggling to keep my eyes open at this point. My whole body hurt. I needed to lie down. Demi picked up on it first and quickly pulled money from her purse, but I covered her wrist with my hand.

"I've got it," I said.

"You two get out of here. I've got a tab going for all my legal expertise. Get your boy home. King and I will walk Tia to your mom's on our way."

"I don't need an escort. I'm in college, remember?" my sister said as Demi and I both hugged her goodbye.

"Too bad. You're on the way, so there's no shaking us," Kingston said. We said our goodbyes, and I waved at Lionel on my way out the door.

"You okay?" Demi asked as we walked the short distance home.

"Yeah. I'm just feeling it today."

"My house or yours?" she asked.

"Let's go to yours. It's closer."

She laughed, considering it was only a few feet closer than mine. But I was about to fall over, and the few feet made a difference at this point.

She unlocked the door, and we made our way upstairs, and I collapsed onto her bed.

Fuck. I was tired.

Joey and Butch were stepping up the workouts. We were down to the wire, and I'd be tapering back a few days before the fight, so this was the final push.

Demi pulled my shoes off, and she lifted my hands to see the bruising across my knuckles before tugging at my tee and seeing the same along my abdomen.

"I know you're tired, but what if I run you a hot shower and help clean you up so we get you in bed?"

I stroked her hair away from her face. "Or you could climb on top of me and ride me into oblivion, and I'll fall asleep to you falling apart around me."

She licked her lips. "As much as I love the sound of that, I can see how tired you are. Let me take care of you tonight. We can catch up on the other stuff tomorrow morning if you're up for it."

"I'm always up for it," I whispered, as I thrust my hips up so she could see how hard I was. But the exhaustion was making it challenging to do anything about it.

She pulled at my hand and helped me to my feet and led me to the bathroom.

I stood there in awe of this girl. She turned on the water, and the bathroom started to fill with steam. She completely undressed me as I leaned against the wall, unable to do much more than that.

She quickly stripped off her clothes and led me into the walk-in shower. *Demi Crawford is the real deal.*

She did exactly what she said she would do. She washed my hair and my body, gently tracing her fingers over the bruised areas. She was quick as she could tell I was fading, and she reached for the faucet to turn off the water.

I grabbed a towel, but she took it from me and pushed up on her tiptoes to towel dry my hair and then made her way down my body, patting me dry before doing the same to herself.

And then we climbed into her bed naked, and I wrapped myself around her and felt completely content.

I had everything I wanted.

Everything I needed.

It was right here in my arms.

I slept hard and deep, and when my alarm went off, I practically knocked the phone to the floor when I stopped it. I glanced over at the beautiful woman nuzzled against me. Her hair was covering her face, and I trailed my fingers down her arm as I shifted her onto her back and moved down the bed beneath the covers.

I had a one-track mind, and I'd gone to sleep without pleasing my woman. I couldn't have that.

I pushed her legs apart and settled there before kissing her lower belly and the insides of her thighs and burying my face between her legs. I let my scruff run along her sensitive skin before my tongue dipped in for a taste.

She groaned and squirmed beneath me, whispering my name.

"I'm right here, baby. Right where I like to start my day."

"We need to go for your run," she said, her voice sleepy.

"First, you're going to come on my lips, and then you and your horse can torture me."

She chuckled, but it was sexy and gruff as she continued to rock against me. I slipped my finger inside, and my lips sucked hard against her clit. Her fingers tangled in my hair as she bucked up against me.

And I fucking loved it.

I slipped another finger inside, and she gasped as I took her right to the edge. I loved every little sound she made.

Every bit of pleasure that came from her sweet body.

"Romeo, please," she begged.

I smiled against her as I pulled my fingers out and slipped my tongue inside, knowing just what she needed.

What she wanted.

I spread her legs wider, hiking them over my shoulders, my hands gripping her ass.

I pressed my thumb to her clit as I continued working my tongue in and out of all that sweetness.

She tightened around me and went right over the edge.

And I stayed right there. Taking care of my girl like I always did.

Like I always would.

twenty-six

. . .

Demi

I WAS SWAMPED AT WORK, and my hours outside of the coffee shop were spent with Romeo, either training or wrapped around one another.

But tonight, Joey had asked Romeo to make sure that none of us were there for practice, which meant they were going to probably push him harder than ever. We were leaving for Las Vegas next week, and he'd be tapering back soon.

I couldn't wait for him to get a break from all of this.

I realized that the entire time that we'd been together, he'd been training for this fight. I wondered what it would be like when we didn't have that going on and we could just relax.

Leo had upped his trash-talking game, and I'd become his favorite topic in most of his posts, all in an effort to get under Romeo's skin. I did my best to ignore it, but he'd been finding photos of me on social media and resharing them. He was a disgusting human being. His favorite topic was that I was going to leave Romeo after he humiliated him in the ring.

It took everything I had not to respond. I wanted to tell him to go to hell. That he was the scum of the earth. But that was what he wanted me to do.

Leo Burns was not only a fighter, but he was a showman.

He wanted to drum up drama before the fight, and it didn't help that people were responding to it.

His posts constantly went viral, and everyone in Magnolia Falls was appalled, yet they were following him and talking about it, so his plan was working.

Romeo only seemed concerned about me. He constantly asked if all of this was too much for me or if I was upset by it. I knew he was angry, but he did his best to keep it from me. The amount of stress that he was dealing with was unbelievable.

All while training for the biggest fight of his life.

There was a knock on the back door, and I moved through the kitchen and opened it to find my father standing there. We weren't on good terms, not after the last time we spoke.

I hadn't bothered to talk to my dad about my visit with Slade. My mother had gone to see him after I'd shared our conversation, and they were working on repairing their relationship. I was far more forgiving of my brother than I was of my father. Slade showed a lot of remorse over what happened, and my father had yet to show any.

"Hey. What are you doing here?" I asked.

"I just took Mom to dinner after our therapy appointment and wanted to stop by and see if you were here."

"I'm here," I said.

"Can I come in?"

"Yes." I stepped back and invited him in, and he took a seat at one of the tables, and I sat across from him. "Of course."

"I wanted to talk to you about Ronny," he said, and I groaned. He was actually the least of my worries at the moment. I'd hoped my dad was coming here tonight to talk about apologizing to Romeo and River.

"Of course, that's what you are most concerned about."

"Demi. I messed up, and I admit that. I didn't realize how serious this was with Ronny. Hell, maybe I didn't want to hear it. But my attorney gave me a heads-up that he's heard some rumblings that Ronny is angry that these other women have come forward now. He blames your boyfriend for this going public."

"You're aware that that's the problem, right? He's so busy pointing the finger at everyone who talked or shared what he did with the wrong person instead of focusing on his own actions. What he did was disgusting. And obviously, I wasn't the first person he'd done it to. Perhaps he should try owning his mistakes and stop trying to find a scapegoat."

"Agreed. But I wanted to give you a heads-up that Sam Simmons heard he's trying to find a legal loophole to blame Romeo for defamation."

I rolled my eyes. "Are you kidding me? He came into my coffee shop. He could have just left, but he chose to start the argument outside, calling everyone names, including me. He shouldn't have been there at all. It's not Romeo's fault that people filmed Ronny having a meltdown. Romeo was protecting me, which I'd think you'd appreciate, since no one else was looking out for me."

"That's why I'm here. I've done a lot of thinking, and you're right. I owe Romeo an apology and a thank-you for what he did for you. It's been—" His voice cracked, and he looked away. Vulnerability was not something I saw often in my father. He'd always been strong. Confident. "It's been hard knowing I've let the people I love down. Your mother doesn't know if she can forgive me. I have to live with what I've done. So, all I can do is try to be better moving forward. I can't change the past, Demi. I'm here to tell you to warn Romeo that Ronny is a spiteful man. He wants to blame someone, and unfortunately, he has his sights set on your boyfriend."

"And what do you suggest we do about this? Can you help him, Dad? Seeing as he was protecting me."

"I have Sam putting out feelers to see what Ronny's next

move is. I told your mother what I'd heard, and she thought I should come straight to you and tell you. I don't know that he will do anything because he has a lot of heat on him at the moment. So, I'm sure his legal team will tell him to stay out of the spotlight and keep to himself until they go to court and deal with these other charges."

"He's such an entitled asshole. Did you know that he is the one who introduced Slade to opioids and to almost every drug that he's taken to date?"

My father looked like he'd just been punched in the gut, his eyes wide as they searched mine. "Who told you that?"

"Slade. We went to see him for a family therapy session."

"We?"

"Romeo went with me so I wouldn't have to be alone. Slade apologized to him. He also told him that he's been haunted by what he did to him and River and that he came to you many times about coming forward to tell the truth."

My father looked down at the floor. I was ready for the lies. For him to tear apart my brother. But he didn't do that. Maybe reality really was setting in, and he was realizing how much he'd lost.

He looked up, eyes welling with emotion. "That sounds about right. I knew it was eating him up inside, but I just didn't know how to make things better."

"He's carried a lot of guilt, Dad. I think it might help if you went there and acknowledged that. Maybe you could both start forgiving yourselves if you take that step."

"How about you? Can you forgive me?"

"I'd like to. But a part of me feels like I don't even know you anymore." A large lump formed in my throat.

"You know me, Demi. I'm just a flawed man who has made some big mistakes. But I've always loved my family. I've loved you since the day you came into this world."

I sighed. "Go see Slade, Dad. He needs you. He's making progress, and it's the first time in a very long time that I think he might be making an actual breakthrough. Let's focus on that for now, okay?" I said, my voice low.

I wasn't ready to forgive him for what he'd done to River and Romeo. For what he'd done to me after I'd turned to him about what happened with Ronny. For the lies and the dishonesty.

I didn't trust my father, and that was something I never thought I'd say.

"I can do that." He pushed to his feet and sniffed a few times. I stood, and he wrapped his arms around me. "I love you, Demi."

"I love you, too, Dad." Because I did.

I just didn't like him very much right now.

I walked him to the door and held up my hand and waved as he climbed into his car. My phone vibrated, and I looked down to see an unknown number, and I cringed.

UNKNOWN NUMBER

Do you know the damage your boyfriend has done to my family? Were you always this disloyal?

I blocked the number and deleted the text.

I wasn't going to add one more thing to Romeo's plate. And I didn't think telling my dad about these texts mattered now. Ronny was in a shit ton of legal trouble, and I was sure he didn't want to bring anything more down on himself. So, I'd wait.

I'd keep this to myself, for now.

———

I glanced over my shoulder to see Romeo gaining ground on us, and I leaned forward, urging Teacup to go faster, as my laughter floated around in the breeze. We were going freaking fast, which meant Romeo was hauling ass.

He'd gotten faster.

Stronger.

When we moved out onto the beach area by the water, I knew he'd pass us because Teacup didn't do well in the sand and rocks.

"Go, go, go!" I shouted as he charged past us on the final stretch. I hopped off my horse and tied her to the tree before jogging to where he'd finished.

He was bent over, heaving, his hands on his knees as he waited to catch his breath.

"Damn. You took another three minutes off your time. You do know that you could be entering a distance race after the training you've done for this fight."

He looked up at me, standing tall. "After this fight, I'm going back to my day job."

I laughed. He'd been very open about this being a onetime thing, and I hoped he meant it. I wasn't looking forward to this fight.

I just wanted him to be okay.

It was the weirdest mix of fear and pride.

"I like the sound of that." I dropped to sit in the sand as he did the same. This was our routine. A few minutes of quiet before our days got busy.

"Yeah? What do you see for us after this fight?"

"What do you mean?" I asked, as he picked up a small rock and pulled his arm back, letting it skim across the top of the turquoise water.

"Well, we've been dealing with all this madness since the first time I kissed you. I want to know what you want when it's just you and me. No training. No Leo. No Ronny. When all the drama stops, what do you want?"

"The same thing that I want with all the drama. You. Just you."

This sexy grin spread across his handsome face. His hair was damp and wavy and falling over his forehead. Dark eyes that I swore could see straight into my soul. "Good answer, Beans."

"How about you?" I asked.

"I only want you. I'm ready to put this behind me. Ready to take my girl to dinner and not be exhausted at the end of the day." He glanced out at the water. "But I also thought about using the money that I'm going to make on an investment property. A home for myself that isn't the size of a postage stamp. I'm sure I can rent out my place to one of the boxers."

"You're going to move?"

"Just to a bigger space." He turned to look at me and tugged me closer. "We spend every night together, so it seems silly to have separate places, doesn't it?"

My breath caught as I processed his words. I tipped my head back and smiled. "Are you asking me to move in with you, Romeo Knight?"

"I want to fall asleep with you every night. I want to wake up with my head buried between your legs every morning. I want to shower with you and watch you blow-dry your hair. I don't know, maybe get a dog?"

My head fell back in laughter. "Look at you, being all domestic. Moving in and getting a dog—those are big steps, Golden Boy."

"What can I say? You've made me want things I never thought I'd want."

"Like what?"

"Like… everything. I see it with you, Demi. I see you walking down the aisle in a beautiful white dress, with those eyes on me. I see us having a family. A future. A life. Not right now, but I see it in our future."

I pushed up and moved onto his lap to face him, one leg on each side so I was straddling him. "I see it all, too. I'm all in."

"Me, too."

"Then it's settled. I'd love to move in with you. I'll probably just use the apartment above the coffee shop for an office space."

"It could be our sex den," he said, tucking the hair behind my ears. "When I sneak over to see you at work, I can take you upstairs and have my way with you."

My teeth sank into my bottom lip. "I can get on board with that."

"Thanks for standing beside me through all of this. For tolerating Leo's bullshit and getting dragged into all the madness that has come with this."

"There's nowhere else I'd want to be standing."

He wrapped his hand behind my head and pulled me down, bringing my lips to his.

And he kissed me like he'd die if he didn't.

He kissed me like I was the air he needed to breathe.

He kissed me like this was forever.

twenty-seven

. . .

Romeo

"THANKS FOR COMING by to see us," my mom said, as Demi said goodbye to my grandmother. "You understand why I can't be there, right?"

"Don't give it a thought. I wouldn't want you there. I know it's hard to watch me fight, and if you don't want to watch it on TV, you don't have to do that either."

I still couldn't wrap my head around the fact that I was going to be fighting on national television. I hoped I didn't make a fool of myself and go out too soon.

"I'll be watching, but I can pace here and keep myself from jumping into that ring with you. Just—" My mother looked away as her hands squeezed mine before her gaze returned to mine. "You don't need to be a hero, Romeo. You agreed to fight this lunatic, and I know you felt pressured to do so. But if it's bad, just pretend you get knocked out and stay down. It's not worth your life, son. We are all endlessly proud of you, regardless of this fight."

I wrapped my arms around her. "Come on, now. I trained awfully hard. I'm going to be fine. Stop worrying."

She sniffed, and I knew I had to get out of here. We were heading to Las Vegas the next morning. We'd be arriving a few days before the fight because we'd have the press conference and the weigh-in the day before, and it would allow us time to get settled. I'd tapered off my workouts, and I just wanted to be out of here.

"All right. You get out of here. I love you. Lincoln is flying Tia there from school, so you make sure she stays out of trouble." She let out a long breath.

"Don't worry about a thing, Mama. I love you."

Demi walked up and hugged my mom, and I hustled us out the door. My hand found hers, and we walked the short distance home. The weather had warmed up, and I was grateful for the fresh air. I'd been spending a lot of time in the gym and in the training space next to the coffee shop, outside of my runs in the morning.

"Your mom was emotional, huh?" Demi asked.

"Yep. She gets that way. It'll be fine."

"It will be." She sighed. "I can't believe we leave tomorrow morning."

"It's about fucking time, right? Leo's got to be exhausted from all his antics." I chuckled, and she did, too.

He was a piece of shit. Talking about stealing my girl. About humiliating me in front of her. I fucking hated the guy. I'd kept my mouth shut for months, and I was ready to get in there and just fight the asshole. Regardless of the outcome, I was ready to face it.

"Agreed. I think the whole world is tired of hearing him run his mouth."

We came to a stop in the alley, and I pulled her close. "I need to go pack a few things for tomorrow, so why don't I meet you upstairs at your place in a little bit?"

"Sure. I'll get organized, too." She pushed up on her toes and kissed me before walking backward toward her place. "We're leaving tomorrow, Golden Boy. All your hard work is going to pay off."

I watched her step inside the building before I made my

way inside mine. I opened the box that had arrived today. Demi and the guys had played a role in designing my fight shorts. They were all black with a white band and gold stitching on the waist where it read *Golden Boy*. On the inside of the shorts, they'd had them embroidered with a few things that would mean something to me. The inside waistband said *Beans and Beefcake*, which still made me laugh every time I read it. My girl and my godson. And then on the backside, the letters *RoD* were stitched there, as well.

I'd taken Demi over to see Cutler earlier today, and she'd given him the RoD tattoo in black Sharpie. He'd strutted through the house like he was some sort of badass. I loved that even at just shy of six years old, he wore those letters proudly. I folded the shorts and the matching black-and-gold robe with my name on it into a separate bag.

Lincoln was flying us all to Las Vegas tomorrow, so we could bring as much luggage as we needed to. I packed up my toiletries and paused in the bathroom to look in the mirror.

I stared at the reflection looking back at me. I was bigger and stronger than I'd been three months ago. I'd worked harder than I'd even known I was capable of.

I'd be leaving it all out there.

I was at peace with whatever happened at this point because there was nothing more that I could do to prepare.

I set my bags by the door, as we'd be back in the morning to grab them. I paused at my dresser and pulled out the letter that I'd written to Demi to have during the fight, just in case she needed it.

She liked to act like nothing bothered her, but I knew differently. I knew she'd been stressed over that fuckface Ronny threatening to come after me. But he had nothing on me. You can't sue someone for calling you out for a crime that you committed. He could come after me all he wanted, but he didn't have a leg to stand on.

I tucked the letter into my bag, grabbed my keys, and headed out the door. I jogged toward Demi's place but caught movement coming from beside me.

A blur of bodies charged at me, all wearing fucking masks, and they swung at me.

Three in total.

One wrapped an arm around my neck as he kneed me in the back.

I elbowed the fucker to my left and heard him howl as I swung and yanked the one on my back off of me. A third dude lunged at me, catching me off guard as I'd prepared for the dude on my right who was back on his feet.

"Leo Burns sent a message that you're going down in the first round, and you better stay down," the dude hissed in my ear as the other tried to wrestle me into a headlock. The third dude was stumbling back toward me as I used my head to ram the guy holding my neck. I heard the crack as he fell to the ground, and I swung at the other dude, who was kicking and punching like a fucking lunatic. As I turned to swing at the asshole who was charging at me again, I saw a blurry vision just as I heard her voice.

Demi.

I spun as fast as I could when I realized she'd come outside.

And before I could stop it, the dude's hand swung back, and she went flying through the air. Her body landed hard against the pavement. I lost my shit, grabbed him by the collar, and threw him across the alley. He landed on a car, and the alarm sounded. His mask was gone, but I didn't have time to see who he was.

"Shit!" one of them shouted as Demi lay lifeless beside him.

I sprinted toward her as the three cowards were cussing and running off like little pussies.

"Demi. Baby." I reached beneath her neck as she lay on the pavement, unconscious. "Demi!"

I leaned down, putting my ear to her nose and mouth. She was breathing. I tried tapping her face as hysteria took over. "Baby, can you hear me?"

Her eyes opened suddenly, and a sound I would never get out of my head escaped her throat. She cried out in absolute pain as I realized her arm was turned in the wrong direction.

"Romeo, what happened?" Pinky shouted. He must have come from his place when he heard the car alarm going off.

"Call 9-1-1," I said, running my hand through my hair, not knowing what to do. Afraid to touch her. Hurt. Her.

I heard him on the phone, and he sounded frantic.

"Tell them to get someone here right fucking now!" I shouted.

"They're on their way," he said, bending down to assess the situation.

"Baby, look at me." I held her face in both of my hands, careful not to move her.

She continued to sob, and I heard the sirens in the distance. "They're almost here. We're going to get you some help. You're going to be okay."

The sounds leaving her mouth shattered me. I couldn't move her for fear of hurting her, so I just lay down on the ground beside her, whispering into her ear. "I'm right here, baby."

She wasn't making any sense outside of the cries of pain that were coming from her lithe body. She seemed to be coming in and out as she'd cry and then go completely silent for twenty to thirty seconds at a time, and then the cries would come again.

"What the fuck is taking so long!" I shouted.

"Here they come, Romeo." Pinky's voice cracked as he bent down to talk to us. "You're okay, Beans. They're going to help you."

I heard the ambulance come to a stop a few feet from me, and the sound of people running our way had me whispering in my girl's ear. "They're here, baby. It's going to be okay. Stay with me."

There were three guys there bending down to look at her as I sat up and told them what happened. She cried out again, and they shifted me out of the way so they could assess her. Before I knew what was happening, there was a gurney there, and they were carefully shifting her onto the bed.

"How long was she unconscious?" one of them asked as I took her hand on the arm that wasn't injured and walked with them as they hurried toward the ambulance.

"I don't know. Maybe thirty seconds. And she seems to be coming in and out of it."

He nodded, and I climbed into the ambulance without asking for permission. They'd need to fight me if they tried to stop me from going with her. I called out to Pinky. "Call the guys, and call her mom."

One of the guys called ahead on the radio to say they had a patient with suspected head trauma and a severe arm injury coming in. He also mentioned her name, as clearly, her family was well-known in Magnolia Falls. I hoped like hell that would get her the best attention possible when we got there.

"Are you hurt?" the other guy asked me as he took her vitals and checked her blood pressure. I rested my head beside her face so I could hear the sound of her breathing.

"I'm fine. She's fucking hurt. You need to help her." I didn't recognize my own voice. The panic. The fear.

Suddenly, nothing else mattered.

All that mattered was her.

We arrived at the hospital quickly, where a team of people were waiting for us. I jumped out as they took the gurney, and I jogged alongside her.

"You need to stay here so we can assess her."

"Fuck!" I shouted in frustration that I couldn't go with her.

One of the paramedics put a hand on my shoulder, and I whipped around, ready to fight him. He held up his hands, eyes wide. "She's going to be okay. Let them take care of her. She's in good hands."

I nodded, running a hand through my hair as I leaned against the wall.

How the fuck did this happen?

Shouting came from the entrance, and I looked up to see River and Kingston running toward me.

"What happened? We just heard from Pinky. Nash and Hayes are on their way. I called Demi's mom, and she was already on her way."

Two police officers approached us, and they bent down to get eye level with me. Kingston handed me a bottle of water, and I chugged it.

"Can you tell us what happened?"

I couldn't wrap my head around any of it.

"I'd run to my place to pack. She was in her apartment. I watched her go inside," I said, my words frantic. I looked up to see Demi's parents and her grandparents right behind them. I pushed to my feet, and Rose lunged at me, wrapping her arms around me.

"Is she okay?" Her words were muffled sobs.

"I don't know. She was in a lot of pain and coming in and out of consciousness. I don't know what the fuck just happened."

"Romeo." Demi's grandfather's voice broke through all the hysteria. He clapped an arm on my shoulder. "Take a breath and slow down. Tell us what happened."

I nodded. River and Kingston were beside me. The two officers stood beside Demi's parents as they all waited for me to speak.

"I was heading over to Demi's place, and three guys jumped me. They came out of nowhere. I had it handled. I had it fucking handled. One guy was already down on the ground." My voice cracked, and I let out a breath. "He was down, but they were coming from every side. And then I saw Demi out of my peripheral, and it was all a blur. I tried to get to her. But before I could do anything, the asshole on the ground went to swing at me and hit Demi instead. She went flying. Landed hard on the ground. She was unconscious for maybe thirty seconds, and then she was crying in pain. I don't know how this fucking happened."

Demi's mom and grandmother were crying now, and everyone else was shaking their heads in disbelief.

"Do you know who these men were?" one of the officers asked.

"They had masks on. One of them lost their mask after he hit Demi, but I didn't get a good look at his face because I was worried about her. But they said they were sending me a message from Leo."

"Jesus Christ," Demi's father hissed as he glared at me.

"What was the message?" the officer asked.

"That I was going down in the first round, and I better stay down."

"That piece of shit," River hissed. "If he's so confident, why in the hell is he having you jumped?"

"It doesn't make any sense," I said.

"Yet you brought my daughter into your mess. You put her in a position to be hurt. Let that sink in," Demi's father said, and my gaze locked with his. I'd hated the man for what he'd done to me and River, but for the first time, I agreed with him.

He was right. I had done this.

I'd brought her into this bullshit mess of mine.

My life was messy. Always had been. But I'd never had to worry about another person before now.

"Spoken like a man who knows what it's like to bring innocent people into their mess, huh?" River growled.

"Don't you go pointing the finger, Jack," Demi's grandfather said to his son-in-law. "We need to make sure our girl is all right. That's what's most important."

"I don't want you near her right now!" Jack shouted as he moved closer to me. "She has no business going to this fight when you've put her in this kind of danger."

"Please stop. We need to go speak to the doctor," Rose said, her voice trembling.

"Agreed. Let's make sure Demi is okay. Pointing the finger at Romeo is not fair. He didn't ask for this," Kingston said, eyes hard as he stared at Demi's father.

"Let's all calm down now," the police officer said. "This isn't anyone's fault but the three men out there on the loose. Let me get some more information from you, Romeo, so we can get our team out searching for these guys."

I nodded, feeling the weight of the world on my shoulders.

I followed him to a corner of the waiting room and answered everything I could to the best of my ability. I'd had a pretty good gauge of their height and weight, but that was about all I had to offer.

"They weren't fighters. I easily had them handled. They were just swinging and trying to take me down. But his arm came back hard, and he was probably twice Demi's size." I shook my head as I buried my face in my hands.

"Why would he send three dudes who don't know how to fight to jump you?" River asked, and I shrugged.

Nothing about tonight made sense.

All that mattered was Demi.

I saw the doctor come out to the waiting room, and I pushed to my feet and walked over.

Her family was standing there, and I moved beside Demi's grandfather. River and Kingston were behind me, and Nash and Hayes had just showed up, as well.

"She's going to be okay. She's got a radial fracture, which will require surgery. We're going to get her in right away. She hit her head hard enough to be knocked unconscious for a few seconds, so we'll be watching that, as well. She's refusing any pain meds and said she has her reasons for that. She also couldn't recall what happened, as she's pretty shaken up."

"Thank you," Jack said, extending his arm. "Can we see her before she goes into surgery?"

"Let's keep it down to one or two visitors, and make it quick. They are getting the OR prepped now, so I'll have the nurse come and get you in a few minutes. But you'll all be able to visit tomorrow, so let's keep tonight brief."

The doctor excused himself, and Rose burst into tears and covered her face with her hands as her father wrapped an arm around her.

"She's going to be just fine."

"How about Rose and I go back and see her, and everyone else can come back in the morning?" Jack said, before turning to me. "And how about you leave for your fight and don't come back?"

"Have you always been an asshole? Or just for the last decade?" River said, stepping into his space.

"Okay, this isn't helping. I think we all know who Demi wants to see. Romeo can go back with me. He's had a traumatic evening, as well, Jack. He needs to see that she's all right."

"How about you come back with me first," Rose said, extending her hand to me. "You can go in when we come back," she said to her husband.

"He's also the reason she's here, but I guess you're still punishing me for mistakes I made almost a decade ago."

"There's been plenty of recent ones, as well," Carson said.

I was too exhausted to engage with them because Jack Crawford was right.

I was the reason that she was here.

And I wouldn't forget that.

twenty-eight

. . .

Demi

MY MOM and Romeo walked through the door, and the tears started all over again.

"Hey, sweetheart." My mom rushed to the side of my bed as Romeo stood back, hands shoved in his pockets, looking like he'd just robbed a bank and was ready to confess. "How are you feeling?"

"I've been better," I croaked.

My gaze moved to my boyfriend, who was just watching me with concern. I answered my mom's questions the best I could, but everything was jumbled, and my head was pounding.

"We've been so worried. You're going back for surgery, and they said we can come back tomorrow. They're going to get you all fixed up, Demi." My mother's words trembled.

"They said I'll be good as new in a few days. I'm fine. Do you think you could give me a minute alone with Romeo?"

"Of course. I'll be back first thing in the morning. I love you, Demi." She kissed my forehead, and I flinched the slightest bit. Everything hurt. My arm, my head, my face.

"Love you, Mama."

She left the room, and I turned my attention to the man

who was clearly in despair, standing just a few feet from me. "Why are you standing so far away?"

"Jesus, Demi. I'm so sorry. You shouldn't have come into that alley, baby."

I tried to remember what happened. My head spun as flashes came back to me. "I heard something. Shouting maybe? And I looked out the window. There were guys with masks dressed in all black, and they were attacking you. I don't remember what happened after that."

He walked over to me and stroked my hand so gently I barely felt it. "I'm so fucking sorry."

A tear landed on my hand, and I realized it was coming from him.

He looked—broken.

"Why are you sorry? You didn't do anything."

"It was a message from Leo. And I dragged you into my shit. And now you're lying in this bed, and you need surgery to fix your arm. I did this to you."

The sadness in his eyes made my chest hurt more than it already did.

"I'm going to be fine. I know we're supposed to leave tomorrow, and I asked Dr. Westman if he could release me early, but he still hasn't answered me."

"You're not going to this fucking fight. I don't want you anywhere near him. Hell, I don't even know if you should be near me anymore." He ran a hand over his face, swiping the moisture from beneath his eyes.

"Don't say that. I want to be there for you."

He shook his head. "No fucking way. We'll talk about it after the fight. But I'm not getting on that plane until I know you're okay. And I'll call the whole fucking thing off if I need to. That fucking guy did this to you. To us."

"You're not calling anything off. You've worked so hard." My words broke on a sob. "You are not seriously breaking up with me in the hospital, are you?"

"Baby, let's just make sure you're okay. That's all that matters right now."

"I'm okay. I'm talking to you, aren't I?" I said, not hiding my irritation. This was ridiculous. He'd been jumped by Leo's guys, and now he thought he was bad for me?

"You're going into surgery to put your fucking arm back together. You hit your head hard enough to get knocked unconscious. Your dad doesn't want me anywhere near the hospital or near you. And I don't fucking blame him, Demi. My life is messy."

"So is mine," I cried, just as my father came rushing into the room, with my mother shouting as she chased after him.

"What the hell is going on in here? Is this your way of helping her? Have you not done enough already?" My father's voice boomed through the room, and my head was pounding so much that I thought it would explode.

"Stop! This is not his fault, Dad. You don't know what you're talking about." My words were jumbled by my cries, and three nurses came rushing into the room.

"Everyone needs to leave now." One of the female nurses pointed at the door as she moved beside me and checked the monitors. "We're taking her back now, and this is not helpful."

Romeo just stared at me as he stood beside the door. And then he bowed his head and left the room.

My heart ached because there was something in his eyes.

Something that told me he believed my father.

And my heart broke a little more with each passing minute.

My parents left the room, and I rolled to my side and let the tears fall.

And they didn't stop until I was in the operating room with a nurse counting down from ten and telling me to relax.

———

I woke up to a blood pressure machine squeezing my arm and two nurses whispering. I'd been woken up every two hours through the night to make sure the concussion hadn't caused more issues, and I'd barely slept. My arm was wrapped and sore, but it hurt less than it had before surgery.

"Can you imagine if that was your boyfriend? He's so freaking hot."

"And he's a boxer and has that sort of bad-boy edge. But did you hear what everyone was saying about how devastated he was when they brought her in last night? He's obsessed with her, apparently."

I kept my eyes closed because the conversation was too good at the moment, and I didn't want to interrupt.

I wanted to hear more.

"Damn. I want a man who loses it if he sees me hurt. And a man who looks like that."

"Excuse me, ladies, but is this a conversation that we should be having with the patient sleeping beside you?" a voice interrupted. She sounded older and much more formal. I wanted to tell her it was totally fine. I liked hearing that Romeo was obsessed with me, and I already knew how hot he was, so I didn't mind listening to them gush over him.

"Sorry," one of them said, clearing her throat, and then they both started laughing, which told me the other woman had left the room.

"How did she possibly hear that?" one voice said.

"It's those eagle ears," the other one said.

"Is she awake yet?" A man's voice entered the room.

"Good morning, Dr. Westman," one of the nurses said, and her voice was very professional now.

I started to stir to let them know I was waking up because I was hoping to get out of here today. I was determined to get to Romeo's fight.

I blinked a few times and opened my eyes.

"Good morning, Demi," Dr. Westman said as he flipped through my chart. "How is the pain this morning?"

"It's tolerable," I said, using my uninjured arm to reach for the controller on the bed to sit up a bit.

"All right. And not being on all those heavy pain meds will help you recover much quicker because you won't be sleeping all day. But we need to keep taking the Tylenol every four hours, all right?" He continued to study the chart.

"Do you think I can be released today? Would I be able to travel if so?"

He set the chart down and studied me. "I heard there was some excitement in here last night. That can't be helpful after all you went through yesterday."

"It's fine. It was my dad making a scene." I shrugged.

Dr. Westman rolled the stool on wheels over to the side of the bed. "You had a pretty major surgery last night, so leaving today is not an option. I'd also like to keep an eye on that concussion, so at the very least, you'll need to stay one more night. You could get out of here sometime tomorrow, providing I like what I see with your recovery."

Romeo's fight wasn't for two days. He had the weigh-in tomorrow and the fight the following night. I could still make it.

"And travel?"

"I wouldn't recommend flying, if that's what you're asking. You took a hit to the head, and you need to be cautious."

I chewed on my thumbnail as I thought about my options. "Okay. But I can be in a car, right?"

Vegas was a couple hours' drive, so I could still make it.

"Demi, that should be the least of your concerns right now. Let's see how you do today. We'll take a look at the test results, and then we can discuss this further tomorrow. You need rest right now. Your body went through some serious trauma, and rest is the best thing for you at the moment."

I nodded. The timing wasn't great for that because I was not missing this fight. It wasn't an option.

"I need to be in Las Vegas in two days," I said, just above a whisper. One of the nurses was still in the room, and her gaze softened as she looked at me. "I was supposed to be on a flight this morning."

"I understand that. But you were attacked last night, and things have changed. It doesn't seem like your boyfriend made that flight either." Dr. Westman pushed to his feet and jotted something down in the chart before walking out the door as I processed his words. How would he know where Romeo was? I glanced around for my phone, suddenly realizing I hadn't had it with me when I'd run outside last night.

"Hey." The nurse walked closer to me. "I'm Maggie, by the way."

"Hi. I'm Demi."

She glanced over her shoulder to make sure no one was listening. "Dr. Westman is right about Romeo. He slept in the waiting room. He was there when I walked in this morning, and everyone said that he slept there."

My chest squeezed. He was supposed to leave this morning. "Could I ask you a favor?"

"Of course."

"Could you go see if he's still here? He should have left for his fight this morning. And I don't have my phone or any way to reach him. Maybe you could ask him to come back here and talk to me?"

"I'd be happy to go check."

I used my fingers to comb through my hair, and I waited for what felt like forever. They brought breakfast to me, and I took one bite of toast and sipped the hot tea that was on the tray. I had no appetite. I was a bundle of nerves after what happened, and my anxiety was off the charts about making sure I got to the fight on time.

Maggie hurried back into the room, glancing over her

shoulder again, but now she appeared to be much more nervous. "Your dad is here, and there's some shouting out in the waiting room. But I was able to speak to Romeo before your dad arrived. He said to tell you that he wasn't leaving town until he knew you were okay and you were going to be released from the hospital. He told me to tell you not to worry about the fight. He had it under control."

A tear rolled down my cheek. "He needs to be there for the weigh-in tomorrow."

"That seemed to be the least of his worries."

"Why isn't he coming back here to see me?"

"I asked if he wanted to come back with me, but he said after the scene in your room last night, he didn't want to make things harder for you. He said he just needs to know that you're okay. And then your dad came in and started screaming when he saw him there, and I ran back here because someone called security."

"My father is unbelievable." I shook my head. He didn't give two shits when his rich friend's son tried to attack me, but Romeo sleeping at the hospital because he was worried about me, that pissed him off?

He was such a hypocrite.

"Thank you so much, Maggie. Can you do one more thing for me, and I'll never bother you again?"

"You can bother me as much as you want. This is the most excitement I've had since I started working here," she said with a smile.

"Could you grab me a piece of paper and a pencil?"

She walked out of the room and came back with a sticky note pad and a pen. "Will this work?"

"This is perfect." I quickly scribbled out a note to Romeo and folded it into a small square. "Could you find a way to get this to him?"

"I'm on it." She left the room before looking back and waggling her brows. "I love this undercover operation."

I chuckled, even though my heart was aching. My father would probably have Romeo escorted out of the hospital because what I'd learned over the last few weeks was obvious —my father was a bully. He would do whatever it took to get the outcome he wanted. And Romeo was not part of the outcome that he wanted for me.

But he was the only outcome that I wanted. And my father was not going to change that.

Maggie walked back into the room with my parents, and she gave me a little thumbs-up from where she stood in front of them, letting me know she'd given him the note.

I nodded in thanks, and she stepped out of the room.

"That boyfriend of yours needs to let you recover. He's making a scene out in the waiting room."

"I'm fairly certain the only one making a scene was you, Jack." My mother's tone was harsher than I'd ever heard it. "I actually spoke to him. He's extremely worried about you, and he spent the night in those chairs because he wanted to be close if anything happened. He's not the bad guy here."

My father's eyes widened. "Am I the bad guy again? Did I cause her to get her arm broken in two places and slam her head against that filthy alley? I'm the one protecting our daughter, Rose. And you better get on board."

My mother moved closer, her jaw clenched and shoulders ramrod straight as she stared at my father. "I've always protected our children. You are the one who needs to get on board. And Romeo Knight is not my enemy, nor is he a danger to Demi. He loves our daughter fiercely, and he would protect her at all costs. I don't believe you can say the same."

I couldn't believe the tension between them, and a part of me wondered, for the first time since everything had come out, if they'd ever be able to repair their relationship.

Maybe all the secrets that had been uncovered were too much for my mom to forgive.

"I've admitted that I made mistakes. Hell, I'm not even

living in my own home, and I'm doing my best to fix that. But you can't keep throwing it in my face if you want to move forward. A crime was committed last night, and I am here to make sure it doesn't happen again."

I shook my head as anger coursed through my veins. "Then go after the guys who jumped him. I love him, and he loves me, and I don't care if you are on board with that. You don't get to tell me who to love, nor do you get to push him out of my life. You may have the power to get him removed from the hospital, but I'll get released, and I'll fix things with him the minute I'm out of here."

My father crossed his arms over his chest and glared at me. "You're not going anywhere until they run those tests and we make sure you're okay."

"You can drag this out as long as you want to. It won't change a thing."

And that was the honest truth.

Because I will never stop loving Romeo.

twenty-nine

. . .

Romeo

EVERYONE WAS ON EDGE. We'd gotten to Las Vegas a day later than planned since I'd waited at the hospital until Peyton let me know that Demi was cleared on all her tests. She'd be released within a few hours, and Lincoln had the plane ready to go.

Joey and Butch were losing their shit that we needed to get our asses there. The weigh-in was in a few hours, and we'd just gotten to the hotel. I was exhausted because I'd barely slept the last two nights, as I'd spent them in a chair in the waiting room of the hospital.

It wasn't the way I planned to go into this fight, but if I were being honest, nothing was going as expected anymore.

The fight was not at the forefront of my thoughts.

I was struggling to manage my anger toward Leo Burns. We'd been able to keep what happened out of the press. It surprised me that he'd not made any of it public. He was still just running his mouth about me going down in round one. But he'd have to cut off my limbs if he thought he'd take me down in round one now. It wasn't happening. I was going to ruin that motherfucker so he'd never fight again.

He'd come for me and ended up hurting my girl.

He'd need a fucking truck to run me over right now if he hoped to take me down that quickly.

I was assuming his piece-of-shit friends who'd jumped me had reported back and let him know they'd hit a fucking woman.

It haunted me that I hadn't gone after them, but Demi had needed me, and I hadn't had a choice at the time. But five minutes alone in an alley now—it would be a different story.

The first time they jumped me, I had not wanted to get hurt before the fight.

Now, I didn't give a fuck about the fight. I wanted to break every bone in their bodies. One by one. Drop them to their knees and make them apologize to her for what they'd done.

Kingston opened the duffle bag and handed me the black tracksuit that I'd be wearing to the weigh-in.

All the guys were wearing black joggers and hoodies that said *Team Golden Boy* on the back.

They'd wear something similar tomorrow, as well.

We'd had fun picking this shit out weeks ago, but now, none of it mattered.

I checked my phone and saw a text from my sister-in-law.

BRINKLEY

Hey, just wanted to let you know that I just picked up Tia from the hangar, and we're on our way to the hospital. I'll text you as soon as she's released.

> You won't leave until she's out of there, right?

BRINKLEY

You have my word. But you may cost me my job if I miss that fight.

> If she doesn't get released by the time of the fight, I won't be fighting. That means something is wrong.

BRINKLEY

I'll keep you posted. Get your head in the game, Romeo. Leo's a loose cannon. Look what he's already done. You need to be safe and focus on the fight. Tia and I will be with Demi.

I've got it covered.

I slipped my phone into my back pocket as Lincoln came to stand in front of me.

"You all right? Let's get changed and get this weigh-in over with."

River, Kingston, Hayes, and Nash were all there, grabbing their clothing and getting changed.

"Yeah. I just talked to Brinks. She's in Magnolia Falls with Tia. They're heading to the hospital."

"Dude, you know how hospitals are. They're just slow about this shit. It always takes longer than they say. Peyton told you that her tests all came back fine. This is probably her dad dragging his feet to keep her from coming to this fight."

"She isn't coming anywhere near this fight or Leo fucking Burns." I tugged my jacket off and reached for the fight tee that I was wearing to the weigh-in.

"Agreed. Brinkley is there, brother. She will make sure everything is okay and get to you as soon as she can. But right now, your fucking head needs to get right. This fight is happening tomorrow. And you've worked your ass off for months. It's time to focus."

I nodded. I knew he was right, but I struggled to shake this off. This anger toward Leo. This anger toward Demi's father, who'd called security at the hospital.

And they hadn't done a fucking thing.

Because I was allowed to be there just as much as he was.

The difference between me and him was that my priority was her. I wasn't going into her room and causing another scene like we'd done the night before. She deserved better. So, I'd stayed in that waiting room—hell, I'd slept there the last two nights, just to be there if anything went wrong. I pulled the note that the nurse had slipped to me yesterday morning out of the pocket of my jeans, and I unfolded it.

Go kick Leo's ass. I love you, Romeo. Nothing will change that. Xx, Beans

That was exactly what I intended to do.

We all got changed and made our way down to the main floor where the weigh-in was taking place in a large arena. There was already a crowd there, and we were taken by security through the back door.

Joey and Butch walked in front of me. Lincoln and River were on each side of me, and Hayes, Nash, and Kingston took up the rear.

We were all quiet. It was game time.

Or what you'd call game time before the real game time. But I was about to be face-to-face with Leo for the first time since all of this started.

Joey glanced over his shoulder just as the doors opened for us to step inside. "You keep your cool. He wants to provoke you. That's why he did what he did. In twenty-four hours, you can unleash all that anger. You've worked too hard to blow it now."

I nodded.

When we stepped inside the room, the crowd went wild. Leo was already there with his team, and they were all wearing bright pink tracksuits.

"I thought you might not show, young Romeo!" Leo shouted from the other side of the stage.

"Your lack of response is driving him fucking crazy. Stay the course," River said, leaning close to my ear.

He was right.

But it was getting more challenging to keep my mouth shut. Especially after what happened to Demi. My hands fisted as the announcer took the microphone and introduced us. I tuned out all the noise and stripped off my hoodie as I stepped onto the scale, ignoring the voice of my enemy, who was relentlessly trying to engage me.

He stepped onto the scale next, throwing his hands in the air like the pathetic showman he was.

He didn't look like the big, bad fighter I'd envisioned.

He looked like a scared little bitch who had done a lot more talking than training.

My jaw ticked as I watched him step off the scale and wink at me.

And then we walked toward one another, standing shoulder to shoulder for photos.

"You're awfully quiet, Romeo," he said. We weren't mic'd, so no one who wasn't standing beside us could hear our conversation, which included Joey and Leo's coach, Tito, and a very large bodyguard hired by the fight promoters to make sure nothing went down today.

"I'll save my talking for tomorrow," I said, as we turned to face one another.

"One round and you're going down," he said, his tone cocky and unapologetic.

I leaned forward, keeping my voice low. "Not happening. And aren't you used to knocking down girls? Using other people to do your dirty work? Be ready because I'm not going down after what you did to Demi. You're going to have to take the last breath from my lungs before that happens."

He pulled back, glanced at the audience, and smirked, but there was confusion in his gaze as he looked at me, leaning forward for my ears only. "Not sure why you're bringing your girl into the mix. I've always had my sights set on you. But if she's looking for an upgrade after I put you in the hospital, I'll be waiting."

I could feel myself on the verge of going completely batshit crazy on this fucker. Joey's hand clasped my shoulder, and I looked up, eyes locked with Leo's. "Good luck with that."

I turned and walked away before things got worse.

"Stay calm. It's getting to him." Joey led me back to our group, and we got our stuff together so we could get ready to go eat, and then I planned on getting some much-needed sleep.

"Hey!" someone shouted as we walked down the back hallway with security. I turned around to see Tito.

I narrowed my gaze, and we all came to a stop.

"What the fuck does he want?" River asked.

"Can I talk to you, Romeo?" Tito said, glancing over his shoulder to make sure no one was around.

What were they up to now?

"Not without me," Joey said.

Lincoln and River were right behind me and Joey, but I held up my hand. Leo wasn't going to send his coach to jump me when I was with a group of guys.

"It's fine," I said, as I moved closer, and he met me halfway.

Joey kept one shoulder right in front of me as if he were ready to dive in if needed. "If he sent you to harass my boy, you better turn around and walk away. You've put him through enough, but he's still here, isn't he? I'm wondering if that was the plan. Make it so he couldn't show?"

Tito's brows cinched. He was a large man in his mid-forties, and he'd been by Leo's side since the beginning. "Leo is a showman. He has hyped this fight for months. I don't always agree with how he does things, but he's brought in a lot of money and a lot of attention to this fight. And you've played your part, Romeo. Staying quiet. Taking the high road. I respect it. But there was something different today, and Leo felt it, too. He doesn't have a fucking clue what you're talking about with hitting girls and bringing your girl into it. That's not his style. He's all about the verbal sparring and then going at it in the ring when it's time. So whatever beef you have with him over your girl, he isn't aware of it."

"Maybe he didn't tell you what he did," I said, my hands fisting every time I thought about Demi on the ground. About the way she cried in pain. "But it went too far this time."

"Romeo, he doesn't make a move without me. Check your facts before you go there. It's not his style."

"Maybe you need to check your facts, Tito," Joey said, moving forward. "Because his girlfriend is as good as they come. You don't see her here, do you? Ask your boy where she is."

Tito threw his hands in the air. "No idea what you're talking about. You got proof?"

"Aside from them saying they had a message from Leo? No. That's all the proof I needed."

Tito's gaze searched mine as he walked backward toward the door. "Come on, now. Why would he tell you it was a message from him?"

"Why would he do half the shit he's done?" River growled from behind me. "The shit he's done to this guy—I wouldn't put anything past him."

"There's one thing he wouldn't do, and that's what you're accusing him of. He wouldn't put his hands on a girl. He has three daughters. I'm telling you, you're off base on this one." He held up a hand. "Let's have a good fight out there tomorrow, all right?"

I scrubbed a hand down my face. I didn't have the energy for any of this. "Planning on it."

He went through the door, and we turned and walked back toward the elevators.

My brain raced because none of it added up to me, if I were being honest. Why would a guy who begged to fight me have me jumped a few days before the fight? Although, the guys he sent weren't fighters, so maybe it was just a scare tactic. I doubted Demi was part of the plan, but she'd ended up there, hadn't she?

And that shit was unforgivable.

"You think he's covering for him, or do you think Tito really doesn't know how dirty his boy plays?" Butch asked.

"I don't have a fucking clue," I said, as we stepped onto the elevators and made our way to our floor.

"Hey," Lincoln called out when we stepped off the elevators. "Brinkley and Tia are there with Demi. They said all her tests were fine. Her dad is causing the holdup and keeps asking for more tests and making things difficult."

"And they're sure that she's okay?"

"She said Demi's aggravated that she hasn't been released. They just ordered takeout, and she's feeling good. Her dad is wielding his power. Probably trying to keep her from showing up here." My brother paused in front of his hotel room door.

"Tell Brinkley to make sure Demi stays home. I don't want her near Leo or any of this drama."

Lincoln nodded. "She knows that. Tia is going to stay with her to watch the fight with your mom and grandmother. Brinkley will catch a flight here tomorrow after Demi gets released, so she can cover the fight for the magazine."

"All right. Thank you."

"Of course," he said.

"That sounds like a good plan. You can figure everything out when you get back home. Now we know your girl is fine. And you've got a fight tomorrow, so let's get our heads in the motherfucking game!" Joey shouted, and everyone cheered.

At the end of the day, I was the reason Demi had been hurt, and I couldn't get past that. That hit was meant for me. And she and I would have to deal with that when I got home.

Loving someone as fiercely as I loved her was one thing.

Hell, I'd fucking kill for that girl. Give my life without hesitation if it meant protecting her.

But that didn't mean that I was right for her.

Demi Crawford deserved better than me.

But right now, I wasn't going to think about it.

I was going to get my head right so I could show up tomorrow and hopefully put my fist through the face of the man who'd hurt her.

That was one thing that was in my control.

Game on, Leo Burns.

thirty

. . .

Demi

THE FACT that I'd spent three freaking nights in this hospital when I should have been released shortly after the surgery had pissed me off beyond belief.

I was fine.

My tests had all come back normal.

I had a broken arm. Lots of people broke their arms, and they didn't spend three nights in the hospital. Yes, I'd hit my head. Also, not my first time hitting my head. My dad was playing games. I'd now realized who he was. He always got his way because he played dirty.

He didn't want me at that fight, and he'd proven his point.

But he'd better buckle up because I was about to break myself out of this hospital and get my ass to that fight.

I was going to be there for Romeo whether my father approved of it or not.

Brinkley, Peyton, and Tia had taken shifts staying here with me. They'd finally admitted that Romeo had asked them to make sure someone was with me at all times. They were keeping him updated on how I was doing.

I never doubted that he loved me.

I knew he needed to be focused on the fight, or I'd snatch

Tia's phone and call him right now. But worrying about me was the last thing he should be doing.

I didn't need my father's permission to go to Las Vegas.

I didn't need Romeo's permission to go to his fight either.

I was a grown-ass woman who could make my own choices.

Unfortunately, I needed Dr. Westman's permission to get the hell out of here.

"How'd you sleep?" Tia asked from the cot beside me as she stretched her arms over her head.

"Not good. It's fight day. We've got to get out of here, Tia. I mean, we are down to the wire."

"Demi, I think you need to just watch the fight on TV here. Your dad is not going to be okay with this. And Romeo doesn't want you at that fight. He doesn't want you anywhere near Leo."

"And I respect their opinions, but I disagree. And I'm going, with or without you guys," I said, just as Brinkley walked into the room with three coffees in her hands.

"What are we talking about?" she asked as she studied me and handed me my drink.

"The fight. I'm going to be there. Where is Dr. Westman? I've had enough."

Brinkley studied me for a long moment and then handed Tia her coffee. "There are two police officers waiting out in the hallway to speak to you. They think they have a lead."

"What the hell is going on? Is everyone trying to stop me from going to that fight?" I tossed my hands into the air.

"I don't think they care about the fight. I think they care about catching the guys who put you in here. And if we can prove Leo did it, then I am all for it."

"Fine. Send them in." I shrugged as the nurse walked into the room. "Maggie, I'm begging you to get Dr. Westman to come here and release me. Please."

She nodded. "He said he was coming here in about fifteen

minutes. So, hang tight. I'll go see where he is."

The two officers came walking in, and I sat on the edge of the bed as they both stood in front of me. "I know we've questioned you a lot about this, but we found some footage that actually came from the cameras that you had installed on your building. Peyton gave us all the tapes, and we've been going through them. We didn't think the angles were going to catch anything, but sure enough, we got a pretty good photo of the man who struck you because his mask had come off when Romeo had thrown him to the ground. We can't see the other two men's faces, but if we can catch one, it'll lead to the others."

"You probably don't know him, but we ran him through the system, and nothing has come up, so he doesn't have a record. It's a long shot, but we wanted to see if you recognized him before we go public with the photo," the female officer said.

"Okay. I'm happy to look at it. Do you have the photo?"

She pulled out a photograph from the file she was holding and handed it to me.

I studied it for just a few seconds before I sucked in a breath. My heart raced, and I couldn't believe what I was seeing. "I know this guy. He went to college with me."

I searched my mind for where we'd met.

And then it all fell into place.

"He's fraternity brothers with Ronny Waterstone. I met him at a frat party once. Oh my God. This wasn't Leo's doing. Ronny was behind this."

"The senator's grandson?" she asked.

"Yes. He must have something to do with this."

"Do you know this guy's name?"

"Darius McDowel. He graduated with me this last year."

"All right. This is exactly what we needed."

"Unbelievable," Brinkley and Tia said at the same time.

"Let's keep this quiet for right now until we bring this guy in for questioning and he ties Ronny to this. We don't want him to have time to cover this up before we can get a confession."

I nodded.

My father had blamed Romeo.

Romeo had blamed himself.

And this had nothing to do with him. Ronny was going to hurt my boyfriend because he was pissed that he'd been exposed.

I was pacing in little circles, and the officers left and said that they'd be in touch.

"Should we call my brother?" Tia asked.

"No," I said. "We're going to that fight, and I'll tell him in person. He needs to be focused right now. Not worried about me or anyone else."

They both nodded.

"So, how do we spring you out of here?" Brinkley asked.

I pulled some clothes out of the bag that my mother had brought me. Tia helped me as I slipped the jeans on beneath my gown and then we hurried into the restroom so she could help me change into the T-shirt before tossing the gown onto my bed. I pulled my tennis shoes on, which Brinkley helped me lace, and I was ready to go just as Dr. Westman stepped into the room.

He raised a brow. "Someone is ready to get out of here."

"I need to leave right now. I'm going to that fight, and no one is going to stop me. So please, do the decent thing and release me."

He looked between me and Brinkley and Tia and tapped his pen against my chart a few times.

Tia took that moment to speak up. "Wings or wheels, Doc? We can fly, because my bougie sister-in-law has access to a plane. But if it isn't safe for the patient to fly, my brother will hunt you down and murder you himself, so if driving is better, just say the word."

"Wow. Threatening my life, are we?" He smirked. "I was coming to release you, Demi. Your father has done all the delaying he can, but you're cleared to leave." He held up his hand as I picked up my duffle bag, ready to get out of here. "No flying. I'm choosing wheels for this one."

Brinkley glanced down at her phone. "We've got time. Looks like we're going on a road trip."

"Give Maggie five minutes to get your paperwork ready. She's as eager as you are, so she'll be quick."

"Thank you," I said, as I gathered all my things and waited for Maggie.

She came flying around the corner, paperwork ready, and I signed on the dotted line. I gave her a big hug, and she promised to come into the coffee shop next week to see me.

All three of us made our way out of the hospital, and Brinkley informed us that we would make it there in plenty of time, pending there was no traffic. But Las Vegas on a Friday night was always crowded, so I was eager to get on the road.

We'd all agreed not to tell Romeo or Lincoln or anyone that we were driving there. Brinkley just told Lincoln that I'd been released, and she was going to help me get settled at home, and she would be there before the fight.

We didn't want Romeo worrying about me coming there, so this was the best option.

As we were rushing out of the hospital, my father was walking toward me, his face red and angry.

"What's this? You've been released? I asked for another MRI."

I glanced over at Brinkley and Tia and asked them to give me one minute.

"I've been cleared, Dad. Two MRIs and a CT scan were more than enough. I'm heading to my place to get unpacked, and then I'm going to go watch the fight with friends. I'm fine." I didn't even feel guilty lying to him now. He'd lied so many times that I doubted he even remembered what the truth was.

And at the end of the day, I no longer trusted him. I didn't trust that he wouldn't tip off Ronny or his family. I didn't trust that he would do something to stop me from going to Las Vegas.

I don't trust my father to have my back.

But Romeo always had, since the moment we'd gotten together.

And I was going to return the favor.

I was going to be there for him the way he'd always been there for me.

My father's gaze searched mine. "You know I love you, right? I just want to keep you safe."

His words didn't hold any weight anymore, but this wasn't the time to take him on.

That day would come.

Today was about Romeo, not my father.

"I do. I love you, too. I'll call you later, okay?"

"All right, sweetheart. I guess I'll head back to the city. Your mom isn't ready for me to come home, and I've been staying at that hotel in town while you've been here."

"Go back to the condo and get some rest." I kissed him on the cheek and hurried to the car, where Brinkley and Tia were waiting for me.

"Brinks was going to pepper-spray him if he tried to pull you into his car," Tia said.

"He's not quite at the level of kidnapping me just yet, but thanks for having my back. Now, let's get on the road," I said, climbing into the passenger seat of Brinkley's rental. Tia had insisted I sit up front so they could keep an eye on me and make sure I didn't pass out, which made me laugh.

"You do realize I passed out because I hit my head on the pavement. I'm not a fainter."

"Yeah. But Dr. McHottypants whispered for us to keep an

eye on you, and I've googled all the concussion symptoms." She held up her phone and turned on her flashlight, nearly blinding me. "Pupils look good."

Brinkley pulled out of the parking lot over a fit of laughter. "Dr. McHottypants is twice your age. Your brothers would lose their shit over you crushing on him."

"He's a silver fox," Tia said. "Hey, I'm excited about this last-minute girls' trip, but I have no clothes with me."

"We have no time to stop. We can shop in Vegas," Brinkley said, as she merged onto the freeway.

We spent the next few hours talking about all that had happened over the last few days. I checked the odds on the fight, and Romeo was a huge underdog, but he'd known that going into this.

My stomach twisted in knots as we got closer, and I kept checking the time.

We'd stopped once to use the bathroom, and Tia had bought enough junk food for a week's-long vacation.

"Okay, so what's the plan?" I asked as we turned down Las Vegas Boulevard, and I slipped my tennis shoes back on.

"We've got my press pass, and I'll text Lincoln to come get us when we get there."

"Okay, that works."

"I hope my brother doesn't lose his shit when he finds out you're here for the fight," Tia said as she bit off another piece of her red licorice.

"I need to let him know in person that I'm okay. That Leo didn't do this. That he should just focus on all the work he's done to prepare for this fight. I was always supposed to be here," I said, feeling butterflies swarm my belly because this was really happening. Everything he'd worked for was happening today.

"He can't get too mad. You've got the sympathy sling on your arm and the whole concussed thing going for you," Tia said.

I chuckled as we turned into the hotel, and Brinkley groaned at all the traffic. "Okay, we need to get up front somehow," she said before she shocked the shit out of me and pulled into a lane that was coned off and drove down with people shouting at her.

"I guess we're doing this," I said when she put the car into park.

"Hey, this lane is closed. You need to get in line!" a guy who was in his early twenties shouted before he jogged toward us and came to a stop right in front of me.

"This here is the girlfriend of Romeo Knight, the guy fighting tonight. This is his sister, and I'm his sister-in-law. And I've got a press pass that says I need to be in there before this starts. How about you be a good guy and help us out?"

He looked between us and held his gaze on me and then nodded slowly. "Yeah, I recognize her from Leo's social media. And wait a minute, aren't you married to that NFL quarterback?"

"Damn straight."

"If I let you go, will you get me both of their signatures?" he asked, as he raised a brow.

"Yes. Done." Brinkley tossed him her keys.

"What's your name?" I asked, already on the move.

"Johnny Cane!" he shouted after us.

"We will be back with autographs, Johnny Cane!" I yelled. We were moving as fast as we could without jostling my arm, as we made our way across several lanes in the valet area now.

"Come on, we've got to get inside first, and then we'll figure out where to go." Brinkley was just ahead of us and she kept turning around and telling me not to run. She led us to the events area and headed straight for the VIP line, which was thankfully much shorter than the other lines.

"Thank goodness your magazine splurges for the good

seats," Tia said. Brinkley pulled her phone out for them to scan the tickets.

We hustled once again, walking briskly, which was not easy without the use of one arm.

We stopped at the escalator, and there was security there.

Brinkley stepped to the side and pulled out her phone and dialed Lincoln. "Hey. I'm here. I need you to do something for me without asking any questions."

She paused and listened. "Very cooperative today, Captain. I need three badges to get down there."

"No. It's not press." She paused again. "What did I say about all the questions? Can you just trust me on this?" More silence. "Love you, too."

I kept looking at the time and glanced over my shoulder to see the crowds of people piling into the auditorium. It finally hit me that we were actually here.

This fight was happening.

"Oh my God. I'm going to throw up," Tia said as she looked around, and her face went completely pale.

"You keep it together, T. They won't let you back there if you start freaking out. And if Romeo sees you upset, he'll worry about you. We're here for him. Got it?" Brinkley's voice was eerily calm, and even I pulled my shit together.

Tia nodded. "Okay."

Lincoln came up the escalator, and his shoulders slumped when he saw the three of us standing there. He nodded at the security guard and flashed the passes. "These three are with me."

The guy scanned the badges and moved aside to let us through.

"What the fuck is this?" Lincoln whisper-hissed under his breath.

"She got released, and there was no stopping her. She needs to see him before he fights." Brinkley reached for his hand, and he shook his head.

"He doesn't want you near Leo," Lincoln said. His eyes met mine now.

"Leo wasn't involved in what happened," I said. "Please, Linc. I need to talk to him."

"All right. I hope we're not making a huge mistake. And, Tia, I thought you didn't want to see the fight live. You look like you're going to be sick."

"How about you take me to a different room? I don't think I should see him right now. I'll wait down here during the fight."

"Good idea." He paused and pushed open a door to a room that had TVs and a couch. He told Tia to wait there. She hugged me and Brinkley goodbye and asked us to text her with updates.

Lincoln shook his head as he led us further down the hallway. A few guys in security shirts moved past us, but it was otherwise quiet down here.

He pushed open the last door and held his hand out for me to go inside. Romeo was getting his hands taped, and he looked up to find me standing there.

He didn't look angry. His gaze softened, and he motioned for Butch to stop taping.

"Can we give them a minute?" Lincoln asked, and all the guys walked past me, each giving me a hug one at a time before they were all out in the hallway. I couldn't wait another second. I ran toward Romeo and threw myself against him on a whoosh, careful of my arm.

His arms gently came around me. "What are you doing here, baby?"

"I needed to be here. With you." Tears were streaming down my face because I was just so happy to be near him.

"You're okay?"

"I'm fine." I used the hand of my uninjured arm to stroke his face. "It wasn't Leo who did this. It had nothing to do with you. The cameras caught a photo of the guy you knocked down. He was a fraternity brother of Ronny's."

His brows pinched together, and he nodded as he listened.

"But none of that matters. Not tonight. You go out there and show how hard you've worked. You have nothing to prove to anyone anymore. You fight this fight for yourself, okay?"

"I can't believe you're here." He pulled me against him again. "I love you so fucking much."

"I know you do." I pulled back and smirked. "I never doubted that. I love you, Golden Boy. And I will be cheering you on tonight."

"If it's too much, you take a pass and come back here and wait for me, okay?"

"It's not too much. Anything you can take, I can take with you. You just go out there and do your thing." I took his hands in mine and kissed his knuckles on each hand. "I believe in you, Romeo Knight."

He nodded, a look of contentment settling on his face. "I'm ready."

"I know you are."

"You're awfully cocky tonight." He leaned down and kissed me. "Now, get out there with Brinkley and take your seats. Let me get gloved up. I'll see you in twelve rounds, baby."

I kissed him one last time. "You will."

Joey came through the door, and everything moved quickly after that. Nash and Hayes escorted Brinkley and me to our seats. We were in the press area off to the side, but we had a good view of the ring. They both hustled back to meet Romeo as they were going to be right there beside the ring as part of the crew.

I said a silent prayer.

But I already knew he was going to be okay.

He had to be.

thirty-one

. . .

Romeo

I WAS READY.

I had my boys beside me.

My coach and my trainer were with me.

And my girl was in the audience.

I thought I'd be pissed that she was there, but I wasn't at all.

She was stubborn and full of fire, and that was one of the things that I loved about her.

I was glad that Leo hadn't been behind what happened, but it didn't change the way I felt about getting into the ring. Leo had pushed for this fight, and he'd dragged my name and Demi's name and the people that I loved through the mud.

I'd kept my head down.

I'd done the work.

I may not have had control of how tough Leo Burns was, but I was not going down without a fight.

I knew that I had the heart to go further than everyone thought. Leo had claimed I'd go down in round one.

The Las Vegas books had given me three rounds max.

Other fighters and sportscasters had agreed with that.

But I planned to stay standing for longer than that.

I'd trained to go longer than that.

"You ready, brother?" Lincoln asked as we waited inside the tunnel to be introduced.

I'd never experienced anything close to the magnitude of this fight. I glanced out to see a packed arena, and I nodded. "I'm ready."

I'd wondered for months what this would be like. If Leo had been right and one punch would do me in. But standing here, taking it all in—I was going to try like hell to take the punches he threw at me.

"Damn straight. You've got this. We're here. Everyone is rooting for you, brother," River said as he bumped me with his shoulder.

"Ride or die. Brothers till the end. Loyalty always. Forever my friend." Kingston clapped me on the shoulder.

I nodded, and Joey shook his head and laughed. "Your dad is watching you right now, and he's probably shitting himself that you got yourself into this mess, but if anyone can handle it, it's you."

The announcer took to the mic. Most of what he said was a blur, but the crowd roared, and a big spotlight shone down on me.

"Let's hear it for Magnolia Falls' Golden Boy, Romeo Knii-iiiiiggghhhttt." He really stretched out my last name, and I started walking forward with all the guys surrounding me, almost like a shield.

We made our way toward the ring, and I heard Kingston laughing his ass off from behind me. It was overwhelming, the crowd, the cheers, the support. I climbed into the ring and glanced over, catching Demi in my peripheral vision.

Like a bee to honey, in a sea of people, my gaze always found hers.

Just a moment in time that said all I needed to know.

She was right there in my corner.

All that I needed.

I held my hand up and waved as people continued to cheer.

And then the announcer asked everyone to quiet down and get ready for the contender, who had a shit ton more accolades than I did. He'd held this belt eighteen months ago before losing it to Gunner Waverly six months ago.

He had a record of 32-1. Much more impressive than mine. I'd had one professional fight, and I'd beaten the one guy that he'd lost to.

What are the fucking chances?

"Leo 'The Flamethrower' Burrrrrrns!" he shouted into the mic, and the crowd cheered in response, along with an equal amount of booing.

Leo had an entourage that was three times the size of mine, and he came walking in with all the confidence in the world.

I'd expected nothing less.

He danced around in his corner, trying to get the crowd riled up before we were both called to the center. We stood close enough that our foreheads nearly touched. His smug look irritated the fuck out of me, but my stomach was also wrenching with nerves at the same time.

I am not going down in the first round.

Not after all the work I'd done. I wanted to wipe that cocky smirk right off his face. Three minutes to remain standing. I could do this.

One round at a time.

He leaned closer to my ear, and I remained perfectly still. "Didn't touch your girl. It's not my style."

When he pulled back, my eyes locked with his. "I know."

"But I'm still going to knock you out in round one."

Not happening.

But I didn't respond. I backed away. Unlike Leo, I would let my skill do the talking. I was focused on staying on my feet. Protecting my head and my eyes and my body. Staying in one fucking piece and fighting smart.

I wanted to get some hits in on him. Let him feel my wrath for once.

We moved to our respective corners, and I sat on the bench placed there for me while Joey shouted a few things at me and Butch shoved the mouthpiece into my mouth.

River, Kingston, Hayes, and Nash were all standing in my corner, right outside the ring.

"Protect your face. He's going to come out with a fury, so be smart. He thinks this is a one-round fight. You're here for the long game." Joey clapped me on the shoulder before stepping out of the ring.

I kneeled down and said a quick prayer, making every effort to settle my nerves.

The sound of the bell had me moving toward the center of the ring just as Leo charged me.

Fast and furious, just as we'd predicted.

I stayed calm. I'd prepared for this. The first hit clipped the bottom of my jaw and stunned me a bit, but I adjusted.

I kept control of my movements. My feet steady, as he continued to swing. He must have fired off twelve shots, but he only landed two that I felt.

The second was a shot to my ribs that hit me with a jolt.

But I'd been hit so many times over the last few months in that exact spot that my body weathered it. When he paused and his steps faltered a bit, I used that as my opening. My left hook landed right where I wanted it to, square in the face, ringing his bell just enough to let him know that he wasn't the only one in this fight.

He shook it off and then started with the antics that I'd expected. He tapped me on top of the head with his glove and danced around like a clown.

The noise from the crowd was deafening, but I stayed focused on Leo.

He lunged forward, landing an uppercut to my body, followed by a powerful hit to the side of my head.

And holy shit—I fucking felt it.

I stumbled a bit, falling back onto the ropes and trying to steady my feet. And he pounced. Came at me and tossed me into the corner, firing off at least a dozen hits to my body and head. I kept my arms up and took the hits, just as the bell rang.

Thank fucking God.

One round.

I'd survived.

I was on my feet.

The ref pulled him back, and he held his hands up and turned to the crowd to get them riled. He was shouting something at me, but I couldn't make it out. Joey pulled me to the corner and pushed me down to sit on the stool.

Butch was squeezing water into my mouth, and the guys were all clapping me on the shoulder.

"One down. Eleven to go," Joey said. "How do you feel?"

"Like I just got punched hard in the head and body multiple times."

Laughter floated around me, and I let out a few quick breaths.

"You're still standing, kid. You're here with one of the best fighters of your time, and you just went one round with him, and you look good."

"Stay calm, Romeo," River said as he leaned in close to my ear. "It's going to get in his head that you just withstood that. Stay the course, brother."

I nodded and clapped my gloves together.

I was ready for more.

I pushed to my feet, and when the bell rang this time, I was moving faster than I had the last time. He was older than me, so he'd tire quicker. He was used to knocking guys out early, and I was going to test that. The longer I made it, the more it would fuck with his head.

Stay present. Focus.

I threw the first punch, which rattled him a bit. He responded like a clown because the man was all about the show. He wound his arm up, egging on the crowd, and then came at me.

Hard.

He connected with the side of my head, and my ear stung like a bitch. I put my chin down and moved, following his pace. And this time when he came at me, I ducked and lunged at him, getting in multiple shots to his body.

And that was the moment that it felt like the fight officially started.

Round two was like nothing I'd ever experienced. We traded hits over and over.

The body. The head. The face.

And when the bell rang, I wasn't in any hurry to get back to my corner, and neither was he. The ref had to tear us apart, and Leo was shouting all sorts of threats my way. I held my arms up in question.

Bring it on, motherfucker.

So much fucking talk, and here I was, still standing.

I dropped down onto the stool as the guys cheered and screamed. But Joey's voice broke through all the noise.

"Two down, Romeo. Stay present. One round at a time. Don't let him distract you."

Butch flashed a light into my eyes and told me to protect my face. I knew that once your eyes were swollen shut, it made fighting really tough. So far, Leo had focused more on my body and my ribs. And I'd prepared for that.

I nodded. Listened. Swished some water around my mouth and spit into the bucket.

The next three rounds were a complete blur.

The hits just kept coming. He was throwing more than I

was, but I was landing mine. I was going for the side of his face and his ribs. We took turns pushing one another into the corner and taking our shots. The more we fought, the more I recalled the tapes of Leo's moves and caught him off guard with my swings.

When the bell rang at the end of round five, I saw something in Leo's eyes.

That cocky smirk was still there, but there was doubt.

Maybe even fear.

But it told me that he was giving me his best, and he was rattled. Maybe tired.

Joey and Butch were there, pulling me to the corner and cleaning up my face as Kingston clapped me on the shoulder.

"You're doing it, brother."

I nodded and tried to catch my breath before taking a swig of water.

"How are you doing?" Joey asked.

"I think he broke a rib. And my ear is ringing. But otherwise, I'm fucking peachy."

Joey held my chin in his grasp, looking me right in the eyes. "We knew it would hurt. It was never supposed to be easy. You're fighting for a motherfucking belt, Romeo. And you're holding your own with this guy. Five down. Seven to go."

I nodded but was also aware that he was getting in more hits than I was. "The guy is fucking strong."

"No doubt about it. But you're still standing. Your goal is to go the distance. No one goes the distance with this guy."

I took one more pull from the water bottle and spit it into the bucket before pushing to my feet.

My legs were feeling it. Hell, my arms were feeling it. My entire body was feeling it.

But I clapped my gloves together when the bell rang, and I moved toward him.

The sound of the crowd faded with each passing round.

Six.

Seven.

Eight.

Nine.

When the bell rang at the end of round ten, the ref had to pull Leo off of me from where he'd been wailing on me with his fists after tossing me into the corner. I hadn't been able to get out, so I'd taken the punches.

Over and over.

I stumbled a bit when the bell rang, and Butch and Joey were there. River was bending down in front of me now, looking up at me.

"You all right?" I could hear the concern in his voice, but I'd be lying if I didn't admit that his face was blurry now. I'd taken a lot of shots to the face during the last few rounds.

But I am still standing.

Ten fucking rounds with this beast, and I had managed to stay up on my feet.

"You've got to protect the eyes, Romeo. He's fading."

"He doesn't seem like he's fading," I said, as Butch put ointment beneath my eyes.

"He's getting tired," River said. "He's panicked that you're still in this thing. Ten fucking rounds. You're a fucking rockstar, Romeo. You've got this."

I nodded.

Two more rounds.

I could do this.

"You need to keep going for the left side of his body and face. He looks as bad as you do, so you're doing something right."

I couldn't laugh because everything hurt.

Every fucking bone in my body hurt.

But when the bell rang this time, I wasn't afraid. All the nerves were gone. I was in the fight of my life.

And I am not going down.

thirty-two

• • •

Demi

I'D BEEN INVOLVED in Romeo's training for months. But nothing could have prepared me for this fight.

I'd watched as he'd taken hit after hit.

The crowd was completely behind Romeo now, as everyone was chanting his name.

A part of me wished they would call the fight, because I couldn't stand to see the way he'd stumbled to his corner after the last round.

Leo was not steady on his feet either.

They were both relentless, though Romeo was taking twice as many hits as Leo.

But the punches Romeo landed seemed to really rock Leo.

They both had to be completely exhausted.

Brinkley's hand was wrapped around mine through every round, and I'd had to bury my face in her neck several times when Romeo had taken several shots to the face.

I felt every blow that he took.

And he just kept going.

Everyone was invested now. The commentators, Ben Kilny and Rod Baker, were screaming as if they could feel each hit, as well.

The sound of the bell had my hands fisting.

Round eleven.

Here we go.

"I don't think one person on the planet thought this fight would go eleven rounds," Ben said into the microphone.

"I'm guessing Romeo and his team were the only ones who expected this. But I don't know how many more hits this guy can take and remain on his feet," Rod said, as Leo circled Romeo.

They were both moving slower. Romeo's right eye was swollen, and Leo was leaning to the left, which told me he was in pain and probably had several broken ribs.

Leo moved in, throwing a punch that landed on the side of Romeo's face, and his mouthpiece shot out as he stumbled into the ropes.

I gasped, along with the thousands of fans packed in the arena. As if we'd all just felt the hit. I squeezed Brinkley's hand so hard my knuckles were white, and we both jumped to our feet.

"Unbelievable. How is this guy still standing?" Rod said, as we all watched the ref talk to Romeo and hand him his mouthpiece.

Tears ran down my face. It was almost too much to bear.

But he held his hands up, letting the ref know that he was okay.

I glanced at his corner, and it was impossible to miss the distraught look on Joey's face.

He wanted them to call the fight.

He shouted something at the ref, and Romeo turned around and shouted something back.

Lincoln looked pissed as he yelled at both Romeo and the ref. He punched the side of the ring in frustration.

"Oh my God," Brinkley whisper-hissed. "Lincoln's losing his shit."

River's gaze locked with mine from a distance, and he gave me a nod. As if he were saying everything was okay.

But I did not miss the pained look on Hayes's, Nash's, and Kingston's faces.

No one thought they should let Romeo continue.

But the ref agreed that he was okay, and that was when I saw it.

Complete panic written all over Leo's face.

He was desperate for them to call the fight.

Because he was also hanging on by a thread.

I squeezed my eyes shut as they finished the rest of the round, and Brinkley grabbed my face when Romeo went to his corner. "Look at me."

I opened my eyes; my vision blurred as the tears were coming fast now.

"Demi, he's a fighter. He's made it eleven rounds. He's still standing. Listen to the people chanting his name. He needs us right now. Do not fall apart. You wanted to be here for him, so you need to be here. Through the good and the bad."

I sniffed and pulled myself together. "Okay. One more round."

"One more round."

And this time when I looked over at his corner, Romeo was looking right at me. One eye was swollen completely shut while the other found mine, and the corners of his lips turned up just the slightest bit. No one else would have noticed, but I did.

He was telling me that he was okay.

Tears streamed down my cheeks as I grasped my heart and shouted his name.

My fierce warrior.

And then he moved to his feet. Joey whispered something into his ear, and he nodded.

The bell rang, and they both moved toward the center of

the ring. The next three minutes would be the longest of my life.

They took turns throwing punches. One after another. They were leaving it all out there. And Romeo was throwing as many as Leo now.

One for one.

As if the exhaustion was too much for more than that.

They'd throw a punch and then stagger as the other landed theirs.

Again and again.

Everyone was on their feet, screaming and shouting.

"I've honestly never seen anything like this before," Ben said, his voice filling the arena through the speakers. "The heart and the determination. It's unbelievable."

It was then that Leo landed a hit that had Romeo stumbling back on his ass, and the entire auditorium gasped in unison.

He was down.

And the countdown started.

"One. Two. Three!" the ref shouted, and Romeo crawled toward the side, reaching for the ropes.

Leo stood, shoulders slumped, and you could see the hope in his eyes that Romeo would stay down.

"Four. Five."

I couldn't breathe as I watched. Joey was telling him to stay down. Lincoln and River both had tears streaming down their faces.

Hayes, Nash, and Kingston had their faces buried in their hands as if they couldn't watch.

And I shouted at the top of my lungs. "Get up, Romeo!"

He'd come this far, and I knew that going the distance was what he'd wanted. He had a minute and a half left to go. As much as I wanted him to stay down, I knew how important it was to him to go the distance. To remain on his feet.

The crowd must have picked up on what I'd said, as they all started chanting those words. *"Get up, Romeo!"*

Over and over.

"Six. Seven."

He reached for the last rope and pushed to his feet as a startling roar filtered around the arena.

"He's on his feet!" Rod shouted into the microphone over the roars of the crowd.

I had both hands over my mouth as I watched him nod at the ref and move toward Leo, who looked completely devastated that this wasn't over.

They both raised their gloves and went at it once again.

Punch after punch.

Hit after hit.

And that was when the shift came.

They weren't going one for one anymore. It was only Romeo throwing the shots now. He pushed Leo into the corner and just kept going.

Leo no longer held up his arms as he slowly started to slide down the ring. The ref pulled Romeo back as Leo fell to the ground in a heap.

The deafening screams were overwhelming, and it was difficult to see through my tears.

The ref started another countdown, but Leo wasn't making any effort to get up. He held his hands up in defeat, but the ref continued to count.

"Seven. Eight. Nine."

I never did hear the number ten because the auditorium exploded in celebration as the guys charged the ring, and Romeo fell against Lincoln and River, as they supported him.

"He did it!" Rod shouted. "I can't believe it."

"What a fight! I don't think anyone expected this outcome," Ben said.

Brinkley and I were hugging, and then I was rushing toward the ring, needing to make sure he was okay. Brinkley was right behind me as we shoved past a few spectators to make our way to his corner.

Hayes and Nash were standing there crying, and River and Kingston were shaking their heads in disbelief.

I hugged Hayes, and he quickly lifted me up as my sling made it near impossible to pull myself up there. River reached over and grabbed me.

"Our boy did it, Beans!" he shouted. "Go congratulate him."

I maneuvered the best I could through the crowd that had gathered in the ring, and I saw him.

My Romeo.

He was searching the crowd for me, and his gaze locked with mine.

Lincoln must have picked up on it because he shoved a few people out of the way, clearing a path for me to his brother.

I lunged at him, and he scooped me up into his arms.

"You did it!" I shouted over the noise as I buried my face in his neck.

"We did it, baby. I love you so fucking much."

"I love you." I didn't know how long he held me there as I sobbed, and everyone congratulated him.

But he wouldn't let go.

He kept me close.

And then I pulled back when they were ready to announce the winner, which everyone already knew was Romeo, due to the knockout.

Brinkley found my hand, and I stood with her and Lincoln as they held up Romeo's arm, and he and Leo actually hugged.

They'd gone to battle, and they'd both fought like hell.

There was a mutual respect now.

The emcee took to the mic and asked Romeo several questions.

He thanked his coach and his team and all the guys and me. He was humble and genuine and honored when they handed him the belt.

"So, what will you do to celebrate, Romeo?" the man asked him.

"Right now, I'd just like to take my girl home."

More cheers came from the crowd as he thanked the man and then made his way to his corner, where we were all waiting for him.

He wrapped his arms around me and tipped my head back and kissed me.

I tangled my hand in his hair and kissed him right back.

I didn't care who was watching.

I was too busy loving Romeo to care about anything else.

My champ.

My heart.

My everything.

thirty-three

. . .

Romeo

WE'D BEEN BACK for over a week, and it had been a three-ring circus in Magnolia Falls. We'd arrived home the day after the fight, and people had lined the streets with signs as they cheered me on.

This entire town had been behind me.

I guess in a way, this fight represented a lot to many people.

A small-town boy doing something unexpected.

Going the distance.

It taught me that you could accomplish anything you wanted to accomplish if you worked hard and stayed the course.

If you had the right people in your corner, which I did.

The next few days were spent recovering, taking a lot of baths with my girl, and enjoying every second of her pampering the hell out of me.

The guys teased me relentlessly about how concerned she'd been, and I sure as hell wasn't complaining.

I'd been the same with her. Worried like hell about her broken arm and insisted she hire more help at the coffee shop so she didn't have to work so much.

This morning, I watched her sleep, running my fingers through her silky hair. She was so goddamned beautiful she took my breath away every time I looked at her.

"Hey," she whispered. "Are you watching me sleep?"

"I am."

Her eyes peeked open, and she blinked a few times. "How do you feel?"

"Pretty damn good. How's the arm?"

"It doesn't hurt anymore. I told you that." She chuckled.

I ran my fingers over her shoulder. "Good."

"Are we still going to see a few houses this morning?"

"Yes. There's one down on the water. It needs a lot of work, but we've got two contractors at our beck and call, and you've got a good eye."

"A good eye, huh?" She pushed up, keeping the sheet around her shoulders as she moved on top of me. Sitting up with one leg on each side and straddling me.

This girl, man.

She was so fucking beautiful.

My hands covered her perfect tits, tweaking her nipples and loving the way her cheeks flushed when I touched her.

"You've got a good eye for design," I said, my voice gruff.

"I think I have a good eye for more than that," she teased. "I picked you out, didn't I?"

"I didn't make it so easy for you in the beginning, did I?"

"No. But that's okay. I'm all about the long game." Her teeth sank into her juicy bottom lip, and I groaned.

I pulled her mouth down to mine. She raised her hips, settling just above me, and she slowly slid down my throbbing cock.

I didn't know how I'd gotten so lucky to find my way to Demi.

I never believed in happily ever after before I met her.

But she'd changed everything.

She pulled back and smiled down at me. I gripped her hips as she started to move.

Slowly at first, but then she found her rhythm, and I thrust into her every time she slid back down.

We were insatiable together, and I fucking loved it.

Loved her.

I tugged her mouth down to mine, my tongue slipping in and out as she continued to ride me.

And I savored every minute.

Kissing her.

My hands roaming her body.

We were both covered in a layer of sweat, and she was begging for her release.

I never was any good at making her wait.

I wanted to give her everything.

My hand slipped between us as I continued driving into her over and over. I circled her clit, and she tightened around me seconds later.

She cried out my name as she squeezed my dick and went over the edge.

I flipped her onto her back in one fluid movement, and I thrust into her three more times before I came so hard, I could barely see straight.

That was the way it always was with us.

And I couldn't get enough.

––––––

We'd seen several houses over the last few days, and Demi's grandfather had asked us to meet him at his house to talk about something important.

I'd grown close to the old man, and I respected him.

He loved his granddaughter fiercely, and he and his wife were good people. I'd misjudged them over the years.

Thinking people with money were all corrupt.

And I'd been wrong.

We'd had dinner with Demi's mother a few days ago, and she was nothing but kind to me. She and my mom had become friends now, as well, and had apparently watched my fight together.

Demi's parents were still not living together, and there didn't seem to be a lot of progress going on there. Demi hadn't spoken to her father since we'd returned. I'd offered to go with her to see him, but she said she wasn't ready to talk to him.

There was a lot of damage there, and it would be up to him to try to repair things.

The one surprise in her family had been Slade. He'd asked her for my number and texted me congratulations after the fight.

We'd gone back and forth a few times. He was leaving rehab in a few days, and I was going with Demi to help her get him settled.

It was what you did when you loved someone.

Most of this shit didn't matter much to me the way it used to.

Maybe it was because I was happy now.

She'd brought this light into my life that had erased a lot of the darkness from my past.

It was hard to be pissed off all the time when you were nauseatingly happy.

That was what River called it when he razzed me all the time.

"Hey, we're here," Demi called out as we walked into her grandparents' home.

"There's the champ," Carson said as he hugged his grand-daughter and then pulled me in for a big bear hug. "It was all that training out here with the horses."

"I think you might be right," I said, as I hugged Demi's grandmother, and we followed them into the kitchen.

We sat around the table, drinking sun tea and talking about the white party for a bit before her grandfather changed the subject.

"I just wanted to give you all an update on what's happening with the men that attacked you that night, Romeo. The one who hit you, as well, Demi," he said, his eyes welling with emotion.

I understood the way he loved her.

There was something about her that made you want to protect her, no matter how badly she wanted to prove that she could take care of herself.

She loved hard, and she was loyal as hell, and the people around her loved her just as fiercely.

"Were they able to tie him to Ronny?" Demi asked, as she reached for her tea.

"His family is scrambling to cover it up; it's just what they do. But with the other women coming forward and you filing that report against him, they are going to be tied up in court for a long time. All three guys were quick to throw Ronny right under the bus, so I don't think he has a chance of walking away from these charges." Demi had officially reported what had happened to her with Ronny and she'd filled out the paperwork, so at the very least, there was documentation about it.

"I don't know what he thought he was going to accomplish by having me jumped," I said, scrubbing my hand over my face. Here was a guy who had everything at his fingertips. Money and opportunity to pursue whatever the hell he wanted, but instead, he was a piece of shit and spent his time trying to cover up the shit he did.

"I think he was having a temper tantrum. He wanted to retaliate against you and thought he could pin it on the other fighter and no one would suspect him. He's a bad guy at his core, and it's catching up to him. I'm just glad that you two are all right."

"He had three guys jump Romeo, and they didn't make a dent in you, did they?" Demi waggled her brows at me.

"Well, that's because my girl came flying out of nowhere to fight them off." I wrapped an arm around her shoulder and kissed her cheek.

Her grandmother placed her hand on her heart and smiled at us. "Did you two go see some more homes?"

"Yeah. I think we found one that we love," Demi said. "It's down by the water. It will need some work, but it has potential."

"It also has a lot of land around it, which means we can get the barn up and going, and she can have Teacup there so she can ride every day if she wants to."

"How about you? Are you going to get a horse so you can ride with her?" Gramps asked with a gruff chuckle. He knew I didn't ride.

"I'm not much of a cowboy. I prefer to be on foot, chasing after her." I shrugged.

More laughter.

We spent the next hour talking and catching up with them, and as we walked to the door and hugged them both goodbye, her grandmother reminded me for the millionth time that she expected to see all of us at the white party.

The thought of wearing a suit made my skin crawl, but Demi had found a dress, and she wanted to surprise me with it the day of the event, so I'd embraced the idea.

And all the guys would be joining us, so I wouldn't be the only one standing out like a sore thumb.

I pulled the helmet over her head and fastened the strap beneath her chin, before helping her onto the back of my bike. I'd take it slow, as she had one arm that wasn't very helpful when it came to wrapping around me. But she'd wanted to feel the breeze in her hair today, so we'd taken my bike out.

We were heading to Whiskey Falls to meet everyone. Nash and King had gone out to the property we'd found and were going to give us some bids for how big this renovation would be.

River and Hayes were stopping by to meet us for a quick bite. Hayes had dropped Cutler off with my mom for the afternoon, as she was working in the garden and, apparently, he liked planting flowers with her.

He'd made Demi come over a few days ago to redo the Sharpie tattoo because it had faded. I'd nearly fallen off my chair when she'd shown me the inside of her wrist, which also had a Sharpie tattoo that said: *Beefcake*.

When we walked into the bar, they were all there. They'd ordered lunch, and they led a chant when I stepped inside.

"Golden Boy. Golden Boy." They got everyone there to join in, which meant there were four other fools saying the same thing as them.

I held my hand up, pleading for them to stop, and Demi just laughed like she always did.

She fit in with my boys like she'd always been there.

They'd ordered a bunch of appetizers, and it was damn good to finally get to eat bar food again. To not have to be so careful about what I put into my body and to not have to work out ten hours a day.

Lionel brought over some extra napkins and clapped me on the shoulder. "Proud of you, Romeo. This whole bar was packed the night of your fight. Thanks for not only winning but for helping me sell a shit ton of liquor within a few hours."

"At least you have your priorities straight," River said, rolling his eyes.

Lionel's gaze moved to Demi, and he scanned her arm. Everyone in town had heard what happened, but she'd continued to brush it off.

"I get mad every time I see you with your arm in that sling," Lionel said.

You and me both.

"Please. You should see the other guy." She waggled her brows.

"Atta girl. You take no shit."

"Exactly," she said.

Lionel walked off, and we filled them in on what we'd heard from her grandfather.

"It's about time that piece-of-shit Ronny is held accountable," River hissed.

"Yeah. You can only run from karma for so long," Kingston said over a mouthful of onion rings.

"Can you please stop talking with your mouth full?" Nash grumped. "Every fucking day, this guy is telling me something over a mouth full of fucking food."

Hayes barked out a laugh. "He's been doing it since we were kids. He's not changing."

"Hey, *he* can hear you two dick weasels talking shit. *He* happens to enjoy life, and when he has something to share, he shares it." Kingston winked at Demi, who couldn't hide her smile.

"So, Cutler made me take him to get sized for a white fucking suit," Nash groaned. "Apparently, your grandmother encouraged him to get a suit for the white party."

"He told me all about it. He said he looks really good in it," Demi said over her laughter.

"Damn. Beefcake is going to show us all up." Kingston held up his phone to show Demi a photo of him in his suit. "I think I'm going with baby blue."

"I like it. It suits you."

"I thought we were wearing black suits, and the women would wear white dresses," I said, grabbing the phone and falling back in laughter at Kingston wearing a baby blue suit that was far too small for him.

"Hey, that's the style. It's called slim fit." He raised a brow and grabbed his phone from my hand. "Grammie said the women wear white and the men just need to be in suits. And that suit spoke to me."

Yes. He was calling Demi's grandparents *Grammie* and *Gramps.* Because this was King that we were talking about.

"It spoke to you, huh? Did it also tell you to turn around and trade it in for a black fucking suit that isn't sized for a toddler?" River asked, and more laughter erupted around the table.

"Trust me. The ladies like my style. You boring fuckers can wear your penguin suits, and I'll be the standout."

"Yeah, you and Beefcake." River smirked.

"I'm happy you're all coming," Demi said.

"We were kind of bullied into it by your grandmother, Beans." Hayes raised a brow at her.

"She's very persuasive," Demi said.

"She's not the only one." I nipped at her ear.

"Oh, for God's sake, wife this girl up already. You two are making me sick." River feigned irritation, but I saw the way the corners of his lips turned up when he watched us.

"Agreed. They're moving in together and renovating a house. Put a ring on it already, am I right, Demi?" Kingston broke out into his best Beyonce imitation and sounded absolutely fucking ridiculous.

I threw my napkin at him and shook my head.

And then I sat back and took it all in.

My brothers.

My girl.

The way life had taken an unexpected turn for the better.

My hand found hers beneath the table, and our fingers intertwined. I leaned close to her ear. "You know I do plan to put a ring on it someday, right?"

"What did it for you?" She leaned closer and whispered into my ear. "Was it the fact that I jumped into a fight for you in the back of the alley, or was it the pumpkin chai?"

I grazed my lips over her ear, watching the way goose bumps spread down her arm.

"I think it's the way you look when you're sleeping," I spoke against her ear.

She pulled back to look at me. Those gorgeous green eyes that always found mine. "What do I look like when I'm sleeping?"

"You look like forever."

Ain't that the fucking truth.

epilogue

· · ·

Demi

THE LAST FEW weeks had been a whirlwind. Romeo and I had bought a home. Well, he'd bought a home with the money he'd earned from his fight, and for whatever reason, he'd insisted that both of our names be on the title.

So, whether he liked it or not, I was insisting on pitching in for the renovations. And we were practically gutting the place now. We were going to make it our own, and I loved everything about it.

Romeo had flown with me to Boston and listened when my brother had opened up about being miserable living there with no family and no friends. It was a tough way to deal with sobriety.

So, Romeo and my grandfather had come up with a plan. Slade would stay in Boston for three months and continue to attend meetings at the rehab there. If he stayed clean, he'd come back to Magnolia Falls. Romeo had agreed to let him rent out his little apartment behind the gym and work at the gym, as well. I didn't know where that generosity came from. Especially after what Slade had done to Romeo and River all those years ago. But somehow, he'd been willing to help Slade under the agreement that he'd take a drug test twice a week.

I knew that he was doing it for me, and it only made me love him more. But if Slade messed up, I would have no problem sending him back to Boston. I was still skeptical, but there was more hope there now than there'd been in a long time.

Maybe because everything was out in the open. There were no secrets where my brother was concerned. He'd owned his mistakes, and he'd been given a second chance.

Now it was up to him what he decided to do with that.

"You look fucking gorgeous," Romeo said, as he pulled me onto his lap.

My boyfriend looked so freaking good in a black suit that my mouth had gone dry when he'd walked into the room all dressed up.

River, Hayes, and Nash were all wearing black suits, as well, but Kingston had stayed true to his desire to wear a baby blue fitted suit, which they'd all razzed him about since we got here.

We were sitting at a table with twinkle lights all around us, eating dinner. Everyone in town was here.

"Thank you," I said, nuzzling my nose against his.

"Damn. I need to find me a woman like Demi," Kingston said.

"Didn't you find one last night?" Nash teased. "Seems like you find yourself a new woman every week."

"Hey now, don't be hating on me like that. I'm just saying, a woman who takes care of me and wants to renovate a house with me sounds appealing."

"You'd make it one week and be bored," River said.

These guys had become family, and there wasn't anything I wouldn't do for them.

"I think when King finds the right woman, he'll be knocked on his ass." I smiled at him because he loved when I took his side when the guys were giving him a hard time.

"And it's such a good ass, too, isn't it?"

"Please make him stop," Hayes groaned. "No one wants to think about your ass."

Everyone was laughing as Cutler made his way over to me. He was wearing a white suit with a blue carnation in the pocket. His hair was slicked back, per usual, and he had on white, shiny dress shoes that Nash had groaned about earlier because they were going to be filthy in a few hours. Cutler moseyed over to me and pulled out the flower.

"What's up, Beefcake?" Kingston said, fist-bumping Cutler.

"I saw you all watching me on the dance floor, so I thought I better come over here."

"We weren't watching you," Nash said with a laugh. "Although I did see you eating a chicken finger on the dance floor, and it caught my eye."

Cutler smirked at his father before turning his attention to me.

"Demi, don't worry about me dancing with Lexi. She goes to my school. She's not my girl."

"Well, she's awfully cute," I said.

"But she's not you, is she?" he said, waggling his brows and matching the swagger of the men that had taken part in raising him.

Romeo leaned forward. "You moving in on my girl, Beefcake?"

"Well, you're the champ now, Uncle Ro, so I'm not going to fight the champ. But if you don't marry her, I'll grow up and marry her myself."

"Shots fired," River said over his laughter, as he high-fived Cutler.

My head fell back in laughter, and I looked up to see my father watching me from the other side of the party. He'd pushed to attend, and my mother didn't want to completely exclude him.

Romeo must have caught it, too, because he leaned close to my ear. "You want me to go with you to speak to him?"

He'd been encouraging me to talk to my dad, as he'd called multiple times since I'd returned from the fight. It shocked me that Romeo wanted me to repair my relationship with my father after the way he'd treated him.

"No. I've got this." I kissed him quickly before leaning down to kiss Cutler on the cheek and walking toward my dad. My long white dress swooshed at my feet.

He was standing alone, which made me feel bad. He'd burned a lot of bridges lately, and my mother didn't know if she could forgive him for all the lies. I'd never imagined a world where my parents weren't together, so it hurt me to think of them both being alone. But at the same time, he'd done some horrible things, and I didn't know if I could forgive him either, so I understood her struggle.

"Hey," I said when I came to a stop in front of him.

"You look beautiful, sweetheart. You aren't wearing the splint anymore. Does that mean you're healing well?"

"Yeah. It's been a few weeks and it's healing nicely. No boxing with Pinky right now, though, or lifting anything heavy for a while."

He nodded. "I'm glad you're okay. I am sorry that I blamed Romeo for what happened when it ended up being Ronny behind the attack."

"You know what, Dad," I said, holding my hand up when he attempted to interrupt me. "You say I'm sorry a lot, but it doesn't mean anything anymore because you do it all again the next time something doesn't go your way."

He looked away, gazing out at the water. "I'm not a perfect man, Demi. But I'm doing the best I can."

"That's not good enough anymore. So, you have two options. You can keep lying and protecting the wrong people, or you can step up for your family. Romeo and I are moving in together. I've never loved anyone like I love him. And you've done some horrible things to the man I love. You need to try to make that right, or you and I will never be okay." I let out a long breath. "And Slade is working hard to move forward, and releasing all those secrets he was carrying helped. But you could go there. You could own your part in what happened. Help your son get his life back."

"I don't know where to start," he said, his eyes locking with mine.

"Well, you've done nothing so far, so anything will be an improvement. Saying I'm sorry to the people you've hurt and following that up by not repeating the same mistakes again would be a good start."

"I don't know if your mom can forgive me," he said.

"I don't either. But the only way to find out is to start being the man she thought she married."

"I don't know how I got so lost along the way." He shrugged.

"Just because you're lost doesn't mean you can't find your way home. I hope you do the work that you need to. Because I miss my father." I pushed up on my tiptoes and kissed him on the cheek.

That was enough for today.

We had a long way to go, and I wasn't certain we'd get there, but I hoped we would.

When I made my way back to Romeo, River was on the phone, and everyone was quiet and watching him. I gave my boyfriend a curious look, and he wrapped an arm around my shoulder.

River ended the call and reached for his drink, taking a long pull. "Lionel had a stroke."

"What the fuck happened?" Kingston said, leaning forward and resting his elbows on his knees.

River ran a hand down his face. "I don't know. That was Doreen calling. Apparently, it happened at the bar when he was getting ready to head over here for the party."

"He's not that old. How the fuck did he have a stroke?" Romeo asked.

River glanced around at each of us, and then he cleared his throat. "He's dating that woman who's a lot younger than him."

"And we're blaming her?" Hayes asked.

"We're blaming the double dose of medication he took, along with a shit ton of supplements to help him with some issues—*down south*."

"Jesus. I never knew good loving could be the death of me." Kingston shivered.

"He's not dying. He's going to be fine. But he's going to be in the hospital for a while and then need physical therapy. He won't be up and moving for a few months."

"What can we do to help?" I asked. "Should we leave and head to the hospital?"

"No visitors until tomorrow. So we can take shifts. I don't know what the fuck will happen with the bar. Doreen said she called Ruby. They're hoping she can come to manage the bar until he gets on his feet." Lionel's daughter, Ruby, hadn't lived in Magnolia Falls for the last few years, but she and Lionel had always been close and she visited when she could.

"Wow. Isn't Ruby Rose the only person that ever beat up the champ?" Kingston said over a fit of laughter as he waggled his brows at Romeo.

"The girl had a mean left hook. And I wasn't about to hit a girl back," he said with a wicked smirk on his face.

"Yeah, she was a bit terrifying when we were young. She hated all of us back in the day. She's an angry little demon. But she does love her dad, I'll give her that." River shook his head.

"Well, someone needs to run that bar, or it'll go under quickly." Hayes took a long pull from his beer bottle.

"I think she'll come home," I said, and everyone turned to

look at me. "Yes. I know Ruby. She used to ride with me out at our barn. She won't let her dad's bar go under."

Romeo nodded. "We'll figure something out if she doesn't come back. We can rally and cover things for him if we need to."

"Agreed." River stood, shaking off the fact that he was clearly upset. He and Lionel were close.

The guys all went to the bar to get another drink, and Romeo pulled me to my feet. "Want to go down by the water and you can tell me about your talk with your dad?"

"Sure." I took his hand, and we walked down to the beach. The water splashed against the shore, and he pulled his coat off and laid it beside him before tugging me down to sit there.

"It was fine. I told him that I didn't really need any more apologies; I needed action. And I made it very clear that you're in my life now. You're my future. If he can't get on board with that, there is no place for him."

"You don't need to do that for me, baby." He pushed the hair away from my face and tucked it behind my ears.

"Yes, I do. And you'd do the same for me. We're a team, right?"

"The best team I know." He smirked and then pulled me to my feet to walk down to the water. "I can't wait to wake up to this sound every day. To the water splashing on the shore."

"I know," I said, as I lifted my long dress and splashed my feet in the water. It was gorgeous out tonight. "It'll be a nice way to start the day."

He tugged me closer and looked down at me. "Well, the best way to start the day is with my head buried between your thighs and my name on your lips. But if the water is splashing against the shore in the background, I wouldn't complain."

I unbuttoned his dress shirt so I could slide my hands up his chiseled abdomen.

"You've got a filthy mouth, Romeo Knight."

"And you fucking love it." He smirked.

"I do. How'd I get so lucky?"

"I'm the lucky one. You gave me what I never thought I'd have."

"What's that?" I asked, as he dropped his forehead against mine. The sun was just going down, and the sky was all sorts of pinks and oranges melded together.

"The kind of love that lasts forever. The kind of love you can't live without once you have it."

I could feel my eyes welling as I reached for his jaw, bringing his lips close to mine.

"Sounds like we're both playing the long game. Forever has a nice ring to it." I brushed my lips against his. "I love you."

"Love you doesn't seem like enough," he whispered against my mouth. "But I'll just keep telling you until we're old and gray."

And his mouth crashed into mine.

I may not have known it at the time, but forever started the day he'd come into my coffee shop.

And I'd been living it every single day since.

The End

Read a special bonus scene with all of your favorites from Magnolia Falls HERE: https://dl.bookfunnel.com/6wwlpxf8q8

If you'd like to see River fall hard and fast for his fierce heroine, you can pre-order Wild River HERE: https://geni.us/wildriver

. . .

Have you met Romeo's brother and sister-in-law, Lincoln and Brinkley before seeing them in Loving Romeo? If you haven't read their story, an enemies-to-lovers, sports romance, On the Shore, you can head over to Cottonwood Cove HERE: https://geni.us/ontheshore

acknowledgments

Greg, Chase & Hannah… Thank you for supporting me and cheering me on every step of the way. You are my reason for all that I do. I love you endlessly!

Willow, there are not enough words to say how thankful I am to have you in my life. Thelma and Louise forever. I'd be lost without you. Love you so much!

Catherine, thank you for your friendship and all of your support! So grateful to be on this journey with you, my sweet friend. Love you forever!

Kandi, my world is such a better place with you in it! I love our chats so much and I am so thankful for YOU! Love you to the moon and back!

Elizabeth O'Roark, Love you. Love your words. Endlessly grateful for your friendship!

Pathi, I am so thankful for your friendship, and for all the support and encouragement! I'd be lost without you! Thank you for believing in me! I love you so much!

Nat, I would be so lost without you now. I am so grateful to have you in my corner and thankful that you keep things running so smoothly. Thank you for all that you do. I love you forever!

Nina, thank you for supporting me and pushing to make my wildest dreams come true. Your friendship means the world to me. I love you forever!

Kim Cermak, thank you for keeping all the things together. You are so patient and kind and you make my life so much easier. I absolutely adore you and am so thankful for you! Love you!

Christine Miller, Kelley Beckham, Sarah Norris, Valentine Grinstead, Amy Dindia and Ratula Roy, I am endlessly thankful for YOU!

Meagan Reynoso, Thank you for beta reading and for all that you do to support me. It means the world to me! I love you so much!

Logan Chisolm, I absolutely adore you and am so grateful for your support and encouragement! Love you!

Doo, Abi, Meagan, Annette, Jennifer, Pathi, Natalie, Caroline and Diana, thank you for being the BEST beta readers EVER! Your feedback means the world to me. I am so thankful for you!!

To all the talented, amazing people who turn my words into a polished final book, I am endlessly grateful for you! Sue Grimshaw (Edits by Sue), Hang Le Design, Sarah Sentz (Enchanted Romance Design), Emily Wittig Designs, Christine Estevez, Ellie McLove (My Brothers Editor), Jaime Ryter (The Ryters Proof), Julie Deaton (Deaton Author Services) and the amazingly talented Madison Maltby, thank you for being so encouraging and supportive!

Crystal Eacker, Thank you for your audio beta listening/reading skills! I absolutely adore you!

Jennifer, thank you for being an endless support system. For running the Facebook group, posting, reviewing and doing whatever is needed for each release. Your friendship means the world to me! Love you!

Paige, I love our chats… from books to home decor to kids and life and visits from the infamous elf, you make my days so much brighter. I love you so much!

Rachel Parker, I am endlessly grateful for your friendship! My forever good luck charm! Love you!

Megan Galt, thank you for always coming through with the most beautiful designs! I'm so grateful for YOU!

Amy, Rebecca, Monica, Jessica, Sammi and Marni, I am so thankful for your support and your friendship!! Thanks for sprinting, for pushing me and supporting me on this journey. Love you!

Gianna Rose, Stephanie Hubenak, Sarah Sentz, Ashley Anastasio, Kayla Compton, Tiara Cobillas, Tori Ann Harris and Erin O'Donnell, thank you for your friendship and your support. It means the world to me!

Mom, thank you for being my biggest cheerleader and reading everything that I write! Love you!

Dad, you really are the reason that I keep chasing my dreams!! Thank you for teaching me to never give up. Love you!

Sandy, thank you for reading and supporting me throughout this journey! Love you!

To the JKL WILLOWS… I am forever grateful to you for your support and encouragement, my sweet friends!! Love you!

To all the bloggers, bookstagrammers and ARC readers who have posted, shared, and supported me—I can't begin to tell you how much it means to me. I love seeing the graphics that you make and the gorgeous posts that you share. I am forever grateful for your support!

To all the readers who take the time to pick up my books and take a chance on my words…THANK YOU for helping to make my dreams come true!!

keep up on new releases

Linktree Laurapavlovauthor
Newsletter Laurapavlov.com

other books by laura pavlov

Magnolia Falls Series
Loving Romeo
Wild River
Forbidden King
Beating Heart
Finding Hayes

Cottonwood Cove Series
Into the Tide
Under the Stars
On the Shore
Before the Sunset
After the Storm

Honey Mountain Series
Always Mine
Ever Mine
Make You Mine
Simply Mine
Only Mine

The Willow Springs Series
Frayed
Tangled
Charmed
Sealed
Claimed

follow me

Website laurapavlov.com
Goodreads @laurapavlov
Instagram @laurapavlovauthor
Facebook @laurapavlovauthor
Pav-Love's Readers @pav-love's readers
Amazon @laurapavlov
BookBub @laurapavlov
TikTok @laurapavlovauthor

Printed in Great Britain
by Amazon

36773265R00199